Maureen Duffy

is a much respected poet, playw   novels, including *That's How It Was*, *The Microcosm*, *Love Child*, *Change*, *I Want to Go to Moscow* and *Illuminations*. She is best known for her 'Metropolitan Trilogy' – three novels set in London: *Wounds*, *Capital* and *Londoners* – and for her novel *Gor Saga* which became the immensely successful BBC drama *First Born*. She has also published a considerable amount of non-fiction, including *The Erotic World of Faery*, an influential biography of Aphra Behn and, most recently, a biography of Purcell. Co-founder of the Writers' Action Group, she is Past President of the Writers' Guild and Chair of the British Copyright Council and the Authors' Licensing and Collecting Society. She lives in west London.

MAUREEN DUFFY

Occam's Razor

Flamingo
An Imprint of HarperCollins*Publishers*

Flamingo
An Imprint of HarperCollins*Publishers*
77–85 Fulham Palace Road,
Hammersmith, London W6 8JB

Published by Flamingo 1994
9 8 7 6 5 4 3 2 1

First published in Great Britain by
Sinclair-Stevenson 1993

Author photograph by Nick Cook

ISBN 0 00 654723 0

Set in Baskerville

Printed in Great Britain by
HarperCollinsManufacturing Glasgow

CONTENTS

'Entia non sunt multiplicanda praeter necessitatem.'
William of Occam, Doctor Singularis
et Invincibilis. d.1349.

PROLOGUE

· *The Pawns* ·

Orazio put out a thin ivory hand and picked up the slim cream bishop and moved it diagonally along the row of black diamonds. '*Scacco!* Check!'

He always spoke the Italian word first, letting fly with both beats and then rounding off with the softer English monosyllable that should have been stronger but for that soft 'e' embodying all its native ambiguity, even though this time he was sure it was mate.

'In fact, mate. I think.'

Pearse looked down at the board running the gamut of possible escapes through his head. 'You're right.'

'Another game? I don't believe you were concentrating.'

'I've things on me mind tonight.' Pearse was breaking not so much a rule, as a custom. Nine years now they had been playing every Friday night and they had never spoken of intimate concerns, only of the weather and the shops that had closed, the High Street slipping quietly into a ghost town where hero and villain could play out their last act under the sun with no one watching from the boardwalk or the blacked-out windows. Sometimes they talked of politics or disasters but nothing nearer those homes they visited alternately, week in, week out, the months and years flowing away with their chequered pattern under the pieces lifted and set down in their formalised moves.

As he had locked his front door behind him that night, doubting whether to take the lift or the stairs, Pearse had known he would play badly. But they had never cancelled a game, except once when the Don was having a gallstone removed. 'My daughter calls me the Don,' Orazio had said to Pearse on the only other occasion when custom had been breached, and that was how Pearse thought of him, though they never used each other's names as a form of address. It was always just 'you'.

The choice between stairs and lift took him to the end of the walkway to resolve. Looking over the balcony he could see into the well that was the grassy courtyard between the three central blocks. Those on the ground floor had little gardens, handkerchiefs of rancid earth that some filled with compost from the garden centre to nurture unwilling flowers, florid hybrid tea roses and gladioli, while others let them run to milkweed and dandelion.

If they were watching, waiting for him, they would be down there or on the stairs. He might walk out of the lift into his maiming or death or he might be ambushed at any turn of the stained concrete flights. That's if they knew him or if they weren't just after the boy. The letter had been addressed to Liam from Dublin. Pearse had opened it because he didn't know where to send it, hadn't known for thirteen years, only knowing from the occasional postcard in the beginning that Liam was still alive and then these had stopped too. So he had opened it.

He'd seen at once what it was: the cut-out capitals, brightly coloured, from magazines. '*THERE IS NO HIDING PLACE FOR TRAITORS.*' He'd taken it to the window in hands from which all sensation had been wiped as though with surgical spirit but which shook a bit causing the paper to blur. They had sent it here, expecting it would find Liam. Therefore they believed, knew him to be alive. Pearse went through into Liam's bedroom to the chart that almost covered one cream-emulsioned wall. Newspaper cuttings, in chronological order, were stuck to the paper with the names picked out of them as headings, printed in large black letters by a felt pen and underlined with the date and place. Those who had died. At first he had noted only the Noonans. Then he had realised Liam would probably have changed his name and perhaps even his looks so that the record had to become a monument no one but himself would ever see, since any neighbour or official coming to the flat need never enter this bedroom, a memorial to the young male dead of both sides, for how could he be sure which side Liam was on now or even, until that morning's post, if he was still at large among the living?

He elected the lift as the lesser horror, to be felt just once as it plummeted, catching the breath out of him, seeming not its usual jerky half-hearted self, rather than suffer the multiple repeated fear of peering round every bend. When the door opened he stood quite still looking into the entrance hall and through the wire-meshed glass exit into the outside world before he stepped through. Would he even recognise them if he saw them? He thought so. They would be different from the usual hangers around beached cars and motorbikes with their wheels in the air, the tinkerers and gossips, the gangs of boys and girls joshing and scuffling with each other, black and brown intermingled with pink skins.

Hadn't they shot the young black soldier who had dared to get engaged to a colleen born, while they were watching television in her parents' house? No, the group by the long low wall that separated the estate from the world was safe, unless they'd become smart and rich enough to contract out to hired labour that would look less conspicuous in this archipelago of the officially deprived.

To get into the street proper, Pearse had to pass through a narrow corridor stinking of piss and decay, one side recessed for a trio of huge round vats for unspecified waste; the other wall and the roof graffitied cement. Even on a bright day it was to enter a chill coffin where a mugger could lurk. Tonight he went through at a scuttle, feeling the knife slip between the ribs, the fist smash his face as he poked it out of the tunnel, a rabbit into the dangerous sunlight.

Then it was only a hundred yards down the side street to the high wall that fortressed the Don's house, with its wrack of broken bottles on top and the iron gates enclosing the courtyard, where the stone figures of lions brooded and the bronze centurion wept verdigris tears that stained his skirt and breast plate. Pearse rang the bell on the entry-phone with his eyes alert for every move and a hand on the iron bars for the moment the buzzer sounded. Then it was into the courtyard with the gate clanging mercifully behind him, an inverse of the only time he had gone to jail for a drunken punch-up a month after Jessie had died. In the darkness eyes flared briefly, greenly: a tail whisked, rat or cat, and was gone.

Beyond the lions and the centurion were the other shadowy figures: a reproduction David, an eagle outspread over a blank shield, a putto that had once peed into a shell basin but was now arrested in soundless dry-run for ever, a bundle of stone rods. But no women, Pearse had once remarked to himself, missing even a glimpse of marble female flesh.

A flight of stone steps led balustraded up to a portico, above which was a faded sign: *Orazio Carbone Antiques and Garden Ornaments*. He leant against the heavy wooden door and it gave, set ready for him from high up in the house.

'Papa,' Orazio's daughter Agnese had once said to him, 'you have the only palazzo in Deverham.' She had liked to bring her friends home for tea in their maroon convent skirts and blazers under their matching felt hats in the days when it was just a house, a home, before it had become a business, 'a warehouse for lumber' as she called it. 'You've turned Mummy's home into a junk shop.'

'I have to do something, and now you have the Castel Grande . . .'

Orazio had named the restaurant after his grandmother's village, the only place where he had been truly happy even as a child, with that lightsomeness of all burdens lifted, all wants supplied, plucked from the branches or the earth, sweet fruits in red and yellow tasting of sun, their juice staining his mouth and fingers; free to pick and cram and there would always be more while his grandmother nodded her approval from where she sat with sunlight carving a white wedge through the open doorway.

So he had filled the rooms with booty brought back from auctions and country fairs and house clearances, anything that caught his eye, and sometimes he had sold them. That was in the beginning. Now they stood under dust-sheets or dust, embalmed for mouse and spider to build among undisturbed. Pearse was aware of their presences as he passed through the house, remnants of other people's lives leading a life of their own together, incomplete without the humans who'd fashioned them, run their hands over them, fitted buttock or bone into them, shaped their purpose. It needed only a sorcerer's apprentice with a mistaken spell to set them trundling away stiff-legged in search of hands that would caress and polish them again.

'How long have we been having our Friday game together?' Pearse asked, knowing the answer but looking for a way through or out.

'Nine years almost. I remember well. We met at the fête, at St Thomas'. The chess tournament to raise money for the boys. We were the only ones left at the end.'

'You won then. You remember how you beat me.'

'You were *distratto*. Like tonight.'

'My wife had died a few months before. Our son broke her heart. I was trying on religion for comfort.'

'We were both new widowers. At least I was not so new.'

After his own wife Catterina had died Orazio had thought that at last he could do all the things he had always wanted, freed of the pretence of upholding himself as husband and father. He had given the management of the Castel Grande to Agnese and her husband, closed the house up and taken a ticket that would allow him the freedom of all the capitals of Western Europe, Amsterdam, Paris, his own Roma, Athens, Madrid. He had sat at cafés, by canals and piazzas, under branches and fountains, skies that smiled and skies that wept, watching young men pass by, unknown, free at last and totally unable to respond or act. Catterina's death hadn't liberated him. He felt nothing: neither grief nor lust. The words of an old song, of the lover who returns to find his beloved dead of the cholera sang through his head as if he was really grieving, but how could he when he'd never really loved, only done what was required of him?

Fenesta che lucive mo non luce.

There had never been a light in the window for either of them. 'You must marry,' his family had said. 'We'll find you a nice village girl. Make a good wife, good cook. Won't run after other men.' She had cried on their wedding night.

He had come back from his fruitless travelling, opened up the house, crammed Catterina's furniture, her glass cabinets of ornaments, the velvet three-piece suite and ormolu tables into one room and closed the door on it, and begun to accumulate, to study the antique-trade magazines, to travel about the country. And he was good at it, had an eye. As he'd built up one of the finest restaurants in West London, so now he bought and sold and made more money. The palazzo was furnished with all the transient richness of old carpets, alabaster statues, ornate carved and gilded candelabras and chiffonniers. Agnese hated them. Her house was modern: spindly black-legged little glass and iron tables ran across the tiled floor to chairs that were moulded into smooth beanbags of red and purple plastic. Scentless flowers stood stiff in specimen vases.

'It's my son,' Pearse said. 'He's in trouble.'

'Ah, children. What can you do? When we were young we did what we were told. Now they tell us what to do. You need a drink, some red wine, *fa sangue*, makes you blood.' He got up from the mahogany table where the chessboard sat with its scatter of elegant shapes. Pearse loved the feel of the pieces when it was their turn to play here. He knew they were old and valuable and had sometimes wondered whether he should invest in a better set himself, but he feared the look of them against his speckled blue plastic table-top would make him uneasy, might even put him off his game, and the Don didn't seem to notice. Now he came back with a bottle and two glasses, his tall thin figure waiterly in its dark immaculate suit. His movements were all controlled, precise. It was impossible to imagine him being clumsy, slopping the wine as he poured it.

Pearse felt his own thick-set body showed up to disadvantage beside this dapper exclamation mark of a man. 'We'd look like the figure ten going down the road together.'

'*Salute!*'

'*Slainte!*' Usually he drank beer but not so much since his experience of a night in the cells and the humiliation of the magistrate's court next morning among the habitual drunks, the girl prostitutes, the debtors and teenage vandals. On cold nights he allowed himself a drop of Irish, Black Bush if he was feeling flush, for its sweetness like the two sugars he always had in his tea. The wine was warm and dark, almost black but soft on the palate reminding him of the feel of a smooth skin.

'Now tell me about your son.'

Presented with the moment, the opening gambit, he didn't know how to move. He doglegged with a knight.

'Liam, that's the boy, got mixed up with some people when he was a student, over in Ireland, and I haven't seen him since. Now it seems the people he was mixed up with are looking for him. I had a letter for him, I opened. From them. They think he's come home to me.'

'And you can't tell the English Police?'

'No, no I can't.'

'You think he will come home?'

'That's what I don't know. If I knew where to find him I could tell him to stay away. They'll be watching out for him.'

'Then there's nothing you can do but watch and wait. So we should drink up.' And the bottle was tilted again.

By the time Pearse got up to leave they had finished it and washed the contents down with a tot of cognac, and he no longer cared as he brazened his way back through the stinking passage, across the gritty lawn and into the lift. Let them be waiting. He wasn't afraid, wasn't that old that he couldn't give them a fight, wasn't going to spend the rest of his life skulking in the shadow. He punched the air. The open walkway was empty, sketched in tones of grey by the moon's soft lead pencil. As Pearse fell asleep he was aware of the distant caterwaul of two toms staking out their territory.

*

Orazio woke at four, drowning. He had sat up after Pearse had gone, savouring another cognac and the words of his namesake beaten into him by the Fathers.

'You of all should remember the form of the Horatian ode, Carbone. Get three.'

He had stood in line for the youngest Jesuit to tolley him with the rest of the wrongdoers, part of the novice's priestly training in control of the passions. Only when he reached the VIth form and succumbed to the charm of Father Torre letting the seductive lines fall from his lips, 'pearls before swine, *ragazzotti*,' did he take in their meaning. 'An old man's lament for his lost youth. A necessary text to study from the stylistic point of view but you will all say three Hail Mary's tonight and I shall say six.'

The Don took down his thumbed school copy now with the bookplate of St Ignatius in the front garnished with fading ink curlicues from his own pen. Orazio Carbone *libro suo, suum librum*, his book; stolen on the last day of the last term because he couldn't bear to part with it, and carried to his grandmother's summer *masseria* for what was to be his last holiday before the war and his last sight of her. Father Torre hadn't seduced him, although he had let his hand linger on Orazio's dark hair for longer than was usual as he bent over his shoulder pointing out a mistake in construction, or in the strong or weak beats of the formal scansion that seemed to bear no relation to the lilt of the line. It was Horace who had filled his waking and sleeping dreams with unclean thoughts, needing continual penance before he could serve as altar boy at Mass.

'Maybe he'll be a priest,' his mother had said, laughing bitterly. 'He doesn't run after the girls like his papa.' It was his papa who had brought his parents to England in the first place when Orazio was still a boy. The scandal had been too great for his grandmother's village not to gossip openly about. 'In England nobody will know you. What does it matter what he does?'

Now Orazio himself was that old man whose pain he had only barely understood when he had first read of the boy from

Liguria who had broken the old poet's heart. Still, he wouldn't sit there weeping the thin tears of age. He had learnt some English ways: control, reticence. 'Don Freddo,' Catterina had once called him. Perhaps she would have preferred it if he had been like his father, although his mother had been unhappy enough. He remembered one terrible Sunday when she had taken the carving knife to his father and he and Catterina had had to hold her until she began to sob and carve the chicken instead. '*L'ammazzaro!*' she had cried repeatedly, attacking the carcass.

Beyond the window he could hear a bird singing up the dawn, a blackbird or even perhaps a nightingale in the nearby cemetery, opened in the nineteenth century when there was still room for the dead to lie among the living and not be carted off to remote suburbs or powdered into the wind. If he slept again would he also dream again, his recurrent dream that he was drowning, drowning, the water flowing in through his mouth and nostrils, blinding and deafening him as he fought to come up, to rise through the opaque layers, not to go down, down forever?

'Papa, I need to talk to you.' The telephone had drilled through the last fumes of cognac as he was drinking his coffee. 'Will you be there this afternoon early? I'll come over.' He was still replacing the receiver when the entry-phone buzzed angrily. He pressed the button without speaking in reply to Mrs Heamans', 'It's me, Mr Carbonny. I'll just go round the back.'

Every Tuesday and Friday Ruby Heamans brought food for the tribe of feral cats who lived among the abandoned statuary in the yard. As she worked she gave him an update on the community. 'That One-Eye's been in a fight again. You'd think he'd learn he can't win with the youngsters. Ear all torn this morning. The little tortoiseshell's got kittens somewhere she's feeding. Thin as a rake and nervous: a sure sign. I'll bring her a bit extra on Friday.'

She cleaned as her mother had with few concessions to

modern gadgetry. If he'd let her she would have filled the air with dust from her broom rather than plugged in and switched on the 'youva'. The money he gave her she spent on her flock, dispersed throughout the area in abandoned yards and small parks sandwiched between main roads where they waited behind the bushes for her coming and going before they would emerge to fall on what she had left, turning their heads sideways to chew and keep look-out at the same time until they grew used to her and allowed her to whisk one into a cat basket, stunned and yowling while the rest fled, to be returned later, neutered, plumped out, its wounds dressed.

Agnese disapproved of Mrs Kittycat as she called her. 'Why do you keep her, Papa? Let me send for a girl from Italy. A *paesana* who would look after you in this big house. Cook for you. She doesn't clean properly. And she smells of cat.'

'I don't want anyone living here. Anyway, girls these days are different. They don't want to cook and clean for old men. They want to earn good money on computers and go dancing with young ones.'

This morning while she ironed his clothes and cleaned the rooms he lived in, he took a plastic bag from the hook behind the kitchen door and set off to shop. First he stood at the bus stop with the rest of the abandoned, diverting himself by reading all the notices in the vet's window, the advertisements for animal portraits and pet walkers, the painful cries of distress for the found and lost, the begging for donations and good homes, among which he recognised Mrs Heamans' own running plea. This week she had a black-and-white kitten, short tail, neutered, male, on offer.

The bus took him past the football ground and the hospital to the cinema where he got off, crossed the road and retraced his route until he reached *Gennaro's Salumeria* where he bought his specialities: slices of the dangling crusty-rinded salamis, olives black and moist as does' eyes, and his cheeses: *buorroni* shaped like a limbless baby with a butter heart, melting camembert, bottles of full blooded Barbara and in season spongy *panone* and chewy *torrone*, sweetmeats for Christmas and Easter.

'Papa, why do you go to that old man? We could get you anything you wanted and more cheaply. The shop is so dark you can't see what you're buying.'

'I've always been there. He needs my custom; we don't. Besides I like to go out, make a little expedition, exercise my freedom of choice and my legs.'

The shop did smell, but of smoked sausage and cheese and olive oil and freshly-ground coffee. It smelt of his childhood, of his grandmother's stone-flagged kitchen, lacking only the scents from outside of sun, pale and dusty earth, of sweet tomatoes drying into thick red paste for pasta, of basil and rosemary.

He looked up at the thicket of dangling meats as he entered.

'Signor Carbone, *come sta?*'

'*Sto bene, grazie. E lei?*'

'*Bene, bene.*'

They shook hands formally as they always did, preserving the courtesies. For a moment for both of them the alien city no longer boomed beyond the doorway. As he made his choices which were always the same, Orazio heard news from the colony, of births, marriages, deaths and those retired 'home' to Italy or visiting children in America. In return he offered such snippets as came his way, mainly in his sister-in-law's letters.

Sometimes Signor Vitale asked his opinion on some external matter, beginning always, 'Excuse me but what do you think . . . ?' Orazio knew what this formula signalled: that he was to give his opinion both as the Don and the graduate of St Ignatius and the international school of Perugia, almost a *dottore*, as the failed priest they all sensed in him. This time it was crack and crime.

'My son writes me in New York you take your life in your hands to walk the street. The other day a boy came in here, looking round nervously, you know, looking to see if I was alone and then he pulled out a knife, demanded money. I was very angry. I took my big knife, this one, and I shouted at him in Italian and started to come from behind here. He turned and ran. Only a kid, a black kid. Will it be as bad here?'

'No, no. Not as bad. The English don't let it. They have their ways. They always work in the end. Remember the riots? Everyone expected them again and again the next summer but they didn't come.'

'Yes, but why not?'

Orazio shrugged. 'Who knows? They put something in the water maybe.' Signore Vitale would laugh now, only half disbelieving him but with his worries lifted all the same.

Pearse woke with a thick head. Last night he had come home like *Cuchullain*, a hero for all time, ready to take on the world. This morning he crept about in search of aspirin and tea. Brandy was no use to a whisky drinker. His mother had kept a half bottle, for medicinal purposes only, in the dresser. Now they said it was the worst thing you could be forcing down someone's throat when they were in shock or fainting. Strangely, though, it seemed to have made his worries go away. He felt calm and unafraid as if it would all be all right in the end. He had to tell himself this was a dangerous state, the way men went to their deaths. He had to plan some kind of campaign, think out the possible developments and what he would do in each case.

Suppose now he should open his door to a knock and they, whoever they were, should be standing there and force their way in. Suppose he should open his door and it should be not them, whoever they were, but the Police, following them or Liam. He took a pull on his cup of strong brown tea the colour of milked bogwater. His trade taught him that all wires led somewhere from a source to an effect and if you wanted to change the effect, light a fire rather than a light bulb, you had to change the ending or put in a junction, divert the energy, trunk it away to another point, control it, channel it to give the result you wanted.

The first thing was to take down the chart in Liam's bedroom or cover it up. It wouldn't do for any of his possible visitors to find that if he was trying to act the innocent. He felt bad about destroying it, as if that would be to wipe all those people away for a second time. He would prefer to cover it, but what with? The Police would come with a search warrant and turn the place over. They'd been once before, years ago, after Liam had been silent for about eighteen months, asking for him. That time, when Jessie was still alive, she'd faced them down with angry tears. 'We wish to God we knew where he was but I'm bloody sure we wouldn't tell you.'

'You're not Irish, Mrs Noonan, are you?'

'You know bloody well I'm not, since you know all about us. Or is one accent the same as another to you?'

'We'll have to ask your husband to come to the station with us to answer some questions.'

'Ask him then, but bring him back unmarked or I'll ask some questions meself.'

'Bit of a handful, your missus?' they'd said to him in the car.

'They've minds of their own, Scots girls.' He'd been afraid inside of violence, of a beating where he couldn't fight back. A few of the neighbours had been about when they'd bundled him away. Jessie wouldn't have liked that but it wasn't uncommon. People were taken away from the estate for all sorts of reasons. This time there would be no one to defend him and his bones ached with the anticipation of bruising. But maybe they'd be more careful; there'd been so many mistakes.

Posters were the thing to cover the chart. He doubted that they'd tear them down to look behind if he did it cleverly enough. He'd go out after he'd eaten his usual two pieces of toast and strawberry jam and see what he could root out. He wondered how the Don was feeling this morning. He always thought of himself as the younger man though he supposed there probably wasn't much in it. The Don'd be more used to red wine and brandy though and mightn't feel so rough. He must beat him next game, concentrate, keep his end up. Their partnership had always worked because they were level-pegging in their skill, turn and turn about. If either ever got the ascendancy the enjoyment would go out of their meetings.

He realised he was thinking of a future, of a chain of Fridays stretching into the distance. That was how people kept going, on hope, disbelieving the present reality of illness, death, terror, imprisonment, whatever it might be, in pursuit of a marsh light, running after the fairy woman Fand to the Land of Promise.

'What use is all that?' Jessie would say. 'What's needed today is science and mathematics, not fairy tales. They don't even make a proper story you can follow and they're full of fighting and bloodshed, not suitable for weans.' So she would read Liam Rumpelstiltskin and Jack and the Beanstalk that taught a child to be practical and resourceful and endure, and the whole of Bruce and the spider, while Pearse led a procession of beautiful women through the boy's head, Deirdre and Grainne, Emer and Mebh, and put a sword in his hand.

'Tell us about when you were a boy, Dada,' Liam would say and Pearse would try to describe again the ships coming in to Arklow harbour, the one-storey thatched house that was more than a cottage, the patchwork quilts and knitted bedspreads his mother and grandmother had worked at to feed them while his father was away long months at sea.

Only now did he wonder what that might have done. He hadn't realised that he and Jessie were engaged in a struggle for the child's imagination, what the Church would have called his soul. As Liam had grown up into adolescence he had retreated into the secrecy of puberty where all adults were the enemy, especially parents, playing football with the boys after school, smoking and swearing to keep his end up with the others. It was a shock when he said he'd got an interview for Queen's.

'Do you have to go over the water?' Jessie had asked. 'Aren't there places in England or Scotland?'

'I want to see what it's like. Anyway, I've applied for Keele and Manchester as well,' he'd said to comfort her and diffuse her hurt.

'You get over there, I'll lose you altogether,' she said, as if with second sight. 'It's only half of you, you know. You've as much of my blood as your father's.'

'It's all the same blood, Mam. The Scots came from Ireland in the first place.'

'And learnt more sense.' She had banged down an angry pot and turned the tap on full so that the water gushed into the bowl and flung up a scalding shower. 'You speak to him; he doesn't listen to me.'

Pearse had found himself cast as peacemaker. 'You're hurting your mother.'

'I can't help it, Dada. Anyway, it's a good university, one of the oldest.'

'So's Edinburgh.'

'That's only for the ex-public school. I'd never get in there.'

Pearse had tried to comfort Jessie. 'He doesn't mean to hurt. He's just young. All this stuff in the papers has got him excited.'

'If he goes over there I'll never see him again. You might, but I won't. I feel it.' As if she already knew, sensed. But how could she have done?

'That's just superstition.'

'No, it's what I feel inside.'

'You're both as obstinate as each other.'

'You did what you wanted, Dada, when you were my age.'

'And I found I'd made a terrible mistake.'

'I'm only going to see what's what. It isn't like going to war as you did.'

He would wash up his breakfast things and go out now to look for posters and sellotape to cover up the chart, buy himself something to eat in the market and drop in for a hair of the dog at the Duke's Head.

'Why we have to drink at a pub with Stinking Billy as its sign,' Jessie would begin, 'when he murdered the Highlanders . . .'

'Because it's the best around,' Pearse always answered, laughing. He missed her this morning with a terrible ache. He had loved her for her toughness, her indomitableness and the red-gold hair that suggested passion.

He picked out a couple of crumpled plastic shopping bags from among the collection festooning the kitchen door, ghosts of purchases past, and inched open the front door on its chain. Nothing went off in his face or slumped into the gap. He slipped the chain and stepped out, turning his back on the world briskly to double-lock the door, and then began the descent, this time by the stairs ('Never use the same route twice') and strode out into a Saturday shopping morning he felt safe in.

The market was jammed as usual, giving him the illusion of cover and safety as he pushed his way gently from stall to stall with its still-life patterning of fruit, vegetables or fish, or the hanging banners and flags of cheap, bright clothes. Humankind in all its variations flowed and jostled around, nudging him like an empty beer can bobbed in and sucked back by the tide on the shoreline under Putney Bridge among the other flotsam. The faces of the passers-by belonged to those the waters pushed to the side, emptied or anxious, questing the length of the street for bargains, intent, suspicious of every price tag, every blemish. 'Do not squeeze me until I'm yours,' the fruit insisted.

He came at last with his carrier of fresh vegetables, potatoes and carrots, tinned peas, a pound of sausages and four pale French apples in a brown paper bag, to the shop where he thought he'd seen posters, and nervously entered the floodlit interior.

It was a house of cards he had stepped into, with the faces turned inward so that the walls were shrill with colours and shapes. Pearse had never before been inside such a shop. Everything around him seemed flimsy and ephemeral, in paper or filmy plastic. A puff of wind or fire would have blown the lot away. He wandered from stand to stand amazed that people should spend their money on such things: cards for every trivial occasion, ribbons, wrapping paper, glassy figurines of animals, and even a display of anthropomorphic penises he recognised with a shock, wearing hats and ties and smoking cigarettes or opening little obscene mouths like the fish on the market stall he'd just passed, gasping still in death. One was playing jack-in-the-box and jumped out at him when he touched the lid. He was hard put not to leap back in his surprise and looked around covertly to see if anyone had noticed his reflexive jerk.

The posters hung from chromed steel arms in racks. He recognised the idols he'd been just too old for: Elvis Presley and James Dean, whose youth was preserved on countless icons forever so that today's boys and girls could go on worshipping saints, who if they'd lived would now be, even if they didn't look it, older than most of their grandparents; Monroe's sugar-mouse flesh and candy-floss hair sagging towards sixty. He watched two girls leafing through the dead. Miniskirts and skimped shorts were back again and their legs were long and brown from a summer holiday beach in Spain or Corfu. Pearse dragged his gaze away. He would look at the cards while they made their drawn-out choice. 'You're turning into a dirty old man.'

By the time Orazio got back, Mrs Heamans had left. He made himself a tomato salad, with fresh basil and black olives, which he ate with crusty bread and camembert. He took a constitutional among the statuary, crumpling up the paper which Ruby Heamans had left as the cats' tablecloth, nibbled almost clean with only a few greasy smears and fishy yellow stains to show where her offerings had been. The colony was shrinking. Ruby had set about it as soon as he had taken her on to clean, after Catterina's death.

'Did you know there's cats in your yard, Mr Carbonny?' He had confessed to having seen an occasional tail, been woken by spring and autumn yowling. 'There's a whole tribe, I shouldn't wonder. Been there for years. You ought to do something about it.'

In Italy cats lived in the squares and courtyards: hollow-flanked, their coats harsh and dull with dust and nits. He had been aware of them, without actually paying them any attention, all his life. What could he do?

'I'll see to it if you don't mind.'

Mind? What should he mind? The next time she came she had a bag, heavy with newspapers and screw-top jars containing a repellent collection of biological specimens, gobbets of fish and meat in jellied gravy which she had taken through the kitchen into the paved back yard where most of the statues stood: the gladiators and togaed philosophers, the mean emperors and lissome ephebes and a galaxy of assorted, but all dimple-buttocked, putti.

'I'm building up their confidence.'

Later at the end of the morning's cleaning she had returned from a trip into the yard with a demented, spitting demon all fangs and claws clapped up in a wire carrier, and a complacent smile on her face. 'There's no need for him to make all that noise. He'll never miss them once he's been done.'

A subdued animal was brought back the following week to bolt out of its cage and disappear through the open door. Gradually they were all done; the females stayed away longer and came back with a shaven patch on their sides ribbed with a double rakehead of stitches. Only One-Eye and the little tortoiseshell had refused to be lured to their own good. Sometimes he thought that when she had finally dealt with these two Mrs Heamans would stop coming to deal with him.

After his brief look round he settled himself for a siesta with the life of Garibaldi which he had been intending to read for years. Such energy, even in his seventies. He must try to see how it was done. The entry-phone woke him from a dream in which he had found himself in the great patriot's army in a confusion of cannon roar, fire and smoke. A cavalryman was poised above him with a sabre, lifted. Agnese's voice crackled into the room.

'*Sto io, Papa!* Let me in.'

The sounds of battle fell away as he pressed the button, picked up the fallen book and smoothed down his sleep-ruffled hair in the mirror. He went into the kitchen to put on the coffee pot, following his daughter in his mind's eye as she toiled upstairs and along the corridor. It was unusual for her to call without warning.

She pushed open the door and began speaking at once. 'Papa, two men came to the Castel Grande yesterday. They said they were looking for you. Stephen was there and asked if he could help them. They said they wanted the proprietor. He said that he and I were the managers. They were very rude: they said they didn't want to deal with women or Englishmen. I came in at this point and asked them what they wanted. They said they wanted to speak to you. I said: 'What do you want my father for?' And they told me to say that some people wanted to talk to you and they would come again. I said that you didn't come to the restaurant any more. And they said: "Tell him he's expected. Tomorrow afternoon." That's today. That's why I wanted to see you this early. Papa, who are they?' At last the words had stopped pouring out.

'You know who they are.' He didn't mean to be, wasn't angry with her, but the naïvety of the question irritated him.

'What should I do? Should we go to the Police?'

'And tell them what? That two men came to see your father?' He heard himself saying to Pearse: 'And you can't tell the English Police?'

'What time did they come?'

'About four-thirty.'

He looked at his watch. It was already gone three.

'Telephone Stephen. Tell him that if they come he must give them my number and ask them to call me. Say I don't go out much.'

'But Papa, then they will come here.'

'If he doesn't give them something they might hurt him or smash the place up. Do it now and then go home. I'll deal with this. Where are the children?'

'Richard is staying with a boy in France. Teresa is with the English grandparents in the Isle of Wight. They come back for school next week.'

Autumn came early here in the North. Suddenly in the middle of August there would be a taste of it in the morning air, a touch of sadness and decline, the roses overblown in the gardens, a too-heavy dew covering the cars with filaments of moisture. Sometimes it seemed as if there was no summer, it was so fleeting, and fall lingered all year. It was then his mind ached most with that memory of his grandmother's *masseria*. He could have bought one himself of course, a little stone house in an acre of garden on a hillside, in Italy, retired there every summer and lived like a *paesano*, even grown fat, but he knew the dream would have perished if he had tried to embody it because the fruit was touched, held, zipped up in the perfect globes of melon and grape, not just by natural light and warmth but by the golden shower of memory and childhood.

When Agnese had gone, kissing him on both cheeks, suddenly affectionate, telling him to look after himself, he walked through the house that had been Catterina's more than his, speculating, trying to plan. All his life he had hated disorder. 'You're more English than the English,' Catterina would say. 'You're happy to have a cold Englishman for a son-in-law.' But she was appeased by the two perfect children, most perfect grand-children, she could spoil, especially Riccardo who was dark-eyed and dark-haired. 'He's a real little Italian.'

The call came just as he had poured his first glass of the evening. The voice had a slight American twang.

'Mr Carbone, we want to talk with you.'

'My daughter told me.'

'We'd like you to come to the Castel Grande.'

'I'm an old man. I don't go out much. You come to see me here if you want to talk business. Better than in the restaurant, more private. Unless you want to talk now.'

'It's not good to do business on the telephone.'

'I agree. So when would you like to come?' He heard his caller say to someone else in Italian, probably for him to overhear, that the old fool was being obstinate.

'*Va bene*. We will come tomorrow at six o'clock.'

'I will give you my address.'

'We know where you live.'

Pearse came home with an armful of rolled posters. He had discovered that in one corner of the shop there was a late summer sale and expensive toys for adults were being knocked down to half-price. He found some Monets of smiling flowery landscapes where women in hats and long dresses meandered through the breast-high grass, sown with poppies and scabious.

Then there were some strange graphics, lines that suggested half an hour's distracted wondering where to move the brush next, and a flock of glinting motorbikes. If anyone asked he could say that they'd been Liam's young choice. He liked the Monets best. They reminded him of the big houses of the Anglo-Irish gentry when he'd visited Cork as a boy, though the flowers would have been flaming purple loosestrife, fluffy bog-cotton and the stiff orange feathers of montbretia that grew wild in the church-yards where they buried their dead apart.

Liam's bedroom was transformed into an art gallery. Pearse stood on the other side by the door and looked at it. His dead were still there underneath intact but overlaid now by these almost gaudy images. The bikers looked back at him from their shining saddles in their black leather armour, confident, hair tousled with speed. Seen from this distance the graphics resolved themselves into agile leaping figures while the long-dust French girls ambled among bees in their perpetual sunshine. He wondered what Liam would think of the pictures.

He would go out now for his hair of the dog. If anyone came seeking him he wouldn't be there. It was putting off the evil day but why not; he needed time. In the little front gardens that he passed the last rose of summer was blooming dustily all alone as she had all season.

The pub was crowded with shoppers, bags stuffed with the produce of the stalls. From time to time, children peered in through the door demanding a toll of Coke and crisps while their parents supped and gossiped.

The walls were hung with every kind of sporting gear, autographed with the flourishes of the famous and not so famous, the remembered and the forgotten, that Terry, the Guv'nor, had gathered over the years. 'How did you come by them all?' Pearse had once asked, indicating the dangling stalactites of cricket bats, football boots, boxing gloves, a hockey stick under the crossed blades of a pair of sculls.

'Picked them up at jumble sales and suchlike. Couldn't bear to see them lying there when they was all good in their day. Had a go like, bust their guts. Only so many can get to the top and that isn't by what you know but who you know, like as not.'

Pearse knew the Guv'nor spoke out of knowledge and perhaps some bitterness since he'd boxed for the Army, been a PE instructor and run a gym when he'd been discharged, before becoming a pub-keeper.

'She said she wouldn't marry me if I kept on with all that.' He nodded at his wife, elegant in electric blue, where she chatted to a couple of privileged customers. 'Said it was too dicey and she didn't want an old man full of holes like a colander. But I still keep me hand in on the quiet, so if you're ever in a bit of a ruck and need a help out, let me know.'

Pearse considered this offer now. 'How's it going?' he asked.

'Mustn't grumble. Never did no good anyway. Weekdays is quiet at the moment. There's no money about so people stop in and watch telly but they get fed up come the weekend and then we do good business.'

It was too soon for Pearse to put out a feeler. 'What're you drinking?'

'I'll have a half later, thanks. Too early yet. Janice,' he called across to the barmaid, 'put a half in the pipe for me from Pearse.'

'So who's going to win the title?'

'Gawd knows and he don't care. There's nobody worth a light. Name one, go on. You can't. The heart's gone out of it. It's not enough to be built like a brick shithouse and box clever. Now you've got to have psychologists and accountants as well as managers and trainers. And you still get knocked about till your brains is addled. At least Julie saved me from that. Thanks for the drink. They're calling me to put another barrel on. I'll see you around.' He took his four-square frame in the short-sleeved shirt and blue cotton trousers, that let every muscle show its bulge through the tight cloth, across to the door that led down to the cellar.

Pearse looked round over the rim of his glass at the other drinkers. Most of them he knew to nod to but nothing of those lives that had become the stuff of soap-opera. From art imitating life in the early days of *Coronation Street*, the positions had been reversed as someone, he thought it was Oscar Wilde, had put it, to life imitating art. Now ordinary lives played and replayed between the twin mirrors of reality and fiction, flesh and film until it was hard to tell which was which. Words given sudden importance by inclusion in a serial at once became everyone's coinage for a time, a demotic worked to an early death by over-use and discarded in favour of some new minting to be as soon rubbed smooth in its turn.

He supposed it had always been so, only now it was more instant, obvious, worldwide. He felt as if he'd been asleep like Rip van Winkle and awakened to find everything changed, except that it no longer took a hundred years. A decade would do it, or even a single year, as the images flickered between fact and fantasy, faster and faster, in continuous spasms of sheet lightning. He had been muffled under a private blanket of grief since Liam had gone and Jessie died while change had rushed on without him, leaving him stranded to wake and rub bleary eyes at the denizens of this brave new world. He wondered if the Don was in the same somnolent state, alone in his house of dust sheets.

A couple of pints of Guinness later Pearse felt capable of coherent thought again. He should try to find Liam before anyone else did. But where to begin? Once before, when Jessie was first ill, he'd taken time off and gone to Belfast in search of their son but with no success. In the end, he'd been forced to return home empty-handed to the despair that was killing her. 'I'll never see him again.' Perhaps he should advertise in the paper, but what paper, and what could he say that only Liam would understand? He would go home now to cook himself some dinner and try to think things through while he turned the sausages in the pan. Now the pubs stayed open all day there was no monitory bell to set you on your way. Looking at his watch he saw it was half-past three already.

As he cooked and ate his food the temporary resolve faded to be replaced by a great lassitude. He began to long for something to happen so that at least he could respond. It was his own blindness that was the killer. Pearse settled himself in a chair to think, and was asleep. He dreamed that he blundered on through a foreign but remembered landscape of scorched hills and rocks, obscurely pursued, and woke sweating. Somewhere a warning shrilled at him. He stumbled out of his chair. It was the telephone. For a moment he didn't recognise the voice, unused to hearing it filtered through the instrument.

'Mr Noonan, you said last night you have a problem. Now I have a problem too. Perhaps we should consider them together. At least it will help us both to talk.'

'Should I come round to you? Or would you prefer to come here?'

'I will come to you tomorrow evening. I will have more to discuss with you then.'

They kept him waiting of course, a trick so childish and obvious that it even made Orazio smile from the depths of his armchair. He had worked out that he was probably safe today. They wanted something which needed his co-operation. At least that was how they were beginning. This was something he had heard about but never had to deal with before. When several of them in the business got together for a drink they would joke about godfathers and the problems of restaurateurs in America, Marseilles and Sydney, where you had to pay protection money or get your place wrecked; about Calabria and the clan; about the rise of black and Chinese groups in imitation and opposition, congratulating themselves on having picked a quiet place to bring up their families where they needn't tangle with the law.

'Enough to satisfy the Health Inspectors and the Weights and Measures . . .'

At his last encounter with some of his former colleagues, a chance meeting buying coffee in Angelucci's, no one had said anything, perhaps because they regarded him as retired. Surely, if others had been asked to 'talk business' he would have heard. Something would have trickled through. Agnese would have mentioned it to him if only to say that he needn't worry, that she and Stephen could handle it. Any attempt on his part to advise or suggest was always brushed aside as if it threatened their management, was a criticism of their competence.

It had begun to rain outside, signifying the end of summer. Orazio could hear it beating on a skylight and pouring down a gutter into a drain. Once or twice he thought he heard a car swish by on the road in the late Sunday afternoon hush. When the bell rang he got up from his chair and went to the entry-phone.

'Yes?'

'We're here, Carbone.'

'I will come down and let you in.'

He had decided to see them not in the room where he dozed in his armchair or watched television with an open bottle and a glass, but in his old office on the ground floor. The Don had spent the day making it look inhabited, getting in extra chairs, putting a bottle of cognac and some glasses in the cabinet and a heavy cut-glass ashtray on the desk. He reckoned there would be two or three of them. He glanced in on his way down. He needed to keep them down here, away from the centre of his life, in order to feel in some degree of control, of himself and his own fear as well as of what was happening.

When he opened the front door there were two of them, the one behind holding a dripping umbrella over the man in front. In the grey evening light they too were grey under the black umbrella.

'Come in please. This way. *Che tempo*. Can I take your coats?'

'This won't take long. I'm a busy man. Tell him, Carlo.'

'Sit down at least.' They sat. 'A cognac?'

'Signor Macello is in a hurry. We have a proposition for you.'

'You won't join me? Excuse me then.' Orazio poured himself a brandy and sipped carefully. It wouldn't do to choke.

'We'll come to the point. We want the use of your accounts. We have some money that needs processing.'

'Excuse me, I don't quite understand. Why me?' He'd wanted

to say: 'To what do I owe this singular honour?' but felt instinctively that humour would be misunderstood.

'We understand from your father's cousin in Chicago that you're known as "the Don".'

His cousin from Chicago had come to Agnese's wedding, the wedding that had cost him a year's profits.

Cousin Cincio, whose name as a boy when they happened to be staying together at their grandmother's Orazio had changed to Ciuco, the donkey; Cincio had drunk a lot and had to be put in a taxi when the reception was finally over and the dancing stopped. He had been happy to come to the wedding, saying that he could do business while he was in England. There'd been no opportunity to ask him how that business had gone, or even what it might be.

'Cincio,' Orazio laughed. 'He gets everything wrong. It's a nick-name, just a private family joke. It means nothing.'

They stared back at him, unimpressed, the rain dripping off their overcoats on to the floor and forming a small lake around the ferrule of the umbrella.

'It doesn't matter how we made our choice. It's made. You have the kind of operation we need: the right size and turnover. Very respectable, classy joint,' Carlo allowed himself a carefully-formulated, slim smile. 'We'll give you a percentage.'

'Excuse me, I still don't understand. It would be very difficult. My son-in-law is in charge of the financial side. It would be impossible to do anything of this nature without him seeing it and asking questions.'

'Give him a piece of it.'

'He's English.'

'Get rid of him.'

'He's my family, my daughter's husband.'

'That's your problem: you should have taken care she married a *paesano*. It doesn't matter to us how you arrange it. The first deposit will be in a month's time. You'll be contacted. Then we'll tell you when and how to pass it on.'

They had stood up then and Orazio had shown them out. On the doorstep the silent boss had extended a hand. 'Macello.

We can do business. Nice place you've got here. Nice place the Castel Grande. This way we get into Europe again through the back door.'

'Why not Italy?'

'Too noisy. No one will suspect this. We call it the English topcoat, *il cappotto inglese*. No one sees what's underneath. It's too thick.'

When he returned to his office the improbability of the whole thing almost made him laugh. He could have dreamed it all up, this nightmare of Hollywood hoods, except for the puddles on the carpet that were turning the previously innocuous pink pile the colour of spilt blood. He looked at the room with fresh eyes. Now that he had opened it up again he would use it as their campaign centre. He had already made up his mind, almost it seemed without a conscious decision. He would fight back with the cunning and the experience life had given him, and Pearse would help him. When he found out what Pearse's problem was they could help each other. They would meet that night and exchange ideas. Orazio felt almost elated.

'Don't worry,' he told Agnese on the telephone, 'I'm dealing with it. You and Stephen just go on as usual.'

'But Papa, what did they want?'

'They're Americans looking for a way into the Common Market, you know, like Japanese cars.' That at least was the truth, though not the whole truth. 'I might do a little business with them. Give me an interest. We'll see.'

The English Police found Pearse first. 'Mr Noonan? Pearse Noonan?' The man on the doorstep flashed some kind of ID under his nose and away like a conjurer while the other stood back leaning against the balustrade and looking about and down.

'Yes?'

'Can we come in?'

Pearse opened the door wider and shut it behind them.

'Have you got your son here, Mr Noonan?'

'No. You can look if you like. You can see there's nowhere to hide anyone.'

The first man nodded to the second who went past Pearse into the kitchen. They heard him open the broom cupboard. Then he came out and went through to the bedrooms to open the wardrobes and push the beds on their castors. He came back and shook his head.

'Have you heard from your son?'

'Not for ten years or so.'

'You know he's on a list of suspected terrorists?'

'I know nothing of his life since he left the University. We didn't keep in touch after my wife died.'

'We have reason to believe he's in this country.'

'Which country would that be?'

The man affected to sigh. 'That he has left Ireland, crossed the water and is now very probably in London.'

'He wouldn't come to me. I told you: we haven't spoken in years.'

'Blood's thicker than water. We believe he's fallen out with his former friends. We want to protect him.'

'Turn him into a supergrass, you mean?'

'If he contacts you, give him that message: that we want to help him. That's all. Give him this number. Tell him he can call it any time.'

Pearse took the piece of card, with the handwritten number trellising the white ground, as if it might be the poisoned chalice itself, and propped it on the mantelpiece.

'I suppose it's no use asking you to let us know if he does contact you?'

'You can ask. I can't stop you.'

'Harbouring a terrorist is a crime in itself.'

'Confucius didn't think so, not if it was your own son.'

'But he was Chinese.'

When they had gone he opened a can of Guinness and tried to calm the thoughts that reared up ungovernably in all directions. Perhaps he should leave the country himself rather than sit here like a fatal magnet drawing Liam and his pursuers towards him.

They were all so sure he was in England that it must be true, yet as surely Liam would realise the flat must be watched and wouldn't try to come there. But who would he turn to for help if not his father? Pearse tried to remember the names of friends Liam had mentioned but it was so long ago. There were the boys and later girls at his comprehensive but as far as Pearse knew none of them had gone on to Belfast with him to the University.

They had lost him so completely at eighteen, he might as well have been drowned on the boat over or fallen out of the sky. After Jessie's death, Pearse had taken irrationally to reading the reports on homeless children, watching the television documentaries in case, when the reporters, social workers, Police flashed their torches into an alleyway, poked a bundle of old clothes into life, Liam's eyes should look up at him blinking out of sleep. Perhaps that was what he ought to do now, take a photograph with him and go looking, ask the people of the alleys and underpasses and waste lots if they had seen Liam, for there was nowhere else he could think of that the boy might hide.

He went over to the oak sideboard and opened the right-hand drawer, hearing the bottles and glasses chink softly together below as he pulled on the hinged metal handle. The sideboard still kept the patina Jessie had polished into it under the film of dust Pearse blew at now, ineffectually. He went into the kitchen and fetched a duster from the unit under the sink and wiped away the reproachful layer, leaving a greasy black line across the yellow cloth. The sideboard was older than Liam, solid dark oak that had belonged originally to Jessie's mother and that had been sent south when she died together with the family photographs, old certificates of births, marriages and deaths, the long slips crumbling at the folds, a ration book from the Second World War, a packet of letters from a mountain pass on the borders of Afghanistan written by a corporal in the Black Watch in 1917, a long-dead brother to his little sister wondering if she'd put her hair up yet, promising her a dress length of blue silk.

They were still there in the drawer but added to, overlain with a further lifetime's snaps, Pearse and Jessie on honeymoon at Scarborough, in the back garden of their first home, a terraced cottage that had been pulled down to make room for the estate where there was to be central heating, running hot water and a lavatory indoors for every household, refinements that private landlords had been unable or unwilling to provide; and Liam. Liam as a baby, a toddler with the sun in his eyes, in a first school photograph and every year after, solo or with his class, with his parents, whichever wasn't pointing the camera, on holiday; on his last day at school with other now lanky young men in shrunken uniforms fooling with caps and cricket bats while the girls formed a chorus line behind. But Liam at university? Missing. There was nothing in the collection that Pearse could show with any conviction that it bore a resemblance to the man Liam now was.

Perhaps they were all wrong and he wasn't in London at all. Perhaps he had gone north to Scotland, to lose himself in Glasgow or Edinburgh, except that there was nobody up there to help him as far as Pearse knew. The most Liam could do was disguise himself in the anonymity of the city. Pearse looked again at the larking teenagers, standing quite still with the picture in his hand as if he could will it to give up some secret he knew it must hold.

He felt a need for action. To walk the streets, even without a recognisable photograph, would be a relief with the illusion that he was doing something. Or he could call the Don. How much though should he tell him? He had never trusted anyone else before. There were things he had never even told Jessie. Well, he would see what the Don had to say for himself.

'Your place or mine?' he heard his own voice asking.

'Perhaps now this place would be better. There's more space here. I think we may need a place to think in, to plan. About eight?'

'I'll be there.'

He felt easier about leaving the flat now that the Police had been. Those others, whoever they were, if they were watching, would have seen his two visitors and known who they were, would believe that they were watching too. Pearse went to his window overlooking the courtyard and stared out at the shoals of sky the colour of a ring his grandmother had worn, milky clouds of cream and duck-egg blue and green like the sea off Kerrera. He and Jessie had gone there once on a ferry from Oban, the only day of their week's holiday it hadn't rained, and walked the rim of the island looking down at the yellow-lichened rocks where the sea boiled like flawed glass till they were giddy and almost missed the boat back.

'What's that called, Granma?'

'That's an opal, my dear. It's a semi-precious stone and unlucky for anyone to wear whose birthstone it isn't.'

'Is it all right for you, Granma?'

'Yes, it's all right for me.'

It all seemed so long ago. He had been born into a world where the little people danced on the hills and now they danced behind a screen in everybody's living room, showing off their lives that were bloodless reflections of human life. He dragged his thoughts back. That was no way to be thinking now.

The watchers might be anywhere, in another flat, in a parked car, walking purposefully through the estate, chatting like lovers on a corner. He put on his jacket and went out. One thing he could do was try to make sure he wasn't followed. Now the rain had stopped, he could take a roundabout route to the Don's, pick up a bottle at the off-licence, saunter, looking in windows, loiter, make a call to himself at the telephone kiosk. Only when he felt he was truly alone would he double back to the big house, checking again as he waited outside the gate to be let in.

The Don met him at the front door but they didn't climb the stairs as usual. Instead, Orazio pushed open a door leading out of the long corridor and showed Pearse into a room with a desk and office chairs. There was a damp patch on the carpet as if an animal had peed there, perhaps one of the cats from the yard, but Pearse's nose didn't back up this interpretation.

'Sit down,' the Don said, 'the chairs are better than they look. A glass of wine?'

'Thanks very much.'

'This used to be my office.'

'It's better than my place. My place is watched, I think.'

'Perhaps this is too, but perhaps not yet.'

They looked at each other for a moment, raising their glasses.

'Here's to us,' Pearse said.

'*A noi.*'

'Now who shall go first? I've already told you a bit about my problem. Perhaps you should begin.'

'We have to trust each other,' the Don said, 'if we are to help each other, to work together.'

'How do we know if we can help each other?'

'Even to have someone to talk to, to discuss with is better. All my life I have been private. Never asked for help before. Perhaps I have been wrong. My wife always said I was too English.'

'I've never really got to the bottom, I mean, never really liked to ask, what nationality you are.'

'I was born in Italy. I went to school in London. Sometimes I don't know what I am or even which language I'm speaking. I don't always know what language I dream in. Sometimes one, sometimes the other. But inside I think I'm always Italian, *la giù*, at the bottom. At home, we spoke Italian. I had to learn English when I went to school so you can say it's my second language. And you?'

'I never learned the Gaelic. It's a language lost to me.'

The Don topped up their glasses. 'Today two men came to see me here in this room.' Pearse found himself drinking too fast and too deep as usual. 'That's where their umbrella rested.' He pointed to the darkened roundel of carpet. 'They were Americans. Italian Americans. I think they are drug dealers. They want to use my restaurant to launder money.'

'Now you've lost me. How could they do that?'

'They would pass the money through my accounts so that it is given a legal existence. Then I will pay it back to them whenever they say, probably through Switzerland or even Italy.'

'But won't it be noticed if your takings suddenly show a big rise?'

'There are always ways to disguise these things. You have heard of creative accounting? And in any case, by the time the Inland Revenue notices they will probably have moved on. I imagine I am not the only one. They could have approached dozens of businesses with Italian owners, offering a percentage for co-operation.'

'And if you don't co-operate?'

'They will send in the heavies and wreck the place with thousands of pounds' damage and loss of customers. If not worse. They may threaten my family, my grandchildren even.'

'Kidnap?' For once Pearse was glad he had no such hostages for the taking.

'Why not? Perhaps they wouldn't do it but they would threaten, and you can never be sure. Now you know my problem.'

Pearse knew it was his turn now. He took a mouthful of gamey wine. 'The Police came to see me today. They're looking for my son, too, just like the others I told you about. They think he's in this country. They want to offer him protection, they say. That means turn him around, use him. Maybe he would co-operate with them. I don't know. I don't know where he is or what he wants, only that they all want him. Anyway, I played the thick Paddy. I told them nothing. What are you going to do?'

'First I shall open a new account for this money they want to give me. I will seem to go along with them. It will give me time to think and keep them away from my family and the business. What will you do?'

'I have to find Liam, my son, before anyone else does, but if I go looking for him I'm afraid I might lead them, either of them, straight to him.'

'I could look. No one would suspect me. I would need a photograph. Where would I begin?'

'I had a vague idea of going round the places where the homeless hang out.'

'Why should he be there, among them?'

'Because there's nowhere else for him to go. Or at least I can't come up with anywhere. Oh, I've thought and thought; gone round and round like the poor hamster in the wheel. We'd no friends who would hide him; no one from his school was his mate who he'd go to. He was always a bit on his own. Got on well enough with the others but never had a best friend he brought home. Took after the both of us too much. We were never great mixers. And people disappear all the time, youngsters. That's where they go: the streets. He'd blend in there. I've always looked for him whenever they show those programmes on the telly, ever since we lost touch.'

The Don nodded his head.

'But for a photograph I've only an old one and he was playing the fool in that. The truth is I might not even recognise me own son.'

'So then you have no advantage over me. See, our collaboration has begun already.'

'But what could I do for you?'

The Don sipped at his glass. 'You can lend me your name, your identity for my bank account. I will open it in your name.'

'Why not invent a new name, a whole person if you want to keep it away from your family?'

'That would be confusing and if anything happened to me no one would know how to get at the money. That could be disastrous for my family. Will you do it?'

'But isn't it all illegal? Isn't it fraud and things like that? You can be put away for a long time.'

'It is illegal. But what they're doing is immoral. And I have no choice. I'm forced into it. Duress is different from intention. And it's only money. No one is killed or broken. Just counters passing. They all play their games with counters in the City, on the stockmarket and the racecourse, between governments. We would be doing nothing but moving the counters.'

Pearse took a swallow at the piece of cold potato that seemed to have stuck in his gullet while he considered. Then: 'You're on,' he said.

The Don brought a piece of paper and a biro out of his desk. 'What's your first name, Mr Noonan?'

'Pearse.'

'Like this?'

'No, with an "s" not a "c".'

'Like this?'

Pearse stared at his own name, in signature but not in his own hand. Some part of him felt suddenly usurped as if he had died a little. Yet he saw the brilliance of it. If anyone enquired he could say with perfect truth that it wasn't his and produce his own with a flourish of complete conviction before their eyes. The Don was signing his name again on a fresh sheet of paper.

'You must keep this and practise it. Then if it's ever needed . . . But hide it carefully.'

Pearse took the sheet of paper and folded it in four. The Don's characters sloped forward fluently where his own were rounded and upright. He would have liked to think he could get it off so pat he could destroy the template but he doubted whether he ever would. He would make a tracing and try to train his hand that way.

'I shall go to some discreet foreign bank. When I have opened the account I'll let you know which and where. I shall need your date of birth. Perhaps it would be best to set up a box number for the address. When were you born?' And when Pearse told him: 'Then we are within a few months of each other.' But he didn't let on which way.

Pearse walked back through empty streets with the red wine threatening to drown him in its bloody tide. Next time he'd take some cans of Guinness with him. That's if there was a next time. He'd come away curiously empty-handed from what he still thought of as 'the old man's house', with nothing to occupy him but the tracing and retracing of his own false name. The transaction demanded trust from both of them. What was to stop the Don assuming all of him, blotting him out? What was to stop himself withdrawing the money and disappearing to begin his life again? Only Liam. Liam was his

hostage. He needed the Don to find him. But when he had . . . ?
Or if he failed? He couldn't think any more. Pearse stepped into
the lift that stank to him tonight of piss and acidified metal. If
anyone was waiting for him above there was nothing he could
do about it. The wine was rising on a wave of bile. He fitted
his key shakily into the lock and staggered into the bathroom
leaving the front door open behind him.

As he hung over the cold whiteness of the pan with the
plastic seat threatening to crash down and brain him if he
didn't hold it up, he thought that humankind is never so
vulnerable as when it's uncontrollably spewing its guts up,
arse in the air. He pulled down the plastic handle and stood up
to hang his head over the washbasin and purse his lips round
the cold tap, rinsing and flushing the taste away before letting
the sweet chill wash down his throat. Wasn't it the cruellest
quirk of nature that conception should be accompanied by
that bitter morning sickness he remembered Jessie sweating
over, and how he'd wipe the draggled hair from her forehead
with a flannel daubed with eau-de-cologne so that afterwards,
when Liam was born, she couldn't abide the sight of even the
bottle in the place.

Only then did he remember the still-open door and close
it before falling onto the double bed.

Left alone, Orazio took the dregs of the wine and the two
glasses up to his kitchen where he washed Pearse's glass and
stood it on the rack to drain while he emptied the remains of the
bottle into his own and switched on the television. He hoped the
Irishman was reliable. He drank a lot. That might be a danger.
He was intelligent, Orazio could tell from his chess-playing, but
not so well-educated: the softer Benedictines rather than the
tough intellectual school of the Jesuits.

A wildlife documentary chased across the screen while he
waited for the news with the sound turned down. Handsome,
striped in navy and cream, killer whales tossed an innocent seal
pup in the air with their sycamore-key tails, before crunching
on it, as one of Ruby Heamans' cats might play with a mouse.
The seals scuba-diving through shrouding veils of water closed

their jaws on silver blades of mackerel whose bellies were stuffed with penknife sprat. Sea eagles scooped up the young of puffin to disgorge into their own gaping chicks. Wasps laid eggs in ladybirds to eat a way out, when they were hatched, through the stylish jackets of the aphid munchers. Nothing was wasted. It was Occam's razor, as he had been taught at school, made flesh and blood. *Entia non sunt multiplicanda praeter necessitatum.* And there was no necessity for multiplication, for adding to. Give or take a sweeping or so of interstellar gas and the odd asteroid, the earth was stable. No matter how much it seemed to increase its numbers of populations, its weight would stay the same until the moment when it began to burn and give off its gases fast enough to escape: until meltdown. Meanwhile, it endlessly recycled. The elements of dinosaurs were the constituents of late-twentieth-century leaf and limb. Earth's guiding principle was Occam's razor of cruel economy and the god who had set it going, devised this blade-sharp simplicity, was an indifferent mechanic for whom the individual bundles of re-used materials could have no meaning as they coalesced briefly and then fell apart to reassemble, endlessly, as long as time ran.

It was the first time in forty-five years that Orazio hadn't shaved in the morning. The pepper and salt on his chin was like rubbed-in dirt by the time Ruby Heamans rang the bell. 'I'm going shopping,' he said. He had looked through his wardrobe that morning and decided everything was too good for his purposes. His own neatness defeated him. His suits hung straight, cleaned and pressed from their hangers. These weren't clothes he could seek out the homeless in. He would have been a walking insult.

There were a couple of charity shops in the market street, where he'd seen racks of clothes beyond the windows, with people sorting through them, a latterday gleaning or coal picking. Amateur totters scavenged through the cardboard boxes of frayed shirts and rubbed sweaters, bearing the impress of the other bodies that had inhabited them for a time, worn them to eat and drink in, to dance or squabble or slump in a chair.

One window of the first shop was used to display a choice ware, a silver viscose sheath that glittered with promise of a night out, a ghost of the woman who had given up on it: in death, or too stout, too old. It hinted at the hands, her own or another's, that had finally taken it down and brought it here. The other window held a collection of cloudy glasses and knives with loose handles, plated forks scrubbed down to the brassy bone, a faded Japanese paper fan, a brown teapot with a small chip on its spout, a huge white bear new in its cellophane wrapper, the object of a raffle. Inside there were volunteers, cousins-german of Ruby Heamans, to process the goods and collect the small change. And there were the punters, the bargain hunters, and the shelf of thumbed books Orazio turned to first while he gathered his courage to approach the clothes rail. The books were leftovers too: of battles with trigonometry in navy blue hard covers, or with the geography of vanished nations and tribes; perished book club relics of schemes for self-improvement and right, which might be left, thinking on mealy paper with optimistic art deco coverings; and, gilt on pale yellow buttermilk or strawberry milkshake, the names that had once been household words. Then there were the softbacks in their cracked garish laminates, the corners dog-eared, the paper already biscuit-coloured after a couple of years, sucked dry of dream juice by a succession of avid eyes and sweaty fingers. Orazio turned them over distastefully: *sporchi* was so much more pungent than merely 'dirty'. He must stop prevaricating and make himself join the treasure seekers in the middle.

Part of his difficulty was that he was too well-turned-out to be looking for cast-offs. Orazio pushed the wire coat hangers along the rail, pulling a pair of jeans, a jacket, a shirt towards him to inspect and then letting them drop back. The jacket was snatched up even as he loosened his grip, as if his singling it out had made it more desirable. There seemed to be nothing that would remotely fit him. Perhaps he should try the next shop further down the road.

He saw at once that the prices in here were higher, the

clientèle different, mostly young girls. He had read about the children of the rich clothing themselves in charity shops and had thought of it as just a piece of journalism. Now he realised it was simply true. Where the children of the poor shopped in emporia for shining shoddy new, these sought out the eccentrically-styled among the cast-offs. Both looked for the easy throw-away-without-regret in continued pursuit of novelty. The English who had once been the most formal, who had taught him his own rectitude, had become anarchic to the point of the bizarre, keeping only a core at the heart of the City of executive blue- and grey-suited conformity. This shop was even less to his purpose. He must go back to the other one and force himself to make choices.

Pearse woke with a thick head. At some time during the night he had struggled out of sleep and his clothes and sunk back again. His eyes focused blurrily on his watch. It was nine o'clock. What day was it? Yesterday had been Sunday so today must be Monday and he was promised to the widow Pritchard, Lady Nicole Pritchard. He'd said he'd put her in a couple of extra points and mend her record player if he could. It would probably turn out to be no more than the fuse. Pearse drank several cups of his rich brown tea and chewed a piece of toast to steady his hand and his stomach. Then he sorted out his box of tricks and set off for the underground and Huntington Gardens. It was a good thing he had a job to do. It would keep his mind off Liam.

The big shabby house was part of a handsome avenue, tree-lined, porticoed, where Pearse had had his last official job, the gutting of one of the mid-Victorian town houses and its reconstitution for an electronics millionaire to the standards of higher design conformity, an opulent De Mille production of marble and ceramics and gilded bath fittings.

Lady Pritchard opened the door to him.

'I'm sorry if I'm a bit on the late side. I was out drinking with an Italian friend last night. I can't take the red wine. I'm better on the Guinness.'

'Come into the kitchen and I'll make us some coffee.'

She sat him down at the table and switched on the kettle.

'How are they getting on at number twenty?' Pearse asked about his former employment.

'It's up for sale. They've never lived in it. I think he's gone bust. And now they never will. They say an Arab diplomat is after it.'

Pearse knew what the upshot would be. The new owners would rip out the costly interior and refashion it all after their own taste. The baths that had never been lain in would be smashed out with a sledgehammer, the wiring torn from the walls and rerouted from switches that had never had a finger on them but his own. He had seen a working lifetime of glittering waste as waves of fashion flushed through the houses he lighted, tearing at their innards to toss them onto skip and waste tip, delicate plasterwork, carved fireplaces, claw-footed baths, fretted banisters feeding the bonfire on a cold day. He had seen them destroyed and then come round again in replica, lamented and recreated. He supposed it had always been so. Humankind had followed fashion ever since trade began. No doubt the old Pharaohs tarted up their pyramids in a new style every generation but now it was so much faster.

'Seems crazy to me. Spend all that money and never live in a place.' It had stood there in empty perfection for three years at least. He gazed around at Lady Pritchard's kitchen. 'You don't go in for change.'

'I doubt if I've altered anything since Emrys died. Not because of him. He was a difficult man. We only just rubbed along together. But then I'm not easy. He always said it was the music kept us going.' She had been a concert pianist under his conductor's baton.

Pearse looked at the fine bones of her small head in its halo of golden dyed hair and the arthritically-knotted fingers that gripped the handle of her coffee-mug. The stick she needed to lean on heavily as she walked dangled from a loop of tape around her neck. 'That way I can't ever find myself stranded somewhere without it.' They had met when he was working on number twenty and she had called in through the open front door of a house clamorous with building workers to see if someone could get into the home she had locked herself out of. Pearse had obliged, forcing up a window stuck fast with paint.

'You'd better fit a new catch to that now or you'll have someone else getting in,' he had advised her and found himself doing the job on Saturday morning for a fiver which he'd tried to refuse.

'We have to have a proper arrangement if you're going to do jobs for me,' she'd insisted, assuming that this would be a recurring if not perhaps permanent feature of their lives. And that was how it had begun. Now she kept a can of Guinness for him in the cellar just in case. He thought of her as 'the old Lady' with a capital 'L'. The house was a bit like Miss Haversham's, not dirty of course, she had someone to see to that, but as if time had stood still, shabbily declining. 'Like its owner,' she would say with a smile that transfigured her face. The garden was her preferred domain and this morning after he had finished the job she took him out onto the terrace, into the late September sun where she had laid out sandwiches and biscuits and his can of black beer under a trellis of heavy-headed roses.

'You could be anywhere out here,' she said. 'Why go all the way to Chiantishire?' There was a green lawn and a fishpond, where black and gold fish waved leisurely elegant tails, and narrow beds stuffed with flowers in their last bloom of the year, some with seedpods that rattled as they knocked together when a breeze skimmed through them.

She had met Emrys Pritchard when they were both students at the Royal College of Music just before the war and been bowled over by his class-warrior's authority among the boys and girls fresh out of private school. He had taken her to his depressed South Wales mining village and shown her things her comfortable professional upbringing in Lewes hadn't prepared her for. His anger fuelled his study and drove him upwards until, when the war interrupted, he enlisted in the Artists' Rifles and made quick sergeant. They were married on his first leave. When it was all over he'd come home even more full of angry overdrive that had forced her back to her neglected practice, and then on world tours until the British establishment was made to recognise his strength and his reputation and call him home, and her with him.

'I always felt when I sat down to play that I wasn't really good enough but Emrys made me play better than I could. Like Svengali, you know.

'You can't do what isn't in you,' Pearse had said when she had told him this under the influence of a lunchtime glass of white wine, while he downed a second Guinness.

'He didn't want to take the knighthood but the miner's son couldn't refuse it for the conductor, for music. In the end he saw it as "having one back on the buggers",' she laughed, imitating Pritchard's accent. 'He was like a galeforce wind, a vortex that whirled me up and sucked me down so that when he died it was as if I'd had all the breath knocked out of my lungs and had to learn to breathe again, calmly: in, out; in, out.' She orchestrated this with a hand on her bosom which, Pearse suddenly realised, was still firm and round against her small frame.

'Would you play me something?' he had once asked, seeing the lid of the baby grand was up showing the two toothy rows of keys.

'My hands are too stiff. I'd make mistakes.'

'What would that matter?'

'What shall I play you?'

'Do you know any of the Irish songs?'

She thought for a moment and then moved towards the piano stool and sat down. She let the knobbly fingers trickle out notes up and down, flexing themselves in a run that seemed beautiful enough itself to Pearse. Then she began to etch out a tune. 'Ah,' he said, ' "She Moved Through The Fair", that's the finest of them all but wouldn't it make you weep like a child for everything lost?'

'Do you have any news of your son?' she asked now as if

somehow she had a spyhole into his head and could pick out his chief preoccupation from the surrounding chaos.

He wondered how much to tell her. If he spoke, the number of those sharing his problem would double. Jessie had never been a great one for confidences. Keep yourself to yourself had been her watchword. What he'd told the Don had been true. She'd never gossiped or even had women friends after they were married, mates to have a night out with, any more than he'd had, other than casual pub acquaintances. 'Tongue-wagging's just a waste of time.' Something in her upbringing had made it hard for her to talk even to him and Liam, except when grief or anger tore the words out of her, and this had made Pearse draw back too, afraid of appearing a garrulous Paddy. Only when he'd told the boy the stories had his speech flowed.

'He's in a bit of trouble,' he heard himself saying. 'I had the Police call yesterday wanting to talk to him.'

'I thought he was in Ireland.'

'So did I but they think he's here somewhere. They say they want to protect him but I don't know . . .'

'I never quite understood whether he was in the North or the South.'

Pearse watched a red admiral homing in on a clump of blue-fringed Michaelmas daisies whose yellow cushions were the shopping mall for a côterie of butterflies, and brown bees with their miniature chainsaw buzz. 'Neither did I. He was in Belfast for the University. Then he went down to Dublin and after that . . .' They'd had a postcard from Arklow showing the seafront. 'I doubt if this bit has changed much, Dada, but I don't think you'd recognise much else. No more thatched cottages in the town.' But he wouldn't have been living there. It must have been a trip he'd taken. At least it showed he still thought about them.

'About you,' Jessie had said when he'd tried to comfort her with this suggestion. If only there'd been other children. If only the wee girl Jennifer, their first child, hadn't died. Always Jessie had been afraid of losing Liam too when he was a baby, until he went to school and then it was as if the umbilical cord of her concern could be finally cut and the boy set free to run and play, and fall over, to get up again and run on.

'But he hasn't been in touch with you?'

'No, he hasn't. And I don't know how to get hold of him.' He wondered how the Don was making out; if he'd started his quest yet.

'Even if you knew where he was, you couldn't take him home, not with such callers.'

'You're right there.' Pearse laughed and stood up. 'I must be going. Thank you for the bit of lunch.'

Lady Pritchard stood up too, taking her stick from round her neck and preceding him to the door.

'If you find him you could bring him here. After all, there's room enough and nobody would think of that. I have very good relations with the local Police. They often see me across the road. They think I'm a dear old lady and not subversive because I'm not young, or black, or male.'

She had once said to Pearse: 'That first time Emrys took me to his home in South Wales made a socialist of me because I'd never seen anything like the depression there and though they tell us things have changed, I've never seen that they've changed so much or so unchangeably so that they couldn't ever be put back. I mean so much that I have to change with them.'

'That's kind but I couldn't bring trouble on you, involve you in that sort of thing.'

'Nonsense. I'm not involved in enough. Oh, I do my bit for the Musicians' Benevolent Fund but it's hardly exciting. I'd like a bit of excitement again before I die. You just remember that. After all, can you think of a safer place?'

Orazio had to wait until Ruby Heamans had finished and left before he could try on his new old clothes. He thought she'd looked curiously at his stubbled chin and charity plastic bags. Perhaps she suspected incipient senility, the beginning of the long or short slide downhill into oblivion, living or dead. He felt a sense of excitement as he dropped his own clothes from his bony shanks and pulled these strange ones into place. The clothes he had called his own had been a lifelong disguise for the controlled turmoil battened down inside him. Now he saw himself in the long wardrobe mirror, transformed. He would go into the courtyard and scrape dirt under his too-clean fingernails, bark his knuckles on the concrete David's great kneecaps.

What he saw wasn't someone else, only himself set free, in thin grey flannels and a navy blue jacket that hung from his shoulders as from its previous hanger, seemingly with no one inside, a no one he could remake as he wished. The possibilities dazzled him. He could assume other personae simply with a change of clothes. All his life had been an impersonation. Why stop at one? Why not a whole range now that there was no one to see, now that Catterina's pain no longer tied him to just his everyday self?

He mustn't be seen going out and that was a problem he turned over as he chewed on a handful of black olives, carefully defleshing each salty stone before lining it up on the plate and taking another. There was a back gate to the courtyard, disused and bolted for many years in deference to Catterina's fear of intruders. Orazio switched on the cellar light and descended the stairs carefully into the mildew-smelling catacomb. No one would mummify here. They would rot and stink. Perhaps he should ask in his will that he be sent back for burial where he could lie in warm dry earth. He opened a rusty tool chest and brought out a hammer and screwdriver. Maybe he would need pliers too. He added them to the collection and then sought along the row of dusty cans and bottles until he found a small square tin of damp-start, rust dispeller, and carried the lot upstairs, glad to be returned from that grave into even the half-light above. Then he opened the back door and went out into the yard where the afternoon was fading into early crepuscule.

The statues crowded around him, peering over his shoulder, jostling each other to see what he would do. If he'd turned suddenly he might have caught a flicker of movement. One, a dying Gaul, propped himself up in extremis on his plinth barring Orazio's access to the gate. He would have to move him before he could begin undoing the locks. He was too heavy for Orazio to lift. He tried dragging the figure towards him but he didn't budge. He turned with his back against the young warrior and shoved. Finally he took one end and tried to swing him diagonally sideways, cantilevering against the other. He moved, only two inches, but he moved. Orazio tried again, painstakingly, until there was room to insert himself behind and he could lean weakly against the door aware of his pounding heart.

The bolts, top and bottom of the locks, were rusted in hard but the key was still there, though fallen to the ground under the statue and disclosed only by its removal. He wasn't to be defeated now though. He squirted lubricant liberally at each of them and forced himself to wait a full minute before he struck the bolts with the hammer, forcing them back in their sockets and then turned the key with the pliers. Now he paused to listen for footsteps on the other side of the wall. He would have to risk it. He pulled on the latch. At first the door didn't give, sealed in by years of accumulated dirt, lichen and paint, but Orazio heaved again and suddenly the door fell back with him clinging to it and rammed him against the dying Gaul, with a muffled squeal from the jamb as if this tearing-open after so many years was painful to it. Quickly Orazio pulled himself off the statue and poked his head into the street. There was no one about. The piece of waste where the council bin-lorries were parked reeking of their cargoes of refuse was otherwise empty and silent. He re-positioned the door, sliding the bolts to and fro until they ran easily, and then went back into the house to recover with a glass of cognac.

He didn't know if he had the strength to set out now. The Irishman would be wanting news of his son and here Orazio sat, exhausted as much by the novelty of the day as by his physical efforts. If he were to die now sitting in his chair unshaven in his strange clothes, what would people think when they found him; perhaps Agnese, having tried to telephone and receiving no answer, knowing his habits so well, or Ruby Heamans unable to get in, calling the police and finding him there with the glass fallen from his hand. *Non sum qualis eram* he remembered from his old namesake: I'm not the man I was: *non sono più com' ero*.

Was it sensible after all to go out at night in the dark when he would have to stumble around flashing a torch in people's faces, at anonymous bundles that might react aggressively to being disturbed? On the other hand, he could hardly walk through Deverham in daylight in these clothes. He would have to fold them as small as possible and take them out in a carrier bag, find a *gabinetto* somewhere and change inside, one of the new round portables might be best, more private than an ordinary gents'. He thought he had seen one just before the church, near the English bakery that sold the soft cotton-wool bread he never ate. So tonight he should plan his route, rest, go to bed early and begin again in the morning. Somewhere, he remembered, he had read an article on homelessness which gave a convenient list of the main places where those sleeping rough were to be found.

Orazio went to the cupboard where the back numbers of newspapers were stored for Ruby Heamans to bear away. Cat rescue seemed to involve a lot of newspapers and she had long ago trained him not to waste any. He went through them systematically having in his mind's eye the position of the article he was after in the top half of a left-hand page: two long columns on the right, and found it, a fortnight back. Just in time: another day or two and it would have been carried off.

There was the list as he'd remembered it: six areas he would have to search unless he was lucky and found an answer soon. He fetched his London Streetfinder from the sitting-room cabinet where the small store of books lived, mostly from his antique-collecting days, along with an English dictionary, an Italian-English dictionary, some school books of Agnese's and a couple of religious volumes in black and red belonging to Catterina, as well as his own childhood Missal from his days as altarboy, with his name in it, that she had asked him for when he had been going to throw it away.

Now that he looked at them again the listed areas seemed to cover the whole of the centre of London, particularly the mainline stations where travellers came into the city full of hope and got no further than the nearest piece of wasteland or hot air grille in the pavement: Victoria, Waterloo, King's Cross, the Strand. Then there were what might be called landfill sites: Lincoln's Inn Fields, the City, the West End. It could take him days, perhaps weeks to reconnoitre them all. How would Garibaldi have planned such a campaign? A pity he didn't have a thousand to help him.

He turned to the map in the front of the book which showed the whole of London divided into a grid. If he thought of it as a huge target, he could begin with the furthest out of the concentric rings, at the point nearest to home, and work his way in. Or he could begin at the bull's-eye and work his way back. Perhaps he should throw darts at it. That might give him as clear an answer as any other method. No, reason must prevail. If that failed, what else was there? Orazio poured himself another glass and studied the map again. Acknowledging his own limitations he should begin closest to home, work his way towards the centre and give up when he began to flag.

'Everything is ready,' he said a little later into the receiver. 'I begin tomorrow morning.' He wasn't sure if he detected disappointment in Noonan's voice. Orazio went to the stove and put on some water with a stock cube to boil. He would make himself *pastina in brodo*, comforting invalid's food. He shook the little pasta stars into the boiling broth and stirred. Later he set the alarm for five-thirty and went to sleep surprisingly well.

The old round alarm clock woke him on time as it had once woken him every morning to go to the markets to choose the best, only the best, for the Castel Grande; especially the fish whose skins must gleam with freshness, the rubbery jelly of squid and cuttlefish be translucent, the eyes of red mullet and sole be undimmed as sequins, the mussels in tight black buds, the cockles prick-new. An early start would make it less likely that he would be seen by anyone who knew him. Even Ruby Heamans wouldn't be abroad yet although she had often, he knew, visited a couple of her cat sites before she came to him.

The clothes that had so excited him the day before had been stripped of their transforming magic overnight. When he tried them on this morning he saw only himself in the mirror, a destitute ageing self, but himself. Perhaps it was the shirt and the knowledge of his own singlet, pants and socks underneath the façade. Anyone stripping off the outer layer would know he was a fraud but he'd felt his stomach turn at the thought of second-hand underwear, even an alien shirt, ingrained, frayed at collar and cuffs with the friction of another's skin, resting against his own. He slipped a slim flask of cognac into a back pocket and buttoned it down. There was hardly any bulge and the jacket covered it. How much money should he take?

Orazio unstrapped his watch and left it on the bedside table with his wallet. Then he put on his own jacket and trousers and bundled the others into a plastic carrier covering them with a layer of newspaper. He looked down at his shoes, saw they wouldn't do and rummaged in the back of the wardrobe until he found an older pair that had escaped being thrown out. They were covered in that mixture of dust and fluff we and our habitat secrete in a dry sweat, a scurf of discarded cells and fibres, but when he wiped it away they still shone with polishing. He would have to dull them down to anonymity. He fetched a scouring pad and detergent. When their shine was scrubbed away he put a twenty-pound note wrapped in plastic film in the sole of each and slipped them on his bony feet.

In the kitchen he drank three cups of sweetened espresso and ate a couple of pieces of melba toast. Suddenly he saw himself a student again in a Perugia *latteria*, his nose over a big bowl of *caffelatte*, eating a custard cake held in a thin paper square for some long-ago breakfast, the savours filling his nostrils and mouth with a vanished milky sweetness and, further back still, a frothy squirt from his grandmother's goat in a blue bowl he was raising to his lips.

The street outside was still dark, suffused only by the bilious light from the streetlamps craning their necks towards the road. The few people about paid him no attention. Orazio walked briskly down the street where the market would be later, and shut himself in the oval tin and plastic coffin of a portable lavatory where he stripped off and replaced his own jacket and trousers and emerged into a greying world. He would take the bus to Victoria and begin there, look for a coffee stall where he could observe while he sipped. At the bus stop there were mostly women on their way to office-cleaning jobs, who met here every morning laughing and joking to keep out the cold, perhaps mocking him as they chatted together, breaking out in too-loud laughter. He didn't know what women talked about alone together, outside their families. When the bus came he scrambled upstairs out of their reach.

Victoria reminded him of those pre- and post-war journeys before flying became a commonplace, when people, except the very few, still went by train, and boat over the water, and then more train, and the station seethed with excitement and the fear of missed connections, lost luggage, of sitting all night on your suitcase in the corridor, being seasick; when there was still the smack of travel, and the journey was an adventure in itself rather than a frightening whisk from point to point, featureless as airline food. Orazio got off the bus in the station forecourt and began to act his part, shuffling, peering about as if in search of a place to lie down. Passers-by, he noticed, ostentatiously didn't notice him, afraid that at any moment he might stretch out a dirty paw and detain them or even simply thrust it into their line of vision, palm up.

He shambled his way into the echoing station hall and found a coffee machine that gave him a hot bitter liquid tasting of ground acorns, that he took to a station bench. The couple occupying it got up at his approach leaving him alone. He understood the isolation of the destitute. They had expected him at least to smell or be a nuisance. His clothes, his way of life were an affront to their own but also a warning like the damned in the great mediaeval dooms: there but for the grace of thrift, a salary, restraint, you might end up in the red-hot tongs of drink and neglect that would drag you into the fires from which there was no escape. The Fathers had been particularly inventive on the subject of Hell and the wretches who would find themselves there, especially schoolboys.

It was strange to be a watcher when everyone else was on the move, or almost everyone. At least it made things easy. His quarry was those like himself who were still while others flowed round them. Some were staff, perhaps Transport Police. A bundle of an old woman had found another bench and was sorting through her bags of belongings, scavengings. Layers of clothing were wound and pinned about her so that it was impossible to guess her real size and shape. Even her head was tightly bound in a balaclava under a woollen scarf so that she seemed as hairless as a nun.

Quartering the station hall systematically as far as he could see, Orazio finally came to rest on a group of youngsters, *guaglioni* of both sexes, one or two he thought only just past school age smoking and gossiping. Occasionally one would drift away about some business or another would join. The group changed constantly but remained essentially the same like the pieces in a kaleidoscope. The children, for so they mostly seemed to him, had the drawn yet frenetic look of Dickensian waifs or else seemed dulled, inert, stupefied rather than stupid. Most of them were much younger than Liam would be but they might promise a clue. He could follow one of them and try to speak. That would be easier. He couldn't imagine himself tackling the whole group, even in his disguise. But he would have to make a move soon. The station was beginning to fill with rush-hour commuters. Doors slammed, people shoved, scrambled. Soon he wouldn't be able to see anything in the press. He sipped the disgusting brown fluid in its white plastic cup.

He was rewarded eventually by an older boy detaching himself from the group to saunter towards Orazio's bench. For a moment he thought the boy might be going to sit there too or even to speak to him. Perhaps he'd been observed observing too closely. Words in defence formed themselves in his mind: that he wasn't staring, was half-blind, couldn't see so only appeared to be staring. 'Got your eyeful? What you bossing at?' The old playground jibes came back to him. But the boy, thin and fair with a white clown's face, was passing him by. Orazio stood up and put out a hand.

'Excuse me . . .'

The boy swung round alert, suspicious. 'What you want?'

'Do you know Liam, Liam Noonan?'

'What sort of question's that? You fuzz?'

'No, no.'

'What you want then? Got any dosh?'

Dosh, what was that? It might mean anything. Drugs, maybe. He could be deep in trouble and he'd hardly begun.

'No, no.'

'You can't have it then. I don't give it away.'

It was like a foreign language, neither English nor Italian, the language of group or cult, allusive, succinct, excluding the outsider. Yet, although he didn't know the vocabulary or syntax, the meaning was becoming clear.

'Wise up, Dad. You do want it, don't you? But you can't have it for nothing and it costs more for old geezers. You haven't even got the price of a bed.'

'No, no, you're wrong. I'm trying to find Liam, an Irishman, early thirties. He owes me money,' he invented furiously. 'I need it for today, tonight.'

'Why ask me?'

'I have to ask everybody. He told me he came here sometimes.'

'If he did he was having you on. What would an old guy in his thirties be doing here? Once you're over twenty-five that's it. The punters want chicken not scrag. I'll give you a tip. If he's around he'll be dossing down in the Fields or under the arches, Waterloo maybe but not the station. Stations is for people going somewhere, on the make. Get me? Anyway I can't stand here gassing to you. I've got to get me head down. It's been a long night.' And he was gone, carried away by the increasing crowd.

Obviously it was no good hanging on there. The whole station was seething with travellers. Any hope of singling someone out and questioning them had passed and when Orazio turned back towards the group he found that it had all dissolved, sucked into the outward flows from the platforms, and he could no longer distinguish any of its members in the flush of bodies.

He found himself shaking a little. 'Not the stations,' the boy had said: the stations were for trade, rent, for boys and girls, not for grown men and women, unless like the bag lady they'd come to rest temporarily, out of the creeping damp of autumn. Orazio picked up his own plastic bag and got up. He would walk towards Westminster and then take a bus to the Aldwych. He set off out of the station down Victoria Street with its swarms of office workers flowing in both directions, purposeful as ant hordes along a trail. He understood how it would feel not to be part of this movement but purposeless, stock-still in its path or pushed to one side. You would be walked over by the unconscious feet, at best ignored, at worst devoured and the tough or bony bits spat out.

The older way had been to look after each other with that altruism the wildlife programmes sometimes showed in rudimentary forms, when groups of elephants tried to protect and nudge a tottering youngster to its feet or chimpanzees offered food to a sickly member of the tribe, seemingly contrary to the universal law he saw all round him of survival of the fittest, economic evolutionism. He thought of the boys he had brought over at their parents' request, trained as waiters and chefs, given jobs, board and lodging and pocket money too. Now such trainees probably had to pay to learn. He must ask Agnese.

Beside him the office blocks with their skirts of lit shop fronts had fallen away so that he was crossing the open piazza in front of Westminster Cathedral's Byzantine brick. There were benches with an assortment of occupants: some visitors consulting their guide books; others the prone shapes of sleepers. Perhaps Liam Noonan was among them. A coach drew up disgorging more tourists onto the pavement to pop their cameras or sweep the scene with a whirr of their cam-corders before streaming towards the building. The next office cliff closed in on the street, the blank windows of the Department of Trade and Industry, with a cloistered walk under a brutal overhanging rampart that could provide a little shelter from the weather for walkers. In a corner of a disused doorway was a huddled bundle.

Orazio slowed his approach. Should he speak to it? The shape was male but the coat pulled up over the head, hiding the face, made it impossible to tell more. If he didn't ask, didn't risk abuse or making a fool of himself he would never find Liam. He stopped and looked down. Then he bent, stretched out a hand and touched the jacketed shoulder. There was an instant flash of movement. The hand was withdrawn from its cover and black eyes looked up at him in mixed terror and anger. The boy was ready to spring up. Perhaps he had a knife. Orazio stepped back.

'I'm sorry. I'm looking for someone. Liam Noonan. Have you seen him?'

The eyes regarded him for a moment, retreating to dull stones, like drying slate, from the emotions that had briefly fired them. The jacket was pulled up again and the bundle folded back into its corner.

Orazio turned away and walked on towards Westminster. It was all proving more difficult than he could have imagined. He had only faintly grasped the resentment, the withdrawal to a closed world of these fringe-dwellers. He hadn't really thought that what he was doing was dangerous. The Irishman would have been better at it: stronger, closer to this world Orazio was trying to penetrate. He had to have luck. Without it his quest was hopeless and there wasn't even any guarantee that Liam Noonan was hidden among these outcasts. He might be safe in someone's house or flat; hiding out with a girlfriend perhaps. Meanwhile Orazio's own problem hadn't gone away. He would have to give that some time and thought soon.

The pale sunlight filtered through the dusty windows of the top of the doubledecker, warming his knees where it fell across them as the bus crept round Trafalgar Square and up the Strand. He got off at the Waldorf where he had been only once, many years ago, when he was looking at other places to see how he should lay out the Castel Grande. It had still been glamorous then with a painted Thirties theatrical look. Now there was a 'theatre bar' serving snacks and drinks. He turned up Kingsway leaving the dully imposing island of Bush House and the Indian High Commission at his back and walked in his invisible man's cloak of indigence up to the traffic lights where the railings stopped and he could cross at last and follow the sign back again for Lincoln's Inn Fields into what he saw with surprise was called Sardinia Street. He hoped it was a good omen. He had never left Kingsway before to see what lay behind its breadth. He only knew that this was the old legal quarter of the city at the back of the Law Courts. The map had told him Lincoln's Inn Fields was in here somewhere but now he doubted whether this could be the right area as he passed men and women in black courtroom clothes with white ruffles and smart briefcases. How could there be a place for the drunks and the other assorted homeless in the middle of all this?

At the end of the short road he glimpsed the greenness of leaves. Sardinia Street was leading him into a big square with trees and grass in the middle and tall handsome terraces all round. He caught the flash of leaping figures, the sound of a racquet hitting a tennis ball and its explosion off the court. Four young men were playing energetically, calling out to each other as the ball twanged and ricocheted between them. Now he was passing a long block he saw was the Imperial Cancer Research Institute. Opposite on the far side of the square he could read the title of the building that faced it: Equity and Law. But where were the dispossessed? He turned his attention back to the grass and trees, walking towards a gap in the rails surrounding them that ushered in a path across the middle. And suddenly he saw, here and there, unobtrusive at first among the low shrubs, a series of structures made of cardboard and plastic and various kinds of cloth, canvas, blanket, quilt, with one or two tents smart enough for Everest, neatly pegged out, one with a bicycle chained to a neighbouring tree. A figure rose from an older, more ragged tent as he passed, a young man with tousled dark hair and a darkened unwashed face.

'Have you got the time?'

Orazio looked instinctively for his watch but then remembered he'd left it behind and shook his head. Some of the structures, benders he'd read they were called, were grouped together in a village of soft igloos. 'I'm looking for a friend,' Orazio said when he told the young man he hadn't the time.

'Ask them.' The young man nodded towards the clutch of benders where other figures were emerging and a black-and-white collie had begun to bark and gambol about. 'I don't know no one.' His face was sullen and bewildered. Orazio walked on, spotting more shacks among the distant trees and a wooden structure like a disused bandstand where two or three men were gathered. From a long forgotten geography lesson he retrieved the word yurt, the name for the felt huts lived in by some tribes of steppe nomads.

As he approached the men he caught the sweetish rancid smell of unwashed bodies in slept-in clothes.

'Does anyone here know Liam Noonan?'

'Who wants him?'

'I do.'

'And who might you be when you're at home?' The bald man with the moustache, in a shiny navy suit, had taken on the role of spokesman. The others laughed and stamped their feet.

'Just a friend.'

'A nark. A rozzer in civvies, more like.'

'Just a friend. I've got a message for him.'

'A ball and chain.' The man looked at Orazio angrily. Then as suddenly he seemed to relent. 'He ain't here. I know everyone on this manor. He'd be an Irishman by the sound of his handle. There's only one Irish here. That's Mick. How old's this Noonan?'

'Thirty-something.'

'Mick's fifty, going on sixty. 'Tain't him. Try the Crypt. They might know.'

'The Crypt?'

'Down St Martin's. Trafalgar Square. Where you been dragged up?'

'Thanks. I'll try that.' He wondered whether he should offer him money but decided it would be out of character. Instead, Orazio touched his hand to his forehead in salute and moved on. He sensed no violence in the men, not physical violence but an anger, a verbal aggression that made him wary. Later they would be mollified by drink, he imagined, later still shouting and staggering their own way back to crawl into their hovels and collapse. He wondered about the neat tent with the parked bicycle. That was more how he imagined Liam might be. But he didn't know. He realised he knew nothing about him except that he had once been clever, a bright boy who went to university.

For a moment he risked half-turning to look back at the men but they had gone back to their own concerns and the one in the shiny navy suit was shouting at the collie to curb its exuberant to-and-fro. Something about the whole episode had the familiarity of the revisited but he couldn't remember from where. Not the internment camp. That had been quite different. And then he remembered. He saw himself reading Italian Literature for Higher Schools. The book must be still there on his shelf with the missals and the dictionaries. At least it should be though he hadn't seen it the other day. What he was remembering, the angry man who gnawed upon himself, wasn't real. He was one of the damned in Dante's *Inferno*. The whole group might have sprung out of those dark cantos.

He retraced his steps to where he had got off the bus and then walked down the Strand until he could turn up towards St Martin's-in-the-Fields. Suddenly he was in the middle of a craft fair of stalls glowing with Oriental and Asian stuffs and jewels, a bazaar brightening the grey morning. He went from one to the other wondering if he should buy something for Agnese and then, remembering his disguise and that most of his money apart from a few coins was in his shoes, shuffled away before he could be accused of loitering with intent, towards the side of the church where an arch gaped above stone steps, a hell-mouth where the damned might descend.

As they were doing, Orazio saw, and found himself in his turn going down into a long stone cavern lit by neon strips with benches where men and even a few women stood or sat sipping on paper cups. At the far end the crowd was denser and he couldn't see what was happening but he guessed that food and drink were being dispensed. In front of him was a man dressed all in faded green, topped by a green forage cap. Behind him Orazio could hear other feet beginning to descend. He would be boxed in, unable to escape, entombed in this vault of shadowy strangers. He felt panic threatening to engulf him. He couldn't go on. He turned and began to climb up again towards the daylight, aware that he was passing a glass door on his right that opened into some kind of office where he might have asked about Liam Noonan. But it was no good. He had to get out, Lazarus-like, out of this tomb before the chill despair from the walls ate into his flesh and bone.

'Have they done? Are they closing?' a man called out to him at the top.

'No, no. Not yet.'

He stumbled round to the front of the church. His heart was knocking in his chest so that he couldn't breathe and there was a sea-shell roar in his ears. He must sit down somewhere. He turned into the church itself through heavy wooden doors pushed open by visitors who paused to admire the ceiling, the monuments. Orazio was grateful for the warmth and light. He sank back in a deep wooden pew and rested his head in his hands while he waited for his heart to steady.

Above all, he longed for the comfort of hot coffee but the sign he had passed advertising a café in the crypt seemed only to mock. He had begun to feel like the outcast he was impersonating, unfit to go among ordinary people, to sit at a table with them. He must find a hamburger stall where he could stand unnoticed and where the small change in his pocket would be enough to buy him something hot. The day was passing and all he had managed to do was eliminate a couple of possibilities from his search. Feeling better for his rest, he stood up and was able to look about and take in his surroundings.

Like the benders half-hidden by the bushes in Lincoln's Inn Fields, there were prone shapes here and there in the church, obscured by the pews, ignored by the tourists. They slept hunched in on themselves, holding themselves together and apart from the rest of the world so that it shouldn't touch them, as if the more still and drawn tight like a closed fist they could be, the less likely they were to be noticed, the less vulnerable. Suddenly one sat up and stared around wildly under a ragged thatch of uncombed yellow hair. Afraid that he might be seen looking and his interest taken offence at, Orazio made for the door and out into the autumn sunlight. He must go to Waterloo and begin again there. He went down the steps of St Martin's and set off back up the Strand until he came to Waterloo Bridge and turned on to its broad carriageway across the Thames.

Although the air seemed quite still, a breeze pushed at his face once he was out over the river's surface. Looking up and downstream he was almost surprised to see the familiar skyline intact beside the water that glittered with catspaw flurries as if a Botticellian Venus were about to rise and walk on the waves or sail her shell towards Westminster. The bulk of the National Theatre and its dependants straddled the South Bank making the Royal Festival Hall seem almost delicate. It had been there when he had decided to come back, lured partly by the huge loans it was rumoured the English banks would give to anyone wanting to start a business. And because his father was ill, might not live, or so he threatened.

'Come back. As long as I'm alive I'll train you. Then you can start your own place. What you going to do otherwise? Become a teacher or a priest?' He had lived long after he had sent Orazio back to Italy again to marry Catterina. 'If you ain't a priest or a woman you got to marry. Can't be *giovanotto* all your life. Living in your mother's house.'

Yet he knew that when he came back with Catterina and set up a home with her his mother's heart would break, left alone with his father, and she had died within a year relinquishing his father to his chain-smoking mistress with the chesty cough and harsh laughter that spilled out of the painted clown's mouth, who nevertheless coyly shied away now that the old man was irrefutably available. Now it was his and Catterina's turn to provide the Sunday dinner and listen to the rambling discourse, the banalities about life and the family. And money. How Orazio should make it and not spend it, should buy this or that run-down business or terrace of crumbling homes with their miserable, aggrieved tenants. It had seemed as if he had been given immortality, the father forever, until one day there had been a telephone call to the Castel Grande for Orazio. His father had been found dead, fallen into the electric fire, charred. Sometimes he almost believed in retribution from beyond the grave, his mother's frail hand stretching out of the shadows to topple his father.

It was the river flowing under his feet that had brought back all these memories with its commonplace yet irresistible metaphor for time. They said, folklore said, that when a man was drowning his whole life passed before his eyes, yet when he'd been drowning Orazio had experienced no such gaudy procession. Perhaps that was because he hadn't drowned, therefore hadn't been drowning. Like the survival of the fittest. If you survived and others didn't, whether you were a dinosaur or dodo, it was because you were the fittest. If you didn't you weren't. The outcome was the premise; the razor of simplicity. He had been one of the fittest. Not the only one, of course. Others had bubbled up through the oily waters. But one. He had been one.

Now we struggled to keep alive those, human and non-human, who were no longer fit according to nature's inexorables. We decided whom we would like to be fit and tried to make it so. The real successes who could get on very nicely without us or rather with us, land gulls, rats, fleas, we poisoned and gassed in Biblical tens of thousands yet they still multiplied while those we actively nurtured, pandas, chimpanzees, terns, swallowtails, trembled always on the edge of extinction, and we too flourished, until some river cut a swathe through the human population and our fitness was taken from us by a micro-organism too insignificant for the naked eye. Sometimes sitting with his glass of wine in front of the little bathyscope window onto those other worlds Orazio would almost laugh out loud. It was like being God looking down on human affairs or a mortal peering into the fairy ring. We thought we knew so much, were fooled by our own success but in the end the great survivor, the fittest among these mammals who had lived on after the flagship Tyrannosaurus went down in mysterious circumstances, might be the naked mole rat, like us in its disgusting pink birthday suit, whose social organisation most nearly resembled the ants' but who could outlast nuclear heat in its underground burrow. He pictured a world in which everything had been blown away until mole rats emerged to set up their communes, unmolested now above the ground, grow fur and teach their children an unrelenting work ethic.

Gazing down into the water he had drifted away from his purpose. The sun had gone behind a cloud-screen and no longer warmed him. He must move while he still could. There were steps leading from the bridge and he went down them on legs that had begun to stiffen while he had leant on the rail staring upstream towards St Paul's and the National Westminster Bank Tower overshadowing it. Now he was in a netherworld, below the viaducts for road and rail and the underbellies of buildings, where young skateboarders wheeled and swooped, upending their slim chariots with a skilled flick to hop a kerb or reverse their flight. He would go towards the station where he remembered a bank of arches on the left, and narrow streets where the light filtered down as through murky water. But first he must find a coffee stall and then a gents', and his bag with his own clothes in it had grown unaccountably heavy.

Orazio laced the thin coffee when he got it with a dash of cognac from his hipflask and used the warming cocktail to wash down a couple of buns whose sparse currants were like the squashed flies of Garibaldi biscuits without the fruity flavour, but safer he reckoned than the dubious fillings of the rolls his restaurateur's eye recognised as made up the night before. He sat for a while on a station bench in the high echoing classical hall gathering strength to go down again, submerge himself in an alien element in search of that information that now seemed so elusive, so nebulous that he began to doubt its existence. He had entered a dream but because he wasn't asleep there was no waking up.

'I can stop,' he thought suddenly, 'at any moment I choose. I shall go home now. Call it a day and begin again in the morning.' The Irishman would be disappointed, of course, but he would have to be patient for a little longer. After ten years what could another day matter?

'Should I take over from you tomorrow?' Pearse asked when Orazio told him.

'No, no. I've got the hang of it now. I'll make an early start so as to have a good long day.' But as soon as he put the telephone down he realised from today's events that too early a start was pointless. With nowhere to go his quarry would skulk in bed, in a foetid snug, as long as possible.

He set out late next morning with his clothes in their bag and chanced the tube to Waterloo where he changed in the gents'. He left the station and began to walk again, glad of the downward ramp, turning immediately right at the bottom into a narrow lane with one side formed by the arching roofs of the railway bridge above that trembled and thundered constantly as the trains passed overhead. The arches might have been the gothic bays of some brick cathedral, windowless and gloomy where men in grimed grey clothes sat or sprawled, their bottles in their hands or empty on the ground beside them. Orazio realised he had been descending an invisible spiral. Now he wondered if he had reached the bottom at last. He peered into the first recess but there were only sleepers he didn't dare disturb and he moved on to the second.

Two men sat in conversation on the ground among the litter that looked as if it had been stranded there by an invisible tide.

One of the men who had a look of a broken sailor was talking in a slurred fierce voice, heavily accented. Orazio recognised the accent as Scottish, probably from Glasgow, but the meaning of the speech was impenetrable to him. The other who was younger and seemed less drunk nodded in agreement with parts of the monologue from time to time.

He stood still in the entrance waiting for a pause in the flow.

'Who are you then?' the Scot suddenly focused on Orazio. 'Why are you poking in on our conversation?' He was trying to rise, an empty green wine bottle held by the neck.

'Take it easy, Mac,' the other man restrained him. 'He's harmless.'

'How would I ken that? What do ye's want?' The effort to stand had fortunately proved too much but the menace remained.

'I'm looking for someone. An Irishman.'

'What do ye's want him for? Ye're no the busies or the social?'

'No, no. Nothing like that. Just a friend.'

'Ask Gerry.' With a quick swing of mood the Scotsman nodded towards the other man. 'He knows all of we. He'll tell you if he kens the Mick.'

'Who are you looking for?' the other man asked now.

Orazio became wary at once. This one he'd already noticed wasn't drunk. He suspected he was like himself, pretending, but for what reason? Perhaps the man was himself from the Police or 'the social'.

He decided to parade a drunken aggression in his turn. 'Why should I tell you? How do I know who you are?'

'If you want help you have to trust someone.' The man shrugged.

He considered. It was true. Without help he was getting nowhere. If this man was Police he wouldn't know where Liam was, only that someone was looking for him. But if he knew then he couldn't be Police or those others because then Liam would already be in custody or dead. He had to chance it.

'I'm looking for Liam Noonan. He's about thirty. A friend wants to help him.'

'How can he know this is a real friend?'

'He can telephone and ask. I'll give you a number.' He took a piece of paper from his pocket on which he'd printed his own telephone number. 'Tell him he'll need to know his date of birth and his mother's name for identification.'

The man took the slip of paper and folded it away into an inside pocket of his jacket. 'If I come across him I'll tell him.'

Orazio's head swam with the triumphal dash of adrenalin through his veins. He felt he might faint and had to lean against the grimy, cobwebby wall of the arch for a moment. There was no point in enquiring further. He was convinced that in however tenuous a way he had found Liam. He felt it, and sensed too that all further search would be fruitless. He remembered his grandmother's creed of resignation in the face of *il destino. Non c'è niente da fare. Pazienza.* Now he could only wait, hope that Liam would telephone for although he recognised that there was nothing more to do, would Pearse understand that? Or would he want to hurry to Waterloo and search wildly on his own? Orazio would have to convince him that would be pointless but he sensed he would have difficulty, a difficulty he understood and could sympathise with: the need to act, to be in motion, to influence events, not waiting passively for a call that might never come. He knew how hard it would be for the father in Pearse.

'You won't forget?'

'I said if I saw him.'

'Bugger off,' the Scotsman intervened suddenly. 'I'm sick of your gob.'

Orazio ducked out of the archway and turned back towards Waterloo. He would find another of the enclosed lavatories he realised now must be intended for the disabled and make himself presentable for the journey home. Already he could see his key in the lock, hear the excitement in the Irishman's voice as he told him, feel the smooth pleasure of a full glass in his hand. Now he must give his own affairs some attention. Tomorrow he would set up the new bank account in Noonan's name.

*

The news that the search for Liam was to be delayed had thrown Pearse's planned evening. He got his jacket and went out on to the walkway where bulbs were missing here and there leaving deep black recesses between those lights which were still letting out their sickly pallor, and which made any face illuminated by them look ill too, drawn in charcoal hatchings that too clearly showed up the bone beneath the skin.

He wanted as a background people who didn't know him, not the Guv'nor's gossip but an anonymous backdrop that would make him feel less alone. There was an Irish pub in Pimlico he used sometimes, not speaking to anyone, where he could sit in the corner and listen and observe without involvement. It was still early when he got off the bus in Buckingham Palace Road and crossed the bridge over the railway behind Victoria Station where ghost streets of flat elegantly-proportioned houses lay empty like film sets waiting for the cameras and cast, given up to parked cars. He seemed to be the only pedestrian but when he reached the pub he could hear music coming from it before he pushed open the swing door and was sucked into its beery mouth. A couple of pints later he felt himself begin to relax.

Karaoke was the latest craze advertised everywhere but he couldn't see any difference from the old-fashioned sing-song except that the musical backing was mechanical not live. Tonight was Karaoke Night, singalong night for those bold enough not to mind making fools of themselves. Even when drunk Pearse was too conscious of himself, too wary to step up to a microphone, though he knew all the tunes and words and could sing them when he was alone. There had been musical evenings at home in Arklow with his mother playing the piano. Once after he'd first persuaded her to play for him he'd told Lady Pritchard about those evenings and how his mother could play anything with only her convent lessons from the nuns and without music too.

'She must have had a natural talent for it. What a pity she couldn't have taken it further,' Lady Pritchard had said.

There would have been a lot of natural talent washing around then. Pearse remembered that everyone sang or whistled about the streets or on the job or could coax a tune out of fiddle, pennywhistle or squeezebox. Now they had all fallen silent in front of the professionals they could bring into their own living rooms with just a switch flicked. Yet something was missing and on holiday they would go to live seaside shows and sing choruses or demand a chance to perform in bars and clubs as in this latest manifestation. The desire to sing out, to be part of something, never quite went away. It took different forms and expressions: sometimes it was the feet that sang, jiving away the night. When he and Jessie had first met they had been great ones for the dance hall. She followed perfectly wherever he led until suddenly she would break from him to swirl on her own, knowing when she was ready he would be exactly in time with his hand out to scoop her to him again and go on with their harmony. The quickstep had been their favourite.

By the time he was on his third pint, the Irish songs had begun. Dublin was in the green again, Paddy was digging for gold in the street and biassed angels sprinkled their stardust on a little bit of Heaven. Pearse found himself growing increasingly angry. What did any of it mean or rather, couldn't the people there opening their lips to form the sentimental sounds see what it had led to? Then again, he told himself, it was guilt that made him feel that way. He'd sought them out for comfort. They hadn't come after him. They were strangers in a strange land that was now more familiar to them than their own which was growing away from their memories tossed into the European melting pot.

He went to the bar for a refill and as he turned back to thread his way through to his previous seat the voices began on 'The Wild Colonial Boy'. Pearse stood there with the black pint under its cream head in his hand. He supposed that was how Liam had seen himself. He wanted to hurl the glass and its contents across the bar, to make them stop and listen as he shouted at them that it was a lie and the oldest lie, and then let them tear him to pieces.

In the morning he couldn't remember much after that, whether he'd done or said anything foolish, how he'd got home. He must have made it somehow for there he was, and undressed too, in his bed. He lay there for some time looking at the spillage of light outlining the closed curtains, before he put back the covers and lowered his feet over the side of the bed. He still had his socks on; he was glad of that. He hated his elderly feet with the warpings and abrasions of a lifetime. He remembered them pale-brown and fleet running along the water's edge, the striations of wet ribbed sand firm and warm under the soles, the solid thud of hard-packed shore pounded, the small plashings in the clear salt wavelets of the outgoing tide and then the stomp, stomp, stomp as he chased it down the beach until he was in up to the bottoms of his grey flannel shorts. Further along his toes would slither and cling to the weed-slippery rocks where if you fell, like an old broken umbrella of a cormorant going over, you would bash your brains out on the flinty humps below. Only the birds always made it to the water thrusting their handle heads up again. But the danger itself was irresistible. All his life after, shoes had pinched him so that he walked about indoors often in his socks because he couldn't abide the old man's notion of slippers. Jessie had only laughed and indulged him as other women wouldn't have. 'If you can't walk about in your own home in your socks, where can you?'

He drew back the curtains just a crack so that the light wouldn't hurt his eyes and looked at his watch. It was nearly nine o'clock. The Don was probably well on his way by now. Another day of waiting, of inactivity lay ahead of Pearse. How could he make it pass? He began to wish he'd never agreed to the plan. The Don got all the fun of playing gumshoe while Pearse twiddled his thumbs unable to help his own son. Smiling painfully to himself, he acknowledged the hangover symptoms of self-pity and withdrawal. He must pull himself together, find something to occupy his mind and hands. He would buy flowers and take a trip to the cemetery. But first he would force himself to swallow his usual breakfast of tea and toast. That was the best cure for the morning after, follow your usual routine and get out into the air.

There were three flower stalls in the market, one with cut-price special offers, usually gladioli or chrysanthemums, advertised as 'Glads' and 'Mums', sometimes 'Pot Mums' when the flowers weren't cut; a stall with more variety where you could make up a mixed sheaf of tight bud roses that didn't last, iris and lacy gypsophila or the first greenly hopeful daffodils from the Scillies; and the plant stall that followed the changing seasons with its choice of bulbs, strips of fragile annuals: roses, clematis and honeysuckle; hebe and skimmia and pieris; pungent or sweet herbs in cellophane with a label of potting instructions, lavender, mint and parsley, thyme and sage. He sometimes wondered who bought from this country cornucopia since the front gardens he passed showed little sign of it. It must be for the back gardens, Pearse thought suddenly, that you couldn't see from the street, full of leaf and flower and scent, oases in the cracks between brick and concrete. He looked back at the block behind him and saw that those flats with balconies often had a leafy fringe with the last flamboyant geranium heads looking down into the street. There were men he knew to pass the time of day with, who had allotments and cycled off towards the park where there were dozens of narrow strips behind a wire mesh fence, between the park and the river beside the old football ground. He and Jessie had sometimes taken a bus that way to walk in the old palace ground and along the towpath. Once she'd said, 'Wouldn't you like a wee bit of ground to grow things in?' And he'd laughed and said he wasn't the gardening kind: he left that to the English.

Perhaps she would've liked him to bring her back fresh vegetables and flowers he'd grown, and all that time he hadn't understood. He hesitated now in front of the stall. There was nothing he could make of this sudden knowledge. It was all too late. What could he do now but make sentimental gestures of atonement? People were buying bulbs from open boxes, with idealised pictures of their eventual blooms above them, small brown grenades that would explode into succulent leaves and trumpets, bells, cups of mauve and white, yellow and pink while the ground still ached with frost.

He would buy some now and an old kitchen fork he'd seen on a junk stall further back to dig with. What sort should he get? What had been Jessie's favourite colour? Blue and white. 'I have to be careful because of the red hair,' he heard her say. He could buy some of those white daffodils, Ice Follies, and the blue crocus or even a bold hyacinth but he somehow fancied they were for indoors. Jessie used to bring one home from the market sometimes and it would sit on the kitchen windowsill, filling the whole flat with its scent until it grew too leggy, the heavy head toppled and the heavy smell turned acid with decay. She'd hated to throw them out even so. 'And it was only fifty pence the day,' as if Pearse begrudged her the extravagance.

Plants were better than flowers that would soon wither and die out there. Last time he'd gone, at Easter, he'd found a few dry sticks in the vase from his previous visit. There were little pinks still in flower on the stall, white with a dark red centre. He bought a couple of these to go along with the bulbs and a sprig of lavender in a tiny pot. Then he went back for the old fork.

With his purchases dangling in their bag he caught a bus to the end of Deverham Palace Road and walked on to the cemetery gates. A notice inside said they were closed during the school dinner hour in term-time, presumably to keep children from skylarking among the graves and dropping the wraps of their takeaways, chip and crisp papers and Coke cans, unless there was a more sinister reason. The by-laws neatly printed on the other side hinted at mysterious forbidden practices that might not take place: assignations, vandalism, witchcraft, dog walking. He'd never noticed the list before but by the date at the bottom it wasn't new, neither was its portentous wording that echoed with the sonorities of some Victorian council chamber.

In the distance a small tractor mower was at work, running over the verges, and the graves that had lost their raised profiles and markers and lay flat under a green tweed. Otherwise the paths between the lime trees were empty. No one but himself seemed to have come to visit the dead. He was glad Jessie had been a Protestant and therefore able to be buried here. It had made her seem not so far lost to him even though he didn't visit often, not often enough, but it helped him to think of her just down the road and he could talk to her more easily in the months after her death than if she'd been halfway across London. A pair of brilliant birds, like English parakeets in pink and blue, hopped away from him across the grass. They must be jays. He'd never seen them in the city before but there might be all kinds of denizens in this green pocket.

The place was very ordered: Deverham's dead lay tidily, many of them local boys who'd been killed in the First World War. Their headstones with the regimental badges incised above the names had been cleaned, or perhaps replaced, recently so that they seemed as if they'd only been put up yesterday, uniform in their neat ranks, instead of before Pearse was born. It was life that was haphazard and awry, Pearse thought. Here and there his eye picked out family graves, with gaps of a quarter of a century between buryings: Mum and Dad reunited at last. He knew there was room for him beside Jessie but although he loved her, the idea turned his stomach and if he thought about it too much, he knew he might begin to resent the mute call from down there where he was crouched, tidying the plot, raking at the weeds with the old fork and poking the papery bulbs into holes. 'The boy's back, Jessie,' he said to her. 'That's what they say, anyway.'

And she answered as she always did: 'You don't know that for sure; you're just speculating on what you want to think,' as he arranged the lavender bush and the two little pinks above her. He felt the damp chill beginning to creep into his bones in spite of the autumn sunlight. He'd pick up a hair of the dog on his way home. Now that the pubs stayed open all day there wasn't any rush to beat the clock. Pearse wrapped the old fork in the plastic bag and put it in his pocket. Then he gathered the weeds and the little brown shiny pots that had held the plants, and stood up. 'Okay, Jess?' She didn't answer and he turned away looking for the litter basket.

'There's a bloke and a girl bin in 'ere asking for you, the Guv'nor said as he pulled his pint. 'I said you hadn't bin in for a bit. You know, stumm.' And he touched a forefinger to the side of his nose. 'Irish, I think they was. They asked if I knew where you lived and I said I never. Which is God's truth and no lie.'

But they know, Pearse thought, they know because of the letter. Or was it Liam looking for him? The Guv'nor hadn't known Liam. But no, that couldn't be it. Liam knew where he lived, of course. Then how did they know where he drank? Unless they'd simply been going from pub to pub. Why would they need to do that? To lay an ambush, waylay him going home. Like now? He must be careful and not drink too much, be steady on his feet and alert.

The Guv'nor was speaking again, back from the other end of the bar where he'd gone to serve a round. 'You all right, mate? Remember what I said: if you ever need a hand . . .'

'Thanks. I'll remember. If there's anything I can't handle . . .' In this world turned upside-down he found himself part of, who knew when such an offer might come handy and anyway he didn't want to offend the Guv'nor who had scented trouble, had sniffed it out on Pearse months ago as if it was an invisible, betraying scent his clothes and skin gave off.

These two now who'd been asking for him were presumably looking not for him but for Liam. They would try to frighten Pearse into telling them where the boy was and when he said he didn't know they wouldn't believe him. Again he considered whether he could contact the Police and tell them. These two might have faces the English Police would know already, and maybe they could take them off his back. But hadn't he already rejected that course as too dangerous? If he took their help he would be technically, in the eyes of those others, a traitor too, as they'd called Liam, and therefore fair game. Jessie's grave had told him he wasn't ready to die yet. And even if he lived he'd be in hock to the British Police for the rest of his life. No, he'd been right in his first judgement. There was no going back on that.

What then should he do? Suddenly it came to him that by now his phone was probably tapped, so he must stop the Don telephoning him with anything he might have found out. Pearse should ring him from the pub and let him know that Pearse's own phone probably wasn't safe. But when the coins had dropped and he had dialled there was no answer except the endlessly ringing tone. The Don must still be out on his quest. Pearse would have to put a note through his door. Then he realised the outer gate would be shut and prevent him even reaching the door. He would have to try again later, from a call box. Meanwhile, he should go home now without drinking any more and get some food inside him. He wouldn't go back by the stinking alley. That was too dangerous. He'd go the long way round, by the open street.

He saw them as he rounded the corner and knew at once who they were, though to anyone else's eye they would have looked like any young couple rowing. They had stationed themselves where they could watch both the mouth of the alley and the corner he was turning. Pearse dodged back out of sight at once to give himself time to think, to decide whether he should go and confront them in the road or duck back down a side turning and try to make it home from the other direction. If he didn't present himself here, now, they would come to the flat where he would be trapped. They might force their way in and murder him in his own kitchen. He was safer out in broad daylight before the whole world. He took a deep breath and stepped back round the corner, trying to walk as if he suspected nothing, was perhaps a little oiled, a bit unsteady. The man and woman moved to intercept him. She was fair-haired, young enough to be his daughter; the man was dark with a beard showing a fleck or two of silver.

'Pearse Noonan?'

'That's me.'

'We're friends of Liam, Mr Noonan. Is he at home?'

'Everyone's asking for Liam. You know it's strange. I haven't seen the boy for over ten years, not heard from him almost as long and suddenly everybody's asking me if he's at home.'

'Everyone?' The girl spoke now.

'There was a couple of English fellers the other day and now you two. Why should he come home? There's nothing for him here. His mother's gone and he never came back to bury her, so why would he bother now?' He would be in tears at his own words soon.

'If you do see him, would you give him this letter?' the man said, holding out an envelope.

'I'll do that. I'll put it safely in me wallet so's not to lose it. I'm a bit forgetful, you know. But I can't forget it there because I'll see it every time I go for me money.'

'You won't lose it?'

'No, no. It'll be as safe as a maid in a convent. I'll tell him you were asking for him.'

'Those other two, what were they wanting?'

'They didn't say. Said it was a matter of business. They looked like bookies to me. Maybe he's been playing the horses. Even a college boy might be silly enough for that, do you think? Anyway, if you see him tell him his Dada would like a call. I shan't hold it against him about his mother's funeral. Forget the past. I'd like to see him again.'

They were growing bored with his ramblings just as he wanted; the girl swinging impatiently on her heel.

'We'd best be going,' she said now to the man.

'Yes, yes. Well, Mr Noonan, nice meeting you. Don't forget the letter.'

'No, no. I'll remember it fine for sure.' He hoped he wasn't overacting.

The man lifted his hand in farewell: the girl had already turned away.

Sick and trembling, Pearse forced himself to continue his shuffle home, resisting the desire to turn and watch the others go, or break into a trot, aware of the vulnerability of his back, if they hadn't believed him, to a quick bullet tearing through his spine. Too weak to drag himself up the concrete stairs he almost fell into the lift and was carried upwards leaning against the side, slowly regaining his breath as he realised that, unless the English Police were waiting at his front door, he was safe for the moment.

Yet once inside he knew he couldn't rest. He had to reach the Don. As soon as he thought they had gone he must go out in search of a safe telephone. He would have to turn left outside his front door instead of right as he did on his way to the shops or pub, duck below the parapet, hoping none of his neighbours chose that moment to appear on the walkway and wonder who he was hiding from, and scurry along to the far end, down the staircase there and out through a neglected fire exit towards Ashcroft Road where he could pick up a bus to the station. Surely he would find a working telephone there and perhaps by then the Don would have returned to answer his call.

The day was fading fast, the light running out like murky grey bathwater, earlier and earlier down to the shortest stub of St Lucy's. He remembered how his mother used to say with delight that after Old Christmas in January, every day was a cock's stride longer.

He felt dizzy from lack of food and his receding hangover. If the Don still wasn't back he would have to look for a sandwich before he fainted away on the pavement. But there was no need. At the third ring he heard the receiver being lifted.

'I'm in a call-box. I don't think you should telephone me at home or at least not to say anything that shouldn't be overheard. Have you any news?'

'I think so. I think I might have made contact. I'm waiting for a call. I thought you might be it, him. I gave the contact my number. Now all we can do is wait.' He expected the Irishman to break into protests but all Pearse said was:

'I've found somewhere for him to stay. If he does get in touch, tell him. If you ring me make out you're talking about chess.' He dropped a couple more coins into the box. 'Tell me you've worked out a new move. Then I'll come out and ring you back like now. If you don't hear anything from him, you can say you've got to cancel our game. I've no more change just now.' The last coin was running out rapidly before his eyes.

'I'll let you know . . .'

The call, when it came, caught Orazio off guard.

'I hope you're getting on with your arrangements, Carbone. The first package will arrive sooner than expected. We thought we should let you know.'

'*Non si disturba. Tutto va bene.*'

'It better. *Capise'?*'

He understood perfectly, went to pour himself a glass of wine and set up the chess board to pass the time with a game or two, but found he couldn't concentrate and switched on the television searching through the channels until he came to rest among the undersea *fritto misto* of diaphanous squid and shrimp and elegant swordfish. On a plate, lightly coated in batter and sprinkled with lemon, they appeared merely succulent morsels. They had no right to such complex lives, to sex and society, these anonymous bits of tasty plastic and rubber he had so often tossed in a pan of smoking oil. A shrimp disappeared into a cuttlefish maw, and the camera focused on its absorption through a soft contact lens of flesh. At least humans digested their prey decently out of sight.

He was drowsing when the bell woke him, not the expected double of the telephone but one long shrill that for a moment, dazed with sleep, he couldn't identify. Then he realised it wasn't what he was waiting for at all but the doorbell. Perhaps those earlier callers had been suspicious or angry and come to seek him out. Orazio lifted the receiver of the entry-phone.

'Yes?'

Sounds came into the room, half-formed, distorted by the machine, sounds he couldn't interpret. Was it a trick? Perhaps Noonan's son was injured and lying at his gate, or young vandals were mocking him. He had to go and see. Whoever it was he daren't simply let them in. 'Wait,' he said into the machine. 'I'm coming down.'

On his way he picked up a torch and an old pistol from a pair in a wooden case that wouldn't fire but might intimidate. He felt like a pirate or highwayman or a bandit from the mountains. Or Garibaldi. He must remember to take his key.

Closing the front door behind him he flicked on the torch and lit his way down the steps, following the luminous puddle of light across the yard to the gate where he could see a shape still waiting. Was it Liam? Perhaps a messenger from him?

'What do you want? Who are you?'

It was a young male figure in jeans, trainers and a jacket. He was holding up something, pressing it to the bars, a double square of card in a plastic holder. 'I can't see without my glasses.' Orazio played the torch over it but it was a blur. One side had a dark blob that might have been a photograph. 'Tell me what you want.'

The boy seemed to be gesturing towards a suitcase. Then he opened his mouth and pointed inside, shaking his head. Orazio shone the torch up into his face, making the figure cry out as the light struck his eyes and step back. 'I know you. I've seen you somewhere. Where? Who are you? He reached a hand through the bars to seize the boy's jacket but he tore it out of Orazio's grasp with a grunted cry, backing off into the night, followed by the torch beam. He began to run, the suitcase banging awkwardly against his leg.

Orazio kept the beam on him through the gate as if he were trying to pin a dancing moth to a blade of light until the boy was beyond its range and the footsteps died away. He stood for a moment wondering if he should unlock the gate and go after him but it was clear this was no messenger from Liam. Now he was able to think he realised that. How would he have known where to come? He must go indoors again and wait for a call. It was only as he was climbing the stairs to the upper floor that he remembered the boy's face as he had first seen it, looking up briefly in fear from the huddled bundle in the Victoria Street doorway. If only he hadn't forgotten his glasses he might by now have had a name to put to the face.

The suitcase, he now realised, would have been full of dusters, soap, oven gloves and suchlike. He'd seen the charity sellers often, going from house to house, but they'd never come to him before because, he supposed, they assumed no one lived in this dark hulk of a house: it was just a kind of shop. He had read in the local paper that sometimes these tribes of ostensibly charitable teenagers were run by latterday Fagins and that the money collected never reached the assorted good causes these uninspiring goods were hawked for.

The call came an hour later just as his heart and hands had finally steadied. Orazio picked up the receiver. 'Yes?'

'I have a message to call this number.'

'Are you Liam?'

'Maybe. Who is that?'

Orazio realised he had been expecting an Irish voice like Pearse's own, not these light unaccented English tones.

'You don't know my name. I'm a friend of your father, Pearse. He's worried about you. He says you mustn't try to go home or contact him.'

There was a short dry laugh. 'I wasn't thinking of it.'

'He wants to help you, to talk to you.'

'How do I know I can trust you or him?'

'You don't but if you need help you must trust someone.'

'It's better not to trust.' There was a pause. Orazio waited, silent himself. 'What does he want me to do if I can't speak or visit?'

'Is there a number where you can be reached?'

'No, there's no number. Are you the old guy who came seeking for me?'

'I suppose so. Yes. Look, if there's no number can you ring here the same time tomorrow and I'll make sure he's here? That's all I can think of.' Then he added: 'He says he's found somewhere for you to stay. Somewhere safe.'

'I'm sure as hell tired of the streets. All right. I'll phone, but no funny business, no trying to trace the call . . .'

'I'll tell him what you say.'

A couple of minutes later he was dialling. He hoped the Irishman would be sober. 'Mr Noonan, I've been working on a new move. I'd like to show you. I wondered if you could come round tomorrow evening instead of Friday.'

'Can't you tell it to me now?'

'I'd rather show you if you're not busy then.'

'Oh, I've the time. Can't you just give me an inkling now? So I can be thinking of an answer.'

The man was clever, Orazio thought, playing along.

'All right. It's a board of two white pawns, a5 and c6, and their King, g2, against three black, f1, g2 and h3, and their King, a8. White to play and win.'

· *Liam's Script* ·

I don't know when I first realised my father was weak and began to despise him. Perhaps when he started to tell me those old stories my mother hated and tried to counter with her own. It was like mud-wrestling where my mind always slipped out of their grasp whichever tried to hold me. So I tried running round the streets with the other boys but that didn't work either, or only for a time. For all my appearance of rebellion what rubbed off on me was their concern, their puritanism. I was birthmarked a Fifties child. Where others seemed able to escape as we got into our teens, to loosen out those multi-coloured flared new wings and be lifted away on a warm thermal, I couldn't get off the ground. I crawled back into the dark burrow of my bedroom with my books. If I couldn't swing with the rest I had my own world, and the fact that I could play football too stopped me being thought a wet or a swot. Then as I started to read, Dada's stories came back to me. What the school taught was English history and English literature, post-Saxon, post-Norman even more. Before that were the ancient Brits, savages running around in skins and wood or becoming toadies to the Romans. Even Mammy's Scots didn't get a look in. Sometimes there was a mention of kings and princes or saints and I'd get a glimpse of a glittering other life that wasn't the daily round of the manor or monastery but was shot through with excitement, gold and silver thread on silk. I began to look for things on my own, more of Dada's stories though I never told him. That was when I first came across the

Fianna. In those days I didn't even know how to pronounce the word. Dada had always left them out.

At first because of my logical English upbringing and schooling I found the stories hard to follow and I realised he'd tidied them up in the telling. There was so much fantasy mixed in with what must be a residue of fact. I didn't put it that way myself at first, not in those days. I simply accepted it as kids now accept the fantasy of computer games so-called. They aren't games at all of course. They're the old stories from the world's childhood reworked and given new names, that's all, except that instead of fighting the battles in your head, you can press a button and make something happen on the screen in front of you. One day, maybe, if civilisation survives and there are still computers to play with, they'll be calling the antagonists IRA or UVF.

The question that nagged at me then was, where had all the beautiful men and women of that older time gone? How had they come to be replaced by us and our drabness? Even the World Wars were dreary, more a matter of endurance than courage. Think of the trenches of the First, and the war work, rationing, blackout Mammy always talked of in the Second. Now the Fianna, that was different: twenty-five battalions of beautiful young men to defend the High King of Ireland, all comrades and irresistible to women. It was even all right to say they were beautiful. And the girls themselves, so free and every one a stunner. It wasn't till I got to know Tessa that I began to understand there was more to it than that, when she explained how the Church took away the Celtic women's freedom to love and the English took away their freedom to rule and fight, to own land and wealth. It was when I met Tessa that I began to understand my mother better, the anger that was in her, that I'd sensed as a child, fearing it was directed at me.

Up in my bedroom I read the stories with a torch under the bedclothes and hid the books in the bottom of my chest of drawers under my outgrown clothes where I knew my mother never went. I got the books from the library. We'd had a project on the Greek myths at school and when I asked the librarian where I could find some, he directed me to a section on religions of the world, and as I was looking for the Greeks I came across the Irish, and then the rest of the Celts. Then I turned to the ancient history section as the librarian had advised me and began to read that. The Greeks were there and the Celts too. It was hard going and a lot of it I didn't understand. I took the book away to a chair by the radiator in the corner and as I sat there trying to follow a story we'd never been told in school, I suddenly understood about that old lost empire that once stretched south to Ankara and north to Caledonia. But I shouldn't call it an empire because it implies all the hierarchy and bureaucracy the English inherited from the Romans. It was more like a federation of chiefs, kings and peoples based on iron and its power to hew and cut, both trees and men. In 390 BC they even sacked the upstart Rome and a hundred years later they raided Apollo's temple at Delphi and tried to take over Egypt.

I used to walk about the streets of Deverham in a daze, my head ringing with the clang of blade on blade and the clop of horses. Gold and silver cups dazzled me and the armbands and necklaces of beautiful women cast their fire in my eyes as they leant towards me. I was out of this world of mucky streets and sweaty schoolboys. I longed to find that I wasn't my parents' child but had come about by miraculous or at least romantic means, the passing stranger, incest, bestiality, like the old heroes, rather than a common coupling after that meeting at a dance hall my parents always spoke of as if it had been a thing of magic. I would look at my parents sometimes and try to find similarities between us. At least, that was what I told myself I was doing but really I was looking for differences to convince myself I wasn't their child but had been adopted and never told, and that somewhere I had extraordinary natural parents who would bequeath me their gifts of cleverness and beauty. Sometimes I would be so deep sunk in it all I would look up when my name was called and wonder where I was, with my senses still attuned to what seemed a parallel life alongside this one. I knew exactly what they meant in the fairy stories when they said people had been 'spirited away'. For I was reading these too, but even more secretly, for a grown boy of twelve ought to be beyond fairy stories. But I realised that these Irish stories were different, closer to serious things like myth and the old religions than what were usually thought of as just children's fairy stories. If the Greek and Roman myths could be taken seriously then why not these?

Religion was a difficult question in our house. Both my parents had been brought up strictly in their own church but they'd lost it along the way, perhaps because of the war. So when they met it didn't seem a problem until it became a question of where to have the wedding. The neutral ground of the Registry Office solved that one. Next was the problem of christening the children or not. That little big sister I never knew wasn't christened and I think they felt that was why she died. Even though they didn't believe in any formal sort of way, the idea of a punishing god had been hammered into them as children and could surface without warning. I don't know if they discussed it openly. I only know I was christened at the local church and never went there again. I think they avoided St Bernard's, the nearest Catholic church, because my father was afraid the priests would 'get their hooks' into us and there was enough tension in our house without that. Anyway my mother wouldn't have agreed. I once went into St John's where I was christened just to see what it was like. It seemed unlived-in, handsome in a grey late-nineteenth-century way but to me a symbol of the conqueror, the planter. Except that I didn't use those words for them at that time, not even in my head. Not until I met Tessa.

I went to a little Church of England primary school when the time came, where we sang 'All Things Bright and Beautiful' in the morning with our voices half-drowned in the Broadway traffic. It was a low grey-stone and brick building shaped like a mediaeval chapel with a tarmac playground and entrances marked *Boys* and *Girls* and *Infants*. We wore a grey uniform and there were a lot of pictures on the walls, mainly painted by us. The teaching was traditional but we sat at tables together, not in lines of desks, and the teachers were on the whole kind and competent. There wasn't much pressure to learn but most of us could read and write and do fractions by the time we had to move on. Some residual puritanism in my parents must have made them choose me an all-boys comprehensive. There was a new uniform, I was at the bottom instead of being at the top of the school, and it was rougher without the girls. I soon learnt to bash someone quickly, just to show I could and would, and that stopped me being bullied as some kids were, especially if they were fat or dark-skinned, or wore glasses.

I could always run fast, something I got from my mother who had that Scots greyhound leanness while Dada was a lumberer, graceful in his way but not quick and nimble as she was. My speed got me into the football team, first the under-fourteens, then the second eleven. That's when I was happiest: at first, doing a Georgie Best up the middle, the ball as if stuck to my feet by the pace I was going, and then a boot out to pass or ram one in the back of the net. But as I got older and we went further to play away I began to realise what it was about: it was us against them and sometimes, like when we played the Oratory School, I didn't feel very 'us'. 'Load of fucking Micks and nigs,' someone said as we were kitting up. And I thought: 'I'm a Mick,' and said so.

'You wasn't born there. What's your Mum and Dad?' Bateson's head above its grimy vest thrust up through the navy shirt of our strip.

'My Dad's Irish. Me Mum's Scotch.'

'There you are. You're only a half-and-half. A fucking mongrel you are, Noonan. You're nothing.'

I chucked my boots at him still tied by the laces. 'And you're a fucking gippo, Bateson, and a guzzler.' He was dark-haired and -eyed and the only one who could nearly catch me. No one would sit next to him in class or the dinner hall if they could help it because he stank of the unwashed. We'd been at the same junior school where he was always in trouble with the nurse for nits and dirty feet with long hard nails. 'You could grow carrots under there, boy.' He shovelled his free school dinner down him every day as if the plate might be snatched away, and was always first in line for seconds even when it was stew sick or thin leather beef in glue gravy. And as for the sweets: his plate was heaped with stodge pudding lapped by seas of lumpy custard or stacked with layers of brittle treacle tart. His stringy body absorbed it all, converting it into the strange demonic energy for mischief that seemed to possess him. 'You got worms, Batey?' He was always in trouble, found schoolwork tedious and would have been expelled if it hadn't been for the headmaster's refusal to admit failure, and Bateson's ability to run. Then he took up boxing. But at this time it was still football: erratic, sometimes brilliant but on an off-day likely to give away any seemingly safe pass that was made to him.

When the other team came on I looked at them with interest. They were all Catholics but they were English. My opposite number was a young Pele and I had to pull out everything, first to keep up and then to get away. As we came off after the first half Bateson ran past and shoved him. 'Get back up the trees, you black bastard. You don't want an orange: you only eat bananas.' Then he ran away laughing in his ostentatiously raucous way. I hadn't thought about there being black Catholics before. Then I noticed the two team lists pinned up and saw the boy's name was Lynch. I'd had a great-grandmother Lynch on his side, my father had once told me, so I knew it was an Irish name. The game was a goalless draw until five minutes before the end when Bateson tripped Lynch inside our box and they got a penalty.

Afterwards I shoved him back. 'What you do that for, you witless fucker?'

'Going soft on the blackie, Noonan?' He grinned back at me with his creased monkey-face. 'Just because he's got a Mick name like you. Means one of his Mick ancestors screwed a slave cunt so he's half-Irish, another fucking mongrel.'

'Shut your face, gippo.'

'Come on then, hit me.' He stuck his fists up and danced about, tantalisingly, but I knew he was already training at a seedy gym in Hammersmith and anyway my parents had always frowned on serious fighting.

'Any fool can put his fists up when he runs out of reasons,' my mother always said. I knew she remembered drunken punch-ups on Friday pay-nights after closing time when she was a child, and my father too hated violence of any kind though he'd never said why. Maybe it'd been the War that turned him against it.

We'd been in the fifth form nearly a term and it was coming up to Christmas when we were sent for in turn by the careers master. Already we'd been separated into those who were doing CSE and those doing GCE 'O' levels, the group I found myself in without really trying. I doubt if any of us had given our future much consideration at that point, except Bateson who was leaving at sixteen to train seriously. Apparently they thought at the gym in Hammersmith he had a big future. 'I'm going to knock all colours of shit out of them spades. They think they're the only ones who can fight now but I'm going to show them.'

'I suppose that like everyone else I've seen this morning you haven't wasted much time considering what you'd like to do when you leave school, Noonan,' the master said.

'No sir.'

He looked at a file that I supposed contained reports on us all. Usually I was in the top ten for everything except geography where the diagrams always defeated me. I'd spend what seemed hours trying to be neat with a ruler and end up with that most humiliating of marks, B— or even C+.

'The other staff for some reason best known to themselves think you should stay on and do 'A' levels. They also think, though on what evidence it's hard to say, that you are university material. What do you think?'

'I don't know, sir.' It was an unwritten rule that you gave nothing away to the teachers or your parents. We taught each other to keep everything close, to be suspicious of and send up anything that looked like thought or feeling as if we wanted to go on being lost boys forever, knowing that beyond was pain and responsibility, sex and a job. I saw his face register the usual weary hardening that was their response to our wariness and I heard myself saying almost without willing it: 'I'd like to try, sir. Would it cost a lot?'

He looked at my report again with more enthusiasm. 'I see your father's an electrician. You should get a full major county award. Your parents will have to keep you while you're still at school but I expect they could manage that. After all, what would you earn if you left after 'O' levels? Very little. At least girls can get office jobs. It will mean putting more into it than you have so far. The staff think you have the potential but you will have to realise it by hard work.'

I didn't tell my parents about the conversation or even that I'd seen the careers master when I got home but from then on I opted out of the plans to mess around in the evening in the park on our bikes or kicking a ball. I still played for the team and trained but now it was all different. Everything had a purpose: to get to university where no one in my family had ever been before as far as I knew, though I had a cousin, the daughter of my mother's sister, who'd been to teacher training college. I looked at the sixth formers who'd stayed on and were deep in their 'A' levels, the prefects in their strained uniforms showing stretches of bony wrist who only talked to each other in their already deepened voices and were never seen arsing about by the rest of us. I found that now I had a purpose in working, I actually enjoyed the work and could do what was required without too much sweat. *Julius Caesar* was our Shakespeare set book the first year and I enjoyed it. The English teacher took us to see the Brando version which was showing in a season at some art-movie cinema and that made the words really come alive and make sense as if people might really have talked like that, and you could get the meaning of most of what they were saying, once you were over the first few minutes and your ear seemed to be used to it. For the first time I understood the politics of it all, and it didn't seem to me that much had changed.

Then we had to do a selection from Modern British Poetry 1900–1950 and I came across W. B. Yeats. He wasn't one of the poets we had to study; I think they thought he was too difficult, that we wouldn't understand the references.

One day the English master, who always tried to make things as interesting as he could even though he knew most of the class couldn't give a monkey's and just wanted another subject to make up their total, and English Literature was seen as a soft option where if you wrote down something you might pick up a useful C, one day he said we were to choose one of the poets not on the set list and present him to the class with our reasons for settling on that one. I knew who it was going to be because I'd already read through the book, making up my mind about most of the poets on offer.

That night I asked Dada to explain 'Easter 1916' to me. We were sitting at the kitchen table having our tea. 'I'm no good at poetry,' he said.

'You don't have to be. Just tell me what happened.' Mammy was going in and out to the sink and the stove, putting the dishes in to soak and making tea. I sensed her getting angrier as he spoke, telling the story of the uprising that failed and the English reprisals.

'It's all a long time ago,' she said, banging down the brown teapot so that a little slopped out of the spout on to the cloth. 'Before the War, almost before the Great War. They had no right, in the middle of all that while people were dying.'

'Some things can't wait if it's the right moment.'

'Well, it wasn't the right moment because they failed. They were all shot, and they had to wait till 1926 for their independence. And where has it got them? They're still poor. Suppose we were to take over the Glasgow Post Office and hold out for Scotland? What about that? But we know which side our bread's buttered on and so should they have done.'

To deflect her anger I asked him about Cuchullain and Aengus and then he reminded me of the stories he used to tell me and got the book, the child's book of myths and legends, and said I should read it again for myself, and that he had to go out and pay the club and couldn't sit here gassing but I knew it was because of Mammy's disapproval that hung over us like the damp washing on the airer that always dangled above our heads, just under the ceiling. And I couldn't tell him about when I was younger and used to read the library books under the bedclothes and walked about in a daze of those olden times.

Then the day came, before we took our 'O' levels, when we had to put our names down for staying on and so of course I had to tell my parents at last. I don't know how I expected them to react but I was surprised when they were so pleased. And then I mentioned university. 'The careers master said I should get a full grant. It wouldn't cost you anything.'

'University? You crafty little . . . You never told us they thought you were clever.' It was tea-time of course: that was the only time we were together. Dada always left early in the morning and since I'd been grown up, Mammy had a job seeing the children over the school crossing. Anyway, I was always in a rush in the morning, especially once I started to shave. So the only time we sat down together was at tea because at the weekends we were all doing our own thing, Dada often working overtime on Saturday while Mammy shopped and cleaned and I was training or playing still, and Sunday I'd be writing essays or out on my bike while they went out for a walk along the towpath and a drink in some riverside pub. Mammy could never be bothered with the ritual English Sunday dinner. Early on I'd understood that, in spite of the disagreements that in any case weren't so bad until I made them so, they liked best of all being alone or out together. Sometimes I'd hear them through the bedroom wall in the mornings chatting together in bed. I don't know if they had sex by then, maybe when I was out, but they were always talking. I'd wake up to the murmur of it. The two differently-pitched waves of sound alternating, sometimes with a descant of laughter from one of them to the other's words.

So when I said I'd put myself down for Queen's Belfast that was tea-time too. I hadn't realised she would be so upset. I didn't come back for her funeral for a whole host of reasons but one was, and perhaps when I look back it was the strongest of all, that I was afraid I'd killed her and by that time loving Tessa I'd come round to realising that I loved Mammy too.

I applied in October and went over there for an interview in March. I was so surprised by the appearance of the city now the University. I'd expected something dour and industrial and instead it was all wide avenues with fresh leaves out on the trees and yellow and white daffodils in flower under them. And everywhere in the streets were people with redgold hair just like in the stories. When they asked me on the interviewing board why I had chosen Queen's I said I supposed it was because of my Irish half. That seemed to please them and they offered me a place if I got good enough grades in my 'A' levels. I could have flown back without benefit of aeroplane I was that high, but it made things worse at home because I realised as soon as I told my parents I'd been offered a place that Mammy had all along been hoping they'd turn me down. Those last few months I had to work in an atmosphere which alternated loaded silences with the clatter of saucepans and slammed doors. Most of the time I just stayed in my bedroom. They'd put an old dropleaf table in my room for me to work at and once it was up, there was hardly space to sit at it. When I wasn't working I trained and played harder than ever. There was no one I could talk to. Those of us who'd stayed on were wary of each other, keeping everything close and pretending to a confidence in ourselves and our futures I'm sure the rest had as little of as me.

After the exams were over we were free to wait for the results without any classes. It was a hot dry summer and so we lay about in the park that surrounded the school eating ice creams and tossing our Coke tins into dusty bushes. The park had once been a bishop's palace and the grounds were full of exotic trees, the remnant of an arboretum, and peacocks screamed from the lawns around the old walls. We felt ourselves old and exhausted, looking down on the other kids as they shouted and shoved each other, streaming out of the front gates at hometime. When term finally ended and the school wouldn't harbour us any more we should be on our own for the first time, out in the world. I was planning to ride my bike around Britain and had joined the Youth Hostels' Association.

Bateson had gone by now and no word of him filtered back.

The school itself was changing: girls in the sixth form; the first wave of immigrants' children whom we, as prefects, were supposed to keep them from being bullied. I found it hard to see myself as a figure of authority and usually ducked out of laying down the law to the juniors. Jenkins who was head boy took it very seriously and saw me as a skiver, which I was. He had applied for a commission in the army and like me was waiting for the results to decide his future. It seemed to me crazy to go from one institution straight into another and I said so.

He lifted his head from the wispy grass that was burnt to straw and said, 'I expect I'll get sent to Northern Ireland. That's where you're going, isn't it, Noonan? Maybe we'll run into each other,' and he laughed and cocked an imaginary gun at me.

I set off on my bicycle tour, glad to be out of the flat. By the time I got back my parents would be on holiday in Scarborough where they went every other year and there were friends they met who'd join them in the singsongs at the shows and in the pubs. I'd been dragged unwillingly along with them when I was younger and had hated it, feeling nothing but relief when I was finally old enough to say no and opt for school camps or journeys. The school had taken us to France when we were fourteen. It was my first taste of wine and garlic. Like everyone else I played the unimpressed British teenager abroad but inside I was in a state of continual excitement. Secretly I wondered if the rest had been as interested as I was and like me weren't saying so but covering up with our usual rags and ribaldry. Biking round Britain I felt the same, full of superior energy that ordinary people didn't possess. After all, wasn't I about to go to university, the first in the family, among a mere ten per cent of the population? And I was going abroad. That's how I thought of it. I pushed myself as hard as I could go, covering eighty miles a day, riding on into the long summer dusks and reaching the next hostel at the last minute.

When I let myself back into the empty flat after hauling my bike up the concrete stairs, the envelope was waiting for me. I'd done well enough for Queen's though not as well as I'd hoped. My grant was assured and soon there was a letter from the University itself that proved it was all true, full of information and reading lists and invitations to Freshers' Evenings. I dreaded my parents' return and my mother's face when I told her but in the end it wasn't so bad. Either Dada had talked her round, or the sun and the sea air had had their relaxing way with her and she didn't fly at me or go quiet and withdraw into herself but talked about new clothes to go in, money to tide me over till the grant came through and where I'd be living.

When she sent me off alone because Dada was at work she only asked me to write but I could see tears standing in her eyes and her cheek seemed very soft and flat like a chamois duster when I kissed it. She said she'd see about having the phone put in and then I could ring sometimes. She'd always resisted before, saying there was no one who couldn't be reached by letter and if we'd had one the neighbours would be knocking on the door day and night whenever they had to call the doctor or the Gas Board.

My first weeks were lonely and strange though I pretended everything was under control. The great surprise was that there were girls everywhere, not like the girls at school. Here, there were girls running and gossiping and sitting opposite you over cups of coffee which they stirred while their faces, their eyes looked into yours and you had to look steadfastly back. You were allowed to look down to stir your own cup but then you must look up and engage again in a kind of struggle like ocular arm-wrestling that I wasn't used to. I still hadn't had a girl although I'd pretended of course to all kinds of mysterious encounters whenever there was a bull session. Sometimes it had crossed my mind that everyone else was pretending too. These Queen's girls had ribbed sweaters that clung tight to their breasts, and their skirts either swirled to their ankles or were yanked above the knee showing smooth thighs. Only Tessa wore jeans.

Afterwards she said she'd noticed me at once and had only been waiting for the right moment. She'd decided it had come when I was sitting alone in the cafeteria because I'd been putting my name down for a try-out for the football teams on Saturday. Usually we went about in a protective gang that was our year, and our main subject, against the rest. Mine was humanities and I was currently discovering James Joyce and Seamus Heaney who'd both been on the reading list. I had a copy of *Wintering Out* from the college library open on the table in front of me among the crumbs and coffee rings.

'Hello.' The girl put down her cup and plate with a slice of baked beans on toast that seemed to sustain life almost exclusively, except for an occasional buttered bun. 'Is anyone sitting here? What're you reading?' I showed her the cover. 'He was a lecturer here, till last year I think it was.'

'I got this out of the library.'

'Well, they would have it, wouldn't they? Taking care of their own.'

'Have you read it?'

She pulled a face I couldn't interpret. 'Not that one. Some of his earlier stuff. He's too soft for me.'

'Where's he now?'

'Gone to the Republic. Went after Bloody Sunday. Couldn't face it here. Some people say it's running away.' She paused. 'You do know about Bloody Sunday, don't you?'

'I read about it in the papers.'

'I thought it was on British television.'

'We don't have television at home.'

'I thought all the British had television.'

'My mother's talking about getting one.'

Suddenly she put out her hand. 'I'm Tessa Groves. What's your name?'

'Liam Noonan.'

'That's a fine Irish name to go with your fine English accent.'

'It's a London accent.' I felt it was time I said something to keep my end up. 'What's your subject?'

'PPE.'

'Oh.' I wasn't quite sure what this meant but I wasn't going to ask.

'And you'll be doing humanities. Why aren't you a scientist

or a mathematician? Isn't that what boys do? Or a lawyer?'

'I'm doing what I want. I was never any good at Maths. I just about scraped through 'O' level. Anyway, who wants to be a bank manager?'

'I wanted to be an engineer but the Sisters talked me out of it.'

I thought she said 'the Sisters' but I wasn't quite sure what she meant, whether her school or family, but again I didn't ask.

'Have you explored the city yet or have you only found the way from college to your hall?'

'I haven't done much. I've been too busy settling in, apart from running in the morning and going to lectures.' There'd been the horrors of Freshers' Week when we, the chickens, had been invited to one bewildering function after the other in a misguided effort to make us feel part of something. After the first two I'd dropped out.

'Running?' she said, as if I'd said I'd been tossing off.

'To keep in training. I'm down for the trials on Saturday.'

'What trials?'

'Football. I'm hoping to get into the first team. I played for my school.'

'And what was that? Eton or Spewed-Up?'

'Archbishop Edward's. It's an ordinary comprehensive.'

'It sounds like a Prod establishment to me.'

'I don't think it was anything. Just the local state school.'

'And what about you? With a name like that you ought to be a Catholic.'

'I don't think I'm anything either,' I said carefully. 'I don't think it matters what you are. We've got a lot of Rastas and Muslims and that now in Deverham.'

'Here it matters,' she said firmly. 'You'll learn. When you tell people in Belfast your name they'll tell you what you are and you'll find there's no gainsaying it. Anyway I was going to ask if you'd like to join some of us for a drink tonight, if you haven't got to come back early and get your beauty sleep, that is.'

That was how it began. And I suppose I'll never know now whether she really fancied me or had just spotted a potential recruit. But if so what vulnerability was I giving off, or did she just try everyone in turn and I simply hadn't noticed? Maybe I was the first and when she struck paydirt at once she just concentrated on me. Sometimes I think she really loved me.

We went to a pub that evening in the Falls Road. It was all very jolly with a microphone and singing and the beer flowing freely. When I began joining in the songs after a few pints Tessa said, 'Hey, how come you know all the words better than me?'

'My Dad sings them.' I hadn't realised how much I knew, how much I'd taken in. Sometimes, when I was still really small, I'd be left outside with a bag of crisps and a bottle of pop while my parents were in the bar. I'd hear the singing from inside, growing louder whenever one of them stuck their head round the door to ask if I was all right.

Tessa seemed to know a good handful of people in the bar. 'Where are you from?' one of them asked me.

'I'm from London but my father's from Arklow,' I said, wanting to be accepted.

'How long has he been over there?'

'Oh, a long time. Thirty years or so,' I calculated quickly.

'But he still thinks of himself as an Irishman?'

'Yes, yes he does. He never lost his accent.'

'What's his job?'

'He's an electrician.'

'Ah, we could do with more of them. And you, how do you see yourself?'

'Me? I'm a citizen of the world,' I said, laughing and raising my glass, but he didn't laugh and raise his in return. He said something I didn't understand to Tessa, and I realised he was speaking in Gaelic, and felt shut-out and a stirring of jealousy.

He put out his hand. 'I'm Kevin Dooley. Welcome to the front line.'

I shook his hand. 'You do know this is a war Liam? They have told you that over there?' I thought suddenly of Jenkins who must be doing his training now somewhere in England.

'People know there's trouble. I don't think most of them understand what it's about.'

'And do you then?'

'I'm learning.'

But my chief concern was Tessa. She saw me back to hall, saying she lived in digs in the city but didn't trust me to find my way back with a skinful. It's true I was pretty tanked-up. I'd never drunk so much in one go, apart from our sixth form farewell party when we'd smuggled in bottles of wine and got pissed in the prefects' room that last afternoon so that I had to walk home clinging on to my bike for support. Outside the hall on the steps I wanted to kiss her but was put off by the lights streaming out of the hallway and the fact that my lips seemed to have gone numb. But soon after that she offered to show me some of the countryside and we took a bus up above the city and got off to walk while she pointed out this and that landmark and I looked mostly at her.

'Don't you find it beautiful, Ireland?' she was saying.

'So are you,' and I bent down and kissed her. For a moment I thought she was going to pull away, and then she seemed to catch fire and kissed me back and I hung on and held her tight, her body the length of mine until a sudden hot swell had me hard against her. She unclutched a hand from round my neck and slid it down to my flies. For a moment I thought she was going to undo them there and then. I knew I wouldn't have been able to hold it but she just stroked the swelling cloth.

'Well, well,' she said. 'The British boy likes me.'

'I'm not a British boy.' I felt the old man begin to lose interest.

'What are you then?'

'I don't have to be anything except me.'

'And what's "me"? That's the difference between us. Over there you think you can just be you but in Ireland we know it isn't as simple.'

'That's just politics.'

'There you are, you see. On the mainland you all behave

as if politics is nothing to do with you and goes on without you, instead of being part of everything.'

'What about religion?'

'I'm not religious. I mean I don't go to mass or confession or any of that. Here politics is religion and religion is politics.'

By this time every desire, lust, call it what you like, had shrunk away to nothing.

'Can't you just forget it all for a bit?'

'What do you want to do then?'

'Nothing.' I'd gone completely off the boil. Her arguments were as effective as a cold shower.

'All right. I'll race you up the road.' And she set off running. She had a surprise start and she was very nimble but of course I caught her up quickly and grabbed her to me. 'You're very fast,' she said, laughing. For a moment she'd been going to say something else, something sharp and teasing. I saw it go in and out of her face and I couldn't tell if she'd thought better of it, understood that if she got it wrong now I might go away altogether, or if something in me softened her and she put up her face and kissed my cheek. Then she took my arm.

'Come and watch me play.' I'd had a place in the team on the reserve bench for the first match but I'd been promised a trial game next week when we were at home to Loughborough College.

And she did. I played as if the spirit of Georgie Best possessed my feet, and scored after half-time when the game was hanging in the balance. I ran like an old hero who'd been given the gift of speed by the gods because I knew she was watching and I wanted her to cheer for me. When the coach told me I'd got a permanent place I felt as if the rest of life would all be like this with my back being slapped and Tessa ready to take my arm again. That night she let me kiss her a lot and the next day we went out on the bus again. But this time after we'd got off and walked a bit we lay down behind some bushes out of the wind in a flickering autumn sunlight and she let me explore her body.

'You're the wild one. I bet you're a virgin though.'

'Of course not.'

'Well, if you are you'll have to stay one today for I've got the curse.'

I was shocked and excited at the same time. We'd speculated at school about this female phenomenon but none of us, not even those with sisters, really understood it. Still, at least she hadn't pushed me away. She'd held out some sort of promise.

I walked around in a daze now, my whole body alive to her, my thoughts addressing her all the time. We weren't encouraged to have girls in our rooms and she said she couldn't take me back to her digs so all our loving took place in the open air in an Indian summer that seemed laid on specially for us. The next time it looked as though something might happen, she suddenly asked me if I had anything with me as she wasn't wanting to get pregnant. Of course I hadn't. I hadn't given it a thought. Nor did I know how you went about such things in Belfast.

The full-back, Gallagher, was a randy talker, full of smut and stories of how he'd banged this girl and that. I put on my most casual man-of-the-world tone and asked him what he did for johnnies.

'I don't use them.'

'What, never?'

'Well, only if I can't get it without.'

'So what do you do?'

'I bring some back with me.'

'Can you sell us some?'

He laughed. 'Won't she let you have it otherwise?'

I pretended to a knowledge I didn't have. 'She's a Catholic so she can't go on the pill. I don't want her in the club.'

'I'll sell you one packet. Then you're on your own.'

Fortunately when I undid the wrapper I found a mail order address I could write to for more. I looked at the little flesh-coloured balloons in their paper bands, each with a sort of nipple sticking out. Even the sight of them, combined with the thought of Tessa, turned me on so I came just as I was trying to fit one over my prick. I'd have to watch that.

The next time we went for our walk the knowledge of what was in my inside pocket nearly undid me as soon as we lay down. 'What about it?' I said. 'I've got something now.'

She looked at me a little strangely. 'Don't rush me, Liam. Just let it happen if it's going to.' And it did. Afterwards, I wasn't sure how she'd been, whether she'd come or not, because I was so overwhelmed I couldn't pay much attention. It was later it became so important to know what she was feeling too, though at least I managed not to ask but tried to puzzle it out from other things like how she looked and whether she was as keen as me. In between we talked, history and politics, and I met more of her group of friends. One night in December, I said, 'What about this new agreement? Surely that'll change things.'

'It won't last, you'll see. The Prods will never wear it. They don't want to share. They want to keep the power.' The following spring the whole province was paralysed by the Protestant strike. 'You see. They don't want a peaceful solution. Force is the only thing they understand.' I had to agree that that was how it seemed and I found myself gradually taking sides more, Tessa's side of course, but it was the Army, the British Army that is, that finally tipped me over.

I was coming back alone after leaving Tessa at the end of the road when I heard that unmistakable crump of a bomb going off somewhere in the city towards the centre and then as I rounded the corner I ran slap into a foot patrol, soldiers with guns cocked, running and backing and weaving, ducking behind corners and into doorways for cover with only their gun barrels poking out. I just stood still and stared because although I'd been in the city a few months I didn't go much to the centre, and round by the University it was all very quiet and orderly, with children going to school in the mornings in their neat uniforms, better-dressed and behaved than they would have been on their way to Archbishop Edward's. The soldiers came on towards me and I began walking towards the platoon, meaning just to pass through between them and not seeing or hearing anything apart from that thump that would account for their caution, when suddenly two of them turned on me and slammed me face-forwards into the nearest wall shouting at me to get my hands above my head and my legs apart. I could feel a gun barrel ramming me hard and small in the back. I should have felt frightened but at first I didn't. I just thought they were being excessive, over-acting as if we were in a bad movie.

Then they began the questions. 'What's your name? Where've you been? Where are you going? Where do you come from?' When I said I was a student at Queen's and that I came from London they said so did a lot of them, meaning, I supposed, the Provos. My name didn't help either. They'd frisked me straight away for weapons but after the questions they went over me again more carefully and they found a packet of johnnies in my pocket, and accused me of having them to make firebombs, a use that'd never crossed my mind. They shoved me around a lot. One of them was especially rough, saying one of his mates had bought it and he reckoned he was owed 'a bastard'.

'We'll be checking you out,' the NCO in charge said. 'Keep your nose clean, sonny, because we've got you on file now and we can have you in any time.' Then, surprisingly, they let me go. I was seething. I put my hands in my pockets and walked as straight as I could but by now my legs were water and I felt as if at any moment they might change their minds and put a bullet in my back.

When I told Tessa she didn't say: 'I told you so.' She didn't have to. Instead she said, 'It happens all the time.'

'Do you get stopped?'

'Oh yes. Especially when I'm coming back late.'

'The bastards!' I remembered I'd never liked Jenkins. 'Arrogant bastards!'

'They're probably no worse than any other army of occupation.'

After that, I found myself getting in deeper. I didn't make any conscious decisions; it just happened. Sometimes Tessa would go away for a few days. Before, when I'd asked her where, she'd been evasive, now she told me she was training or doing 'a job', though she never told me what. One day she said, 'Kevin says you could come with me next time I go South, if you want to.' So I understood that Kevin was the boss though when I thought about it afterwards I realised I had known already.

We set out for Buncrana on the bus from Belfast through Derry one Saturday when summer had driven football away. For the first time we'd be able to sleep together all night in a bed in a little boarding house Tessa knew. We were going to the seaside, taking a holiday. I felt as light as a kid. Once we'd dumped our bags we hired a couple of bikes in the Main Street and set off, ostensibly to explore the countryside, but the ground rose steeply and we were soon pushing the bikes.

'Look back,' Tessa said, pausing for breath. When I did, I'd never seen anything like the glitter of the sea with the sun on it as if it was a sheet of silver cloth thrown down, with a pale strip of beach, and the hills falling away below and rising up behind. I was suddenly glad I'd come from and to something so beautiful. Then we pushed on, and off, along a track sheltered by bushes and leading down into a hollow where there was a farmhouse with outbuildings, all white-washed and one storey high. This was the training camp. There were three or four people there already. Tessa introduced me. The one who seemed to be the leader was called Fergal. He asked if I'd signed up.

'No, but Kevin said he was all right.'

'He ought to sign.'

I swallowed hard. 'I'll sign,' I said.

'You know we're a proscribed organisation here in the Republic?'

'Yes.'

'No one must witness this except me. Tessa, you wait outside.'

When she had left the room he took a green form from his desk drawer. It seemed to be an oath of allegiance to accept orders and not to betray the organisation or the cause. A bit of me felt it was all games, playing, kid's stuff really, like joining the Masons or some other secret society, but a bit of me was also excited by the cloak and dagger. Fergal produced a Bible too for me to swear on. 'I'd rather just affirm,' I said. 'I don't believe in all that.' After I had done my swearing we shook hands. Tessa was called back in and we gave each other a kiss on the cheek. Then Fergal said, 'I'm glad that's all settled because I've got a proposition for you, Tessa, and now you can take in Liam too. We've been offered training facilities abroad and we need people to go and suss them out. Report back on the set-up. University term must be nearly finished. Would you be free in a couple of weeks' time?' And that was how I found myself on the way to Libya.

Now, of course, I wonder how much of all this was itself a set-up, a play whose script had been written already, including my part, to see whether I was ready yet to speak my lines on cue. But at other times I think that's just the cynical British way of looking at it and that everything happened almost by chance, just as it seemed to do at the time. One thing I'm sure is true: the leaders had decided that the best way to make me really involved was simply to involve me and that this show of confidence in me, under Tessa's watchful eye, was just what was needed to draw me in.

We flew to Paris first, with Tessa looking over her shoulder all the time, convinced that we were being followed, but if we were we managed to shake our tail by diving into the Métro and losing ourselves underground, coming up to book into a little hotel in the rue de L'Abbé Grégoire. Two days later we flew to Tunis and then travelled by bus to Tripoli. It was strange to be looking out at desert from the bus-windows and thinking that Dada had been here too. He didn't talk much about that time but there were photographs of him, his thin chest darkened by the sun above long shorts, boots and socks, his arms round the shoulders of other young men grinning at the camera in front of a dusty pock-marked tank, with white enamel mugs of what must have been tea in their fists.

In Tripoli we were met at the airport and taken to the Libya Palace Hotel where after a bit of argument we were found a room. The next day the same shabby young man turned up to take us to the foreign embassy quarter where the

IRA had been given a house next to the Bulgarian Embassy, and almost diplomatic status. We were received by one of the diplomats and told that arrangements had been made for us to travel into the Sahara and assess the training facilities at a couple of camps used mainly by the *fedayeen* of the PLO. We would be picked up from our hotel and flown in a military plane to a desert airstrip where another truck would take us on. The first camp we would visit was Wair-al-Kabir. 'It will be best if you dress as like the others at the camps as possible. Normally women don't go there. They train at the Women's Military Academy here in Tripoli but we have said you are a very experienced officer and your opinion is crucial so they are making an exception. However it might be a nice gesture if you covered your head. Fortunately the scarf is a revolutionary green.' And he laughed.

The next morning the shabby young man drove us to the airport and out to a distant runway where a small turbo-prop was waiting. Once aboard and strapped in we were given a parcel each and told to change at the back of the plane when it had taken off so that by the time we touched down again we were dressed in the olive shirts and trousers of the *fedayeen* and Tessa's hair had disappeared under the bright green scarf. There was a Landrover waiting beside the airstrip that was merely a smooth stretch of sand. Its driver and the pilot waved to each other, the gangway steps were unfolded for us and up again. We had barely shaken hands with the driver before the plane was taxiing off, had turned and was rising into the evening sky above limitless acres of sand.

'I am Hussein.'

'Is it far to the camp?'

'No, only an hour, less.'

The desert stretched all around us in every direction and again I thought how it must have been for Dada stranded here perhaps for months on end. Suddenly I wanted to ask him all the questions I hadn't asked before. As the sun went down, flaring briefly across the dunes, the temperature that had nearly cooked us in the little plane began to drop, cooling the sweat under our cotton shirts. The light seemed to be draining into the desert sand that soaked it up as darkness washed down the sky. At last the Landrover came up over a short rise and we could see lights below. I looked back marvelling how the driver could find his way at all in the endless sand.

He pulled up in front of a low building, one of three in a broken square surrounded by a wire fence, whose fourth side was the only way in, and the only road was a jumble of tyre tracks in the sand, narrowed by a smaller hut with a crescent moon on the side where a sentry stood.

'Tonight the lady will sleep in the medical hut,' Hussein indicated the small one beside the track, 'and you will sleep in the dormitory of the young soldiers.' He pointed to one of the long low buildings. Outside the wire I could dimly see another lit building possibly with further dark shapes beyond. 'First you must meet our commander and then we will eat.'

We had only one bag between us so I extracted my washing tackle and gave the bag to Tessa. 'We will meet here in ten minutes,' Hussein said. 'Now I will show you your bed.' He took me into one of the long low buildings and indicated a bunk just inside the door by the wall. Then he pointed out the washroom and left me. It was very gloomy inside and the only light was from a couple of paraffin lamps at either end.

The commander turned out to be an elderly man with neat grey hair and beard who looked more like a religious leader than a soldier. Hussein acted as interpreter while the old man welcomed us and hoped we weren't too tired and that we should find what we wanted. He also said, with an air of great sadness, that he was sorry that the British had betrayed us as they had betrayed the Palestinians because he himself had once stood beside a great Englishman, a friend to the Arabs. I could only think he meant Lawrence of Arabia and realised he must be much older than he looked. He addressed himself to me as if I was the senior and Tessa just my hanger-on, so I thought it best to answer that we were glad to be there and grateful for their hospitality. Then he bowed in dismissal with his hand on his heart and we bowed too.

Next Hussein took us to the mess hall which was like my sleeping quarters but with tables and benches and an open hearth at one end where pots were simmering.

'I have things to do. Please help yourselves to food. I will see you in the morning.'

There was a big pot of coffee keeping hot on a paraffin stove and plates of figs and dates and pitta bread as well as what turned out to be a kind of stew.

'Well, I don't know what the older members would make of all this hob-nobbing with the heathen,' Tessa said as we dunked pieces of flat bread in the stew. 'But the new boys that are running things now will take help from anywhere. I find the male chauvinism a bit hard to swallow. I know there are women in the PLO but where are they?'

'I expect we'll find out more tomorrow. I don't know about you but I'm shattered. What're your sleeping quarters like?'

'It's a camp bed that must be used for the sick or wounded. It's all right.'

'I'm in a bunk by the wall with about twenty others.'

In fact I was so tired I didn't hear those others come in. Only once when I woke briefly in the night was I aware of breathing all around me in the dark and the muted noises of young animals in their sleep. It must have been the call to prayer that woke me again but instead of sitting up and making my presence known I watched my fellow sleepers awaken through half-closed eyes and realised with a shock that these young soldiers were some of them children, at least so it seemed from my going-on twenty years.

When I mentioned it to Tessa later she said, 'So what? We recruit in the schools. I was sixteen when I joined and that was quite late. Romeo and Juliet were only fourteen, you know. I'm more worried about the climate and the nature of the training. There's an awful lot of emphasis on the physical side, which is all right for an army fighting over a large area in a conventional war but isn't much use for urban guerilla warfare.' This was after we'd been shown around and watched the boys practising on a kind of assault course that made army training films look like nature rambles. They also learnt weaponry of every sort and bomb- and mine-laying and disposal. We were able to talk to one of the boys who had some English. He was thirteen, very grown-up and serious in his desire to fight for the Palestinian cause. I found myself feeling warm towards him because of his sense of purpose though his constant bringing of Allah into everything was very off-putting.

After a couple of days there, we were taken on to a tougher camp at El Maya for older *fedayeen*, where there was more of the same but harder. 'I don't think our people could stand the pace in this climate,' Tessa said. 'Maybe we could send a few people here as a goodwill gesture so Gaddafi is still prepared to fund us, but I can't see any real future use in it.'

We didn't tell our hosts of course but simply thanked them for their hospitality and said we'd report back. A bit of me envied the simplicity of their cause. Ours seemed much less well-defined, with dubious borders of how far and what we were really trying to achieve. For I now thought as 'we'. During the next couple of years I crossed a series of frontiers without always realising I'd taken another step and the no-man's-land behind me stretched further and further back until the other side was beyond recall.

I gave up writing home because there was nothing I could say. The leadership wanted me to finish my degree course and somehow I managed to struggle to a second while I thought of nothing except Tessa, who'd been a year ahead and left before me, so I faced the whole of my third year alone. On the day I finished my last exam she was there to meet me on the University steps. 'Now you're free,' she said, taking my arm. 'But I shan't be much longer. I was picked up coming back over the border and they found some stuff on me. If they make it stick I'll go down for six months.'

She seemed very calm about it but I was distraught. 'What will I do without you for six months? I can't manage a week.'

She laughed. 'You'll do as everyone else has done, though it's mainly the women of course who go through it: wait. You mustn't come and see me or write. You have to keep yourself free of suspicion. Make it look as if we've fallen out.'

'What shall I do?'

'They want you to go on a training course and then maybe to the States, fund-raising. A nice clean intellectual like you should charm the dollars out of their pockets.'

I wasn't even allowed to be in court when she was convicted and sentenced. The days while she was away went past in a kind of fog of grief and loss. Once or twice, making sure I wasn't followed, I went down to Armagh just to walk about the streets and look at the prison from a distance, to feel near her. In the middle of it Dada wrote to say Mammy was very ill and asking me to go over and see her. But I couldn't move. I seemed paralysed. Then he wrote again about the funeral but I still couldn't make myself cross the water and go. I made the excuse to myself that it was too close to my going to the States. I don't remember much about that either. It was as if the outside world only impinged on my consciousness when Tessa was there to share it. And then one day without warning there she was, free, looking very pale but with her eyes alight, and everything began again.

We rarely worked together. The leaders in their wisdom had decided that my best use was as a courier. I suppose they still didn't trust me and in a way they've proved right. I haven't talked about specific jobs, partly because I was kept to one side of all that but also because, whatever anyone may think, I'm not a traitor. Not twice anyway; not a turncoat. Some people would say I've betrayed the place I was born in, I know, and if I have I have. But I can't do it a second time, whatever happens, because then it would be betraying myself, and love. That too.

Perhaps if they'd trusted me more or even drawn me in deeper so that I couldn't kid myself I was still personally innocent of blood, I wouldn't have begun to hanker after something else. We worked on the cell principle, and need-to-know, but sometimes I'd be there when someone came back from a job and even though you didn't know exactly what they'd been doing, you'd catch such a whiff of excitement off them as if they were high on something, as they were of course: on the sweet flush of adrenalin. Banking the protection money we raised from clubs and pubs, donations to the cause, doesn't give you the same thrill when you're just a step removed from a Securicor man, but no one's going to try one on you. Once I said to Tessa while we were lying in bed after making love in the room we now shared in a communal flat, 'Why don't we go to the States permanently and get married? Haven't you earned a break? Done enough? We could go on collecting, fund-raising. We wouldn't get out completely.'

She looked at me, not angrily as I might have expected, but with a matter-of-factness that was worse. 'Why would I want to do that? Do you see me as a boring, bored, bourgeois housewife?' And it was true. What other way of life was there for her? It was in her blood. It danced in her veins like some living organism that had invaded and taken over. I couldn't imagine her, however much I tried, living any other way. I could see myself getting some job, maybe even as a teacher, but not Tessa. I thought I could go abroad and work for a voluntary organisation, teach in a foreign country or grow vegetables in Africa, dig irrigation trenches in the desert, but when I ran through this coloured brochure of possibilities it was hard to see Tessa standing smiling beside me with a hoe in her hand.

We lived on luck, touching wood that it wouldn't run out, that we wouldn't be arrested or killed. At least I touched wood. I don't think she thought like that. 'Well, involve me more then. You take all the risks while I sit around like the bored housewife. They should give me more to do.'

She put a finger under my chin. 'Is your self-image suffering then?'

'Shut up! Fuck off!'

Now she studied me more closely, no longer trying to make a joke of it. 'You're really cross. All right, I'll have a word.'

A few days later she said lightly, 'You're to go on a course to fit you for higher things. That's if you show any aptitude for it.' And that was the trouble. I'd watched Dada at work often enough but his patience with little screws and wires only set my teeth on edge. And I couldn't help thinking that what he had spent his days doing was enhancing life, mending so that light and music and power came back into dead machines. My fingers were all thumbs, my hands tended to shake at the wrong moment, just when they needed to be rock-steady, so that I often had to stop and try again which wasted precious time. I emerged from the course more likely to be a danger to myself than any enemy, as the instructor put it unkindly but accurately. If I asked to go out on a job with Tessa I could end up killing us both.

'The cobbler should stick to his last,' Mammy used to say, and they would have agreed with her. All I could do was run fast. Maybe I could have dribbled a grenade up the road and booted it into an Army or RUC post, but I was useless with my hands. No one even had to tell me. I said it myself to Tessa with what I hoped was a wry laugh. I understood the theory all right; it was just the skill, Dada's craftsmanship, that I lacked. I wasn't much good with weapons either but then I didn't have to be. When I went to collect our funds, tithe or danegeld, call it what you like, I always had a heavy with me and no one knew if we were armed or not. That way we could keep up the charade that the donation was always willingly given for the cause. And sometimes that was true.

I also went to America again. By this time Tessa and I had both taken new identities. It made me worry that perhaps it wasn't the first time she'd done this and that the person I loved wasn't Tessa Groves at all, but then I found the idea so upsetting that I dismissed the thought as quickly as I could. Because the name is so much the person, what you murmur inside your head, I found my whole apprehension of reality wavering, growing nebulous. Shakespeare may have thought there's nothing in a name but the Celts have always known otherwise and if you hadn't a name you hadn't a soul; some intrinsic part of you was missing. Nameless, how could you identify yourself even to yourself? There was only the subjective 'I', which everyone has in common, without that objectifying name.

I asked Tessa to come to the States with me, the next time that was, just for the trip. But all I got was that stranger-look she sometimes gave me as if she couldn't remember quite who I was. 'No,' she said, 'I've things to do while you're away.' It worried me sick all the time I was over there, in case she was in even more danger than usual, so much so that I switched my flight to come back a couple of days early. I thought if I wasn't there, something might happen to her, as if I was her talisman who kept her safe.

I didn't tell her about my change of plan because it was a stand-by flight that might not have come off. I didn't even stop to ring her from the airport, I was so eager to get home. I ran upstairs with my bag and pushed open the door to the living room where we all cooked and ate. A couple of the others were sitting at the big kitchen table. They'd been talking but when I came in they stopped suddenly, and then Padraig said loudly as if surprised, 'Hello Liam! You're back early. We weren't expecting you for another couple of days.'

'I couldn't wait to see you all again,' I said, laughing. 'Is Tessa home?'

'She's talking a bit of business with someone, I think. Why don't you have a cup of tea till she gets through?'

I understood what this meant. Secrecy, compartmentalism, as I've said, was part of our lives. I sat down at the table. Padraig put a kettle to boil, asking me about my trip and how New York was looking. He made us all cups of tea and before it was cool enough to drink, Tessa came into the room, closing the door behind her, and stood with her back to it. Usually I'd have got up and gone straight over to her but there was a look about her that stopped me.

'Hi. I came back early.'

'So I can see.'

She was flushed and her hair, which was usually tied back,

hung loose. Then I heard footsteps on the stairs and the front door closing and realised I wasn't to be told who'd been with her in our room.

That was the first time it crossed my mind that she ever slept with anyone else. Now I don't know why I'd never thought of it before. Some protective coating of confidence or arrogance had made me blind: unless that was genuinely the first time she'd betrayed me. But I didn't ask. An instinct for self-preservation made me not want to hear words that might break me into shards like a shattered mirror, with every one a cut-throat dagger.

When I tried to make love to her that night she turned away sleepily. I'd read about the dark night of the soul when there's nothing but doubt and the love object is withdrawn from the lover. I entered that now, not knowing because I didn't want to know, but unable to think of anything else, looking constantly for clues which when I found them I wilfully misinterpreted to prove that we were still fine, that she still loved me. My doubting her spilled over onto everything else. Most of all, I began to doubt what we were doing. The hardline British government seemed impervious to everything thrown at them. They'd survived the deaths at their own party conference, the deaths on our side of the hunger strikers, and mainland bombings. Now the Irish government had entered into an agreement with them that seemed to be sticking and they'd thwarted a big consignment of arms and ammunition from Libya that would have given us real credibility as an army. I found myself increasingly getting into arguments in the pub and over the kitchen table.

'The truth is the people don't want our kind of revolution. If they had ordinary politics here and unification most of them wouldn't even vote Labour.'

'But there isn't unification. And anyway, what do you understand about it? The Irish people aren't like the English: they have more idealism.'

'They want houses and comforts, schools and hospitals and freedom to make individual choices like anyone else.'

'Socialism will give them freedom and unity.'

'Not unless you have religious freedom as well.'

'You're an atheist, Liam.'

'That's right, I am.'

'So how can you understand the Irish people?'

'But it's religion that's made this mess.'

'It's British imperialism.'

'What about Irish imperialism that turned North Britain into Scotland?'

'That's just playing with words.'

'So's prod and taig.'

'Why do you go on then if that's how you feel?'

The only answer I could have given was that Tessa wouldn't come away with me. Then I bumped into Jenkins.

I'd enrolled to do an MA at the University because it gave me some kind of cover and meant I could call in on legitimate business if I needed to, using my own name, not my Army one that I used, for example, to play in the reserves for Derry City as I did now.

'Hello, Noonan,' he said. I recognised him at once though he wasn't in uniform. 'It is you, isn't it?'

For a moment I thought of denying it but then I realised I'd never pull it off. 'Hello, Jenkins,' I said cheerfully and stuck out my hand. We shook. I was shaking inside as well and praying it didn't show. 'Yes, it's me, sort of. As far as anyone can ever be sure.' It sounded like terrorspeak even as I was saying it but he laughed.

'Same old Noonan. Always the intellectual. What're you still doing here? This is my third trick. I thought I might run into you the first time but not now.'

'I signed on to do my MA after having a few years travelling.'

'All right for some,' he said.

'You look well.'

'Mustn't grumble. I got married a couple of years ago when we were in Germany as a matter of fact. A local girl. We've got two kids now.'

'Two?'

'Boy and a girl. Made up for lost time.' His voice had changed. He no longer had the Deverham accent. Now it was received pronunciation; mine too, I supposed. 'You must come and have dinner with us. We can have a good gas about Archbishop Edward's. There aren't many people you can talk to socially out here. It was better in Germany. The people are friendlier.'

I wondered if he felt a bit out of it with his brother officers, some of whom would be from military families and public schools.

'Do you ever hear anything of any of the others from our lot?'

'No, never. I don't really keep up.'

'I don't either. I did read in the paper last time we were over that Bateson had been badly knocked about and had to retire. He's the only one of us who ever made the news.'

'Really?'

'Yes. He was European Welterweight Champion for a bit. Was after the World title when he got biffed.'

'Well done him.' I was wanting to get away.

'When can you come and see us? I'd like you to meet Trudy. Are you married? Do bring your wife or girlfriend.'

'No,' I said, 'there's nobody. Nobody wants the eternal student.' I imagined introducing Tessa to them.

'We'll have to find you a nice girl. German women make cracking wives.' He winked and leered a bit. 'Give me your phone number or let's fix something now.'

I fumbled at my jacket pocket. 'I don't think I've got my diary.'

'Okay: phone number.'

'I'm in digs. It isn't easy with calls.' I could see he wasn't going to give up. 'Give me a date and your number. Then if I find I can't make it when I get hold of my diary, I can ring you.'

He produced a printed card. 'That's it. Got used to carrying them when I was in Germany.' I saw he was now a major. 'Let's make it Saturday. I'm off-duty this weekend, thank God. Seven-thirty. The taxi drivers know how to find it. Must dash.

I'm meeting Trudy for the weekly shop. Joys of the married life!' The address was Harwell Road, Holywood.

Tessa was away that weekend so there was no one to take a real interest in what I was doing or where I was going. The night before she'd left she'd turned away when I tried to touch her. I walked down Divis Street and into Royal Avenue feeling sore and rejected. I found a taxi but when I told him the address he said at once, 'Palace Barracks, is it?'

'That's right.'

'Not my favourite job. You never know who might be watching.' We crossed the river and headed east.

I knew where the barracks was, of course, everyone did, though I'd never been there, never even felt the need to walk by on the other side. I felt sick with excitement now as we drove through the leafy avenues and I knew we were getting near. To the left I caught a glimpse of sea and then we were going up Holywood High Street and we might have been in Bucks or Surrey with the parked BMWs and Landrovers suggesting another way of life.

'I can only take you up to the gates.'

'That's fine.'

We bumped over a row of sleeping policemen and pulled up behind a line of cars waiting to be checked. I got out and, as soon as I'd paid him, the driver swung the car round and headed towards the city. Soldiers in full kit had their eyes trained on the row of idling cars. I walked towards the gates and the gatehouses beyond. My own naïvety shamed me. I hadn't even thought about getting in, about the searches and checks I'd have to go through. I joined the queue to be frisked. 'Name? Who are you going to see? Address . . . ?' And then suddenly, I was inside, following the guard's instructions, strolling under the eye of closed-circuit cameras, past the high perimeter wire with the floodlights that would turn night into day.

'They let you in, then?' Jenkins joked, opening the door of a small brick villa that could have been set down on any undistinguished estate in southern England. 'Trudy's in the kitchen. The kids are asleep so we can have a grown-up evening. Now what will you drink? Whisky, gin and tonic? Trudy . . . Ah, there you are, darling. This is Liam, my old school chum who's having a . . . ?'

'Oh, whisky will be fine.'

She was beautiful with a Nordic filmstar's calm blonde perfection.

'What will you have, darling?' Jenkins asked her.

'I think just a glass of wine now, please.'

She came over to the sofa and sat down beside me. I was aware of her perfume like a tangible manifestation of herself reaching out towards me. I fumbled for something to say, unused to making conversation that wasn't either about politics or immediate practicalities.

'It must be very strange for you being here.'

'We become used to it. They say the schools are very good although fortunately our children are too small for that problem now. But the sea, the beach, is beautiful even in winter and here it is very quiet. It is difficult to believe in the war sometimes.'

'Darling, it isn't a war,' Jenkins corrected her.

'Then what must I call it? You are soldiers. You get killed. There are bombs and bullets. If there is no war there is no need for soldiers, only policemen.'

'They can't manage alone.'

'Then, when it is so much killing and bombs that the police cannot manage it, it becomes a war. What do you think, Liam? Is that an Irish name?' Trudy smiled at me.

'Yes, my father's Irish.'

'But not your mother?'

'My mother's dead. She was a Scot.' As I said it I suddenly felt I might burst into tears.

'And you and Ivor were at school together? What was he like then?'

I looked at Jenkins and wondered what had happened to time. We'd left Archbishop Edward's so many years ago. We might even not have recognised each other, but we had. Jenkins had filled out. He was solid and had that soldier's confident, some would say arrogant, gait that even the squaddies fall into as if by second nature. I was willing to bet he had hair on his chest now too. And she loved him, this stunning creature, as I loved Tessa. She must do, otherwise why would she leave her own country and follow him here and have his children? Was he the same Jenkins inside, as I knew I was still that school-leaver of all that time ago? Yet he had something to show for the last years. I had nothing except my tremulous relationship with Tessa.

'It is very beautiful, Ireland,' Trudy was saying.

'Yes, it is. Especially after Deverham.'

'Oh, it wasn't so bad.' Jenkins took my glass to refill. 'There was the river, the park. Liam used to be a brilliant footballer. Do you still play?'

'No,' I said. It was my other self that played for Derry City. 'I had to give up with a torn cartilage.' I turned to Trudy. 'You should see the rest of it while you're here. It's even better than this part.'

Trudy left us and we reminisced about masters and boys until she called us to eat. Jenkins' parents were both dead. Nothing bound him to Deverham except memory. His only sister was married in Australia. He was drinking in quick gulps, half a glass of gin and tonic at a swallow. Now in the small dining annexe he opened a bottle of wine. 'What most of us wish is that the politicians would sort something out. The lads get sick of these tours. They don't join the Army to get shot at!' He laughed.

'Why do they join?'

'For the job, the pay mostly. The Army looks after you while you're part of it. When I have to leave I still don't know what I'll do. Maybe I'll go to Australia too. But you don't like that idea much, do you, Trudy?'

She smiled and passed a dish of green beans but didn't answer.

'Your "lads" can be a bit obstreperous. I was turned over myself one night.' The drink was making me incautious. I must watch my tongue.

'They're only oiks, pretty harmless. Like we were before we decided to stay on and make something of ourselves. Like poor old Bateson really. Remember how he hated spades? It was a spade that downed him. Anyway we'd all be glad to be sent back to Germany. Except of course that the Germans don't really want us any more. So it's back to Aldershot.'

'You will find a job in Germany,' Trudy said quietly.

'Yes. That's another option of course. Especially now. Maybe the EC will solve Northern Ireland too. Put in a peace-keeping force and get us out.'

What would the Volunteers do without the Brits to hate? And how would the Prods and the Paisleyites respond to a lot of French, and Italian, and German Catholics in sky-blue berets? I couldn't see it happening. And suddenly I saw no end to it, and that Tessa's dream was just that. Even if Jenkins' lads went away there would never be a working man's state in Ireland. The South didn't want it and neither did the people of Ulster, Prod or Taig. I'd seen enough to know as well that the two parts were temperamentally different, and that their coming together would be more painful and difficult than, say, the reunification of Germany. Tessa was wedded not to me or any achievable end but to what she called 'the armed struggle' itself, which was Yeats' 'terrible beauty' and the fatal dark goddess of death and battles in the old myths: the Morrigan who perched on the slain in the form of a crow.

At the end of the evening Jenkins phoned for a taxi and I was carried back to our lodgings. Everyone else was still out. I fell into our double bed and sank into a drunken heavy coma. My only comfort in the morning was that Jenkins must have felt even worse. I turned over groaning and went back to sleep.

It was a week later that Tessa, going through my pockets for change, found Jenkins' card. 'What's this?' she asked, holding it up.

'Oh, it's somewhere I went out to supper while you were away last weekend.' I'd decided at once not to lie.

'With a Brit major in the barracks?'

'We were at school together. I bumped into him in the High Street and he insisted. I thought it would look suspicious if I refused.'

'Do you think I'm stupid or something? Surely you can think up a better story than that.'

'It's true. Look, if it wasn't, would I have left the card there?'

'Maybe you forgot it.' Of course I had, though not the conversation at the Jenkins' table and the doubts it had raised. 'And will you be going again, to keep in touch with your handler, like?'

'If he presses me I'll have to go. Unless I tell him I'm going away.'

'Next time you pay him a visit you can take him a present.'

'I'd never get it past the checkpoint. Anyway, he's got a wife and kids.'

'So had the dead of Bloody Sunday. It's never worried you before. Or didn't you think what all the money you collect goes on?' Her anger and disdain were like hard slaps to the face. I was sick and trembling because it was clear she didn't trust me and therefore, by extension, that she didn't love me. Perhaps she never had. That was even more terrible. 'I shall have to think what to do. I ought to report this.'

'You can do what you like. I don't care.' But I did. Not for my life but for our loss, my loss.

They came and got me the next night, their faces hidden in balaclavas, guns in their hands. A hood was put over my head and I was bundled out and into the boot of a car. I couldn't breathe and the exhaust fumes blew back into my tin coffin. But I didn't struggle or shout. I knew no one would interfere and it was best to save my breath and strength. We drove a long while. I decided we must be going out into the country beyond the city. They might just pull up, shoot me and dump my body in a ditch. Whether the shock and the lack of oxygen had numbed my brain, I don't know, but I felt completely indifferent to what was happening, or to happen, to me. Yet there must have been some instinct for survival still there.

Eventually the car stopped, the boot was opened, I was hauled out and half-carried into a building. They slammed me down on the stone floor of some room and I heard the door locked behind me. I sat up and took off the hood, wondering briefly that they hadn't tied my hands. Perhaps they were going to interrogate me before killing me. As my eyes adjusted to the dark I looked about the room. I heard a car start up outside and then the noise of it fading away. Someone must have left. Perhaps they had simply dumped me here to starve to death. I waited, listening. The house was utterly silent. I had to know. I began to shout and hammer on the door not caring whether it provoked them into coming to put a bullet in my head. When there was no response I set myself to find a way out, not bothering to disguise how much noise I was making. There was a small window in one wall, high above my head. Getting as much of a run as I could, I flung myself up at it and managed to grip hold of the sill. My training and playing made me much stronger than I looked and I was able to haul myself up until I could sit crouched across the wide sill and smash at the glass with my foot until it broke. I lowered myself down into the dark yard and I was free.

The night outside was mercifully starry. I worked out which was north from the Pole Star and began to run east. Whether Belfast was to the north or south, I should at least end up at the coast. Having rested and run alternately all night, by morning, when the sun eventually rose, I saw it glinting on water far off, and came down on a main road with a signpost that told me I was near Comber.

I was sweaty and filthy but I still had my wallet buttoned into my back pocket with enough money to get me to Belfast and out to the airport. I cleaned up as best I could in the washroom and bought myself a stand-by ticket, afraid all the time that someone would be watching for me to stick a gun into my ribs or simply shoot me where I stood. I had no idea what I was going to do or where I should go. I only knew my life there was over and I had to get away.

· *King's Indian* ·

As so often when he started awake out of his drowning dream with the water still flowing into his nostrils, Orazio found he was thinking in Italian. *Sordomuto*: that might be it. The boy could be deaf and dumb. If only he'd been able to read the identity card. He turned over once or twice, conscious of mattress and bedsprings under his barely-padded bones, and finally drifted down into sleep with the boy's face as he'd first seen it cornered by the doorway like an icon in a niche. He could go back there any time and seek him out.

When he woke again he was still tired, leaden-legged. He lowered his thin shanks to the floor and in his dressing gown went to grind himself some fresh coffee, the very smell reviving him as it always did. After Catterina's death he'd had to teach himself so many basic domestic skills, beginning with the preparation of the small, dark, glossy beans, in order not to fall into squalor or become dependent on Agnese. She was on the telephone now.

'Papa, those men . . .'

'Are the children still away?'

'Yes, but we can't go on like this forever. When the new term begins they'll have to come back or go to boarding school.'

'Don't worry. I'm dealing with it.'

He was glad when he had put the receiver down that it wasn't a day for Mrs Heamans. He must go and make his arrangements with the bank and then be ready for the Irishman and his son. Suddenly he felt invigorated. There were things to do. He poured himself a second cup of coffee and went to shave and shower and put on his grey silk suit. That should impress the bank of his choice. He gave his false signature one or two trial flourishes until it flowed off the point of his pen.

The weather had turned again and the air on his face was mild, almost warm. He stood outside the Blue Dolphin fish-and-chip shop, run by a short, tough Turkish-Cypriot and a slim Egyptian whose pale olive of a face could have been painted on an early Christian sarcophagus, staring at its fat jars of pickled gherkins, eggs and onions floating foetally in their cloudy amniotic fluids, and the impossibly golden fillets and steaks waiting in their glass showcase above the hissing vats of chips. All day a dribble of customers, that from time to time became a flood, queued in the warm succulent interior undecorated for many years except by the juicy washes of oily steam. The beckoning smell poured into the street so that there was always the temptation to abandon the wait for a bus and push open the glass door, to come out with 'open', for eating at once, hot from the wrapper, or 'closed', to take home to a warmed plate and decorous knife and fork. Perhaps he should have had such a simple shop instead of the Castel Grande.

He wanted something other than the main high street banks, Orazio thought, a more trusting institution perhaps, less likely to ask awkward questions. He wondered how much would come in the drop. Not too much, he decided. He'd be one among many, the big sum diffused through several outlets, chosen because they would understand what could happen to their businesses and families if they didn't play. And all done without emotion, as an operation: efficient, almost clinical. It wouldn't be enough to dupe them. He might have to go further. Who was the queen? He might have to remove her-him. Was it one of the two who had come to see him, or someone higher? The bank business was just playing for time while he tried to work out some strategy. Yet he didn't feel cast down. He felt almost elated, his brain humming with invention and foresight as it did when he played in a tournament.

The bus was given over to the young and the mainly

female old, with an occasional barely-adult mother restraining a scrambling toddler. He got down at the terminus and set off through the scribbled-over subway with its gnomic or simply unintelligible graffiti. 'Phallus was here', someone had scrawled and for a moment he might have been in some subterranean passage at Pompeii or Herculaneum. He came up in the High Street and began to walk its length looking for suitable banks. Behind him lay the building site which the centre of the borough had become, with its giant mantis cranes preying above the shoppers. Promising more offices and chain stores, it had been conceived in a time of boom and now went on lethargically because no one knew quite how to stop it or who would fill the boxes when they were finished. The heart of the district would be an empty atrium, a mural for the sloganisers, and a dosshouse for the homeless. As he walked, Orazio saw that ahead the shops sprouted antlers of 'for sale' and 'to let' signs and another hand had written on one boarded-up window, 'You are entering the closing-down zone.' Scattered among the empty chain-stores with their lights and music playing to an absent audience were the takeaways for the cheap cuisines of every nationality, in shops that clung to the fringe of the street one room deep. He hadn't realised things had gone this far. The Castel Grande must be suffering too. Why hadn't Agnese told him? It must be adding to her fears. He passed fruit barrows whose carefully-piled colours of lemon, tangerine, rose and apple green were the only manifestations of liveliness in the street. The banks and building societies offered him nothing new but were all the ones he recognised from the television touting of their services. Not what he was looking for. There was nothing, *niente, nulla, nessuna cosa, zero*: Italian had so many more expressions for nullity as if the language itself positively hated the very nature of the nothingness that English caressed in its soft polysyllables.

Then he saw it: the United Irish Bank. Wasn't he a proxy Irishman? What could be more suitable, and with its root, its base in another country? He crossed the road. Could he pass for an Irishman in an Irish bank? Some of the Irish were dark, he'd noticed. He might have had an Italian mother. That could be it. He entered the bank as Pearse Noonan.

In the end it was all very simple. The cheque for two thousand pounds from himself to his new self made it plain sailing. He even dropped some coins in the collecting box for some unreadable charity in strange writing that had girls in traditional costume dancing on the tin. Even in the manager's office he felt no suspicion as he crossed his thin legs and explained he was thinking of retiring across the water and wanted his savings kept separate to maybe purchase a small property. This was his redundancy money after a lifetime in the catering (wasn't the whole country closing down?) and there was more to come. He gave his specimen signatures with aplomb, never lifting the pen from the page until the names stood out clear with all the careless conviction of long practice. The manager bowed him out, shaking hands and addressing him as Mr Noonan.

'Where would you be from?'

Orazio had thought about this one, foreseeing that the question might come up. He had only the faintest impression of Ireland as the travel films and brochures depicted it: a land of scenery, mainly water, in the air, in streams under the waders of fishermen or eating away at the shore. He had decided to play safe with the only city that might be big enough to confer some degree of anonymity. 'Dublin,' he said. 'But it's changing so fast I hardly recognise it.'

'Isn't that the truth and the tragedy of it.'

Then he was out in the mild morning again with the promise of cheque books and cards to come that would set the seal on his new composite identity. Glancing at his reflection in a shop window he wondered whether his old features would still look back at him or whether it might show someone quite new, and was almost surprised when the old face was still there.

Pearse had slept badly until six o'clock when he fell into that late, dream-ridden, heavy doze from which you wake feeling numb and slightly sick, still haunted by nightmare presences. He lay for a bit, not wanting to get up; not knowing how to pass the day until it was time to go to the Don's. He wondered how his mind had made itself up, almost without his noticing, to accept the offer of an asylum for Liam from Lady Pritchard. He should let her know what had happened and what he'd decided, even though he couldn't be sure that Liam would go along with it. Perhaps the boy wouldn't ring at all, had changed his mind and would withdraw deeper underground. There was nothing Pearse could do to stop him. He could only wait, and he wasn't used to waiting. He couldn't stay indoors either where he might have callers again who wouldn't be so easily fobbed off a second time. He would go to the telephone box and let Lady Pritchard know the latest. Then he would take himself to the public library for a bit of a read till the pubs opened. The afternoon he could while away at the bingo. Once his day was mapped out he felt a flood of relief buoy him up. While he ate his breakfast he studied the pieces he had set out following the Don's instructions the night before, curious to see whether the problem was real. He thought the Don was too canny simply to have given him a meaningless jumble that might have been exposed by a careful listener. As soon as the game was laid out he saw that it was indeed a classic. If he hadn't felt it best to be out of the flat he could have enjoyed himself working it through.

In spite of his plans the day dragged. From time to time, too often, he wondered what the Don was doing and how soon he could go there. Not before seven, he reckoned. Nicole Pritchard had seemed pleased by his call, excited at the prospect of being included in whatever might happen. Pearse put the receiver back, relieved at her response. He'd been afraid she'd offered help on the spur of the moment and might have since regretted it. He mustn't have too much to drink midday although, shut out from his own home, driven to pass the time like a tramp, become one of the homeless, it was tempting to seek refuge with the Guv'nor in a few pints. Instead, he forced himself to sit in the gloomy reference library along with the foreign students and others whiling away the hours in the warm, working steadily through the daily papers in their hard plastic covers, and then on to the weeklies and monthlies that told him how to take cuttings, put up shelves, groom a pony or himself, or showed him the world, in glorious technicolour or shrunk to the size of a postage stamp glowing like an elaborate jewel. From the library he walked round to the Broadway where he had just two pints in the Maltsters, not daring to visit the Sally in case he should be tempted further, and then on, to join the rest with time on their hands at the old Roxy for an afternoon's play, eyes down on the card as the lottery numbers were called until he only needed legs eleven for a full house, and suddenly there it was and he'd won ten pounds. He prayed it hadn't used up all his luck for the day.

When the session was over he still had two hours to pass. There was a steamy café where he could get tea and a piece of cake to dawdle over. He'd forgotten what it was like to have nowhere you could go to. When he'd first been demobbed in London he'd lived in lodgings where, after his tea, he'd either had to go out or sit quiet in his room. Noise was frowned on by the elderly couple who'd let the room and provided breakfast and an evening meal. That's when he'd taken to pubbing it most nights at the Bamborough, though not so as to get drunk and make a row coming in but just to pass the time. Then he'd found the Irish Club, the dancing and Jessie. She was working at Smith's clock factory in Cricklewood after a spell at the nursing. They were both lonely. It hadn't taken them long to decide to marry. Since then, even after her death, he'd forgotten what it was like to have nowhere to lay his head, no foxhole or cocooning nest to creep into whenever he needed. As he drank the last of his second cup of tea and got up to go when the café closed, he wondered how long Liam had been living rough. If he strolled, he would get to the Don's at a quarter to seven. Surely that wasn't too early. He must make sure he didn't pick up a tail. It was unlikely, but not worth risking after all his care.

'I'm glad you came early,' the Don said as he let him in. 'At our age we're supposed to have developed patience, be good at waiting, but I seem to be getting worse. What will you drink?'

Pearse took a breath. 'I wonder if you've got a little whisky or even a gin. Or a beer maybe.'

'I've got some whisky I keep for my son-in-law.'

'Just a small one with a lot of water. I have to have my wits clear. Tell me all about it now. How did you get on?'

The feeling of envy came back as he listened to the Don's recital. Not that Orazio laid it on but all the action, the excitement of sleuthing and discovery had been his. The news that the bank account had been opened in Pearse's name was the final touch. He was being painted out, obliterated as he'd covered over the wall chart with the posters. And yet there was no alternative. Pearse comforted himself with the thought that the next moves were his. When the phone rang it was earlier than either of them had expected. The Don answered.

'Yes, he's here. I'll put him on,' and he handed the receiver to Pearse.

'Is that you, Liam?'

'Yes.' Not: 'Yes, Dada,' but the single monosyllable that wasn't enough for identification.

'How do I know that's you?'

'What do you want me to say?' It was an unknown voice that he could no longer recognise. Perhaps it had changed in over a decade. Perhaps he had never really known, had never listened closely enough to imprint it on his memory. It had been a light boy's voice still and although he and Jessie had both kept their own speech, the boy had spoken with the cadences and intonation of the local dialect. This voice was deeper and the accent neutral. He'd half expected a touch of brogue by now.

'Tell me your Mammy's name and your date of birth.'

'January twentieth, fifty-six.'

'Anyone could find that out. Now your Mammy's name.'

'I can't! I can't.'

'Then your sister's name.'

'I never knew her.' There was a pause while Pearse waited, intent. 'She was called Jennifer.'

'That'll do. Where are you?'

'Quite close. In a pub.'

'I'll meet you. You can't come here. People are watching for you.'

'My money's running out.'

'Tell me which pub.'

'The Lord Nelson in the King's Road.'

'I'll be there in half an hour.'

Pearse sat on the upstairs front seat of the bus looking down on the tops of cars and people but not seeing them. If I'd been a bit younger, he thought, I'd have walked it, run it even. 'I'll ring you,' he'd said to the Don, 'and arrange to let you know what's happening. We could meet somewhere tomorrow.'

For once he hadn't had long to fret at the bus stop. Almost he could have wished the journey drawn out, the moment of arrival, of recognition, put off a bit longer but already they were passing World's End and coming to the last bend where the road proper begins its straight run up to Sloane Square, the street where he and Jessie had window-shopped from boutique to boutique in the early Sixties, with Liam in grey shorts and shirt, his grey socks wrinkling down to his brown sandals, running ahead and back again or lingering to admire a display of brightly-coloured bumper boots she always judged too flash.

The bus drew up opposite the stone portico of the Town Hall where he must get off. Then he would have to push his way through the swing door of the pub and peer about among the crowd of youngsters, as they all seemed to be. He saw himself sticking out like the old sore thumb, thickly conspicuous in its overcoat of white bandage, that the butcher in Arklow always seemed to sport as the trappings of his trade. Now it was all supermarket safe and wrapped. Butchery went on elsewhere. He paused in the doorway. Would he even know the boy, be able to pick him out of the crowd? How much had he himself changed? Liam might not recognise him. Pearse had passed in that time from middle to old age. He'd put on weight. He got puffed easily. Jessie had kept him more kempt. He might see the boy turn away in disgust.

It was a big double-fronted pub with nautical knick-knacks decorating the wooden walls and a bar at the far end. Pearse took a couple of steps forward, his view blocked by standing groups of noisy boozers. He would get himself a pint while he tried to look about.

'Hello.'

It was someone he knew and it was a stranger, this man in blue jeans and a donkey jacket. His hair was darker. The touch of auburn bequeathed him by Jessie had drained away. The eyes were wary. The mouth thin. Pearse wanted to reach out towards him and break the separation, the long years apart, but they'd never been a hugging family and this wasn't the place. He put out a hand instead and touched the navy blue sleeve. 'Where are you sitting? What're you drinking?'

'I'm over in the corner.' He jerked his head. 'I managed to keep a place for you. I'll have a pint of Guinness. And Dàda, can I have a packet of crisps, cheese and onion?'

Pearse bought him two packets, pleased at the request. When he fought his way over to the corner table he saw that Liam had only an empty half-pint in front of him. He was probably short of money, perhaps hadn't eaten properly for some time.

'Slainte.' Pearse raised his glass.

'Cheers.'

'You're looking a bit thin.'

'I ran out of money a couple of days ago. Down to my last few pounds. I thought I'd better hang on to them.'

Pearse opened his wallet and drew out a tenner. 'Have that to be going on with.'

'I don't want to take your money.'

'Take it. I've plenty; enough anyway.'

'Who was the old guy on the telephone?'

'A friend. We help each other out. They call him the Don. Where've you been staying?'

'Anywhere. Nowhere.'

'I told you there are people watching for you.'

'Who?'

'There's a couple of British coppers, plainclothes. Say they want to help. Then there's a man and a girl from over the water, promising likewise. They gave me a letter for you.'

'I can guess what it says. Have you opened it?'

'I didn't need. There was another that came through the post. I opened that looking for some news of you.'

'Then you know.'

'I can put two and two together. Don't tell me here, now. The first thing is for you to be off the streets and out of sight. I've found a place no one would think of looking for you. It's just a matter of getting you there. I've first to go and make a phone call. You eat your crisps.'

'It's through that door; in the passage.'

'Bring him over at once,' Nicole Pritchard said. 'He'll be hungry. I'll get us some supper.'

'Drink up.' Pearse swallowed the last of his own pint. 'We're taking a taxi.'

He felt pleasure at the flourish with which he said it as if he'd pulled the rabbit out of the hat or ordered champagne. The last time he'd had a taxi ride had been coming back from the hospital after Jessie's death. It was warm, dim and safe in the cab. It made you feel you were invisible, hidden from the outside gaze.

The taxi turned into the tree-lined avenue of classical façades. 'You're sure this is all right?' Liam asked.

'It's a lady I do jobs for. She's a bit eccentric.' Suddenly Pearse remembered a pair of Anglo-Irish sisters, years ago in the big house outside Arklow where his mother took him once a year in summer for the tea and the games, and the ladies moving amongst the little press of old servants and their families, and local gentry, smiling under their hats, their hands hidden in lacy summer gloves, with little pug dogs bumping around their high-heeled feet like animated cushions. They had been terrible hunters and wild dancers, too sprightly to settle down to marriage. For a moment there he'd been miles away and the driver was asking him the number again.

At first Liam attacked the supper Lady Pritchard set in front of them like a dog at the dinner bowl but soon he grew sleepy, hardly able to lift his knife and fork. In the taxi Pearse had become aware of the smell of the streets about him, coldly rancid.

'No questions tonight,' Nicole Pritchard said. 'You're exhausted. You should get to bed.'

'I'd like a bath more than anything but I've no clothes . . .'

'I think I can find an old shirt or pyjamas of Emrys's. They'll hang on you like a scarecrow but they'll do for tonight.'

'I'll take your clothes away with me,' Pearse said, 'and see what I can look out for you tomorrow. Your mother never threw anything away and you've still much the same build as when you left.'

'Won't you stay the night too? There's plenty of room.'

'I'd best get back. There are things . . . I'll just wait for the clothes. Don't drop off in the bath now.'

Nicole Pritchard left them, to run the bath.

'It's best if you don't know too much, Dada.'

'I have to know something if I'm to help.'

' "Need-to-know", Dada, that's what they work under. It's safest.'

Although he was tired too, it was a long time before Pearse could get to sleep. He had binned the boy's clothes as beyond salvation. With a wrench of pain he found, as he had expected, that when he pulled open the drawers of Liam's old dark varnished chest there was underwear neatly put away with clean folded shirts not touched since Jessie had laid them there. He took the clothes out and shook them before laying them out on the bed. They smelt faintly of something he couldn't identify but it might have been death. In the morning he would buy a pair of jeans in the market, and there was a sweater of his own that would do. The practicalities kept him busy till bedtime. Then the uncertainties began.

Orazio knew there would be a message that day as soon as

he unwrapped the little key from the tissue paper inside the envelope that had been all this morning's post.

'Charing Cross,' the voice said. 'Are you ready?'

'*Sono pronto.*'

'In a month you'll be sent instructions to forward the goods. You will make the cheque out to the name you're given and send it at once to the stated address by express post. If it hasn't arrived within three days you will be visited. You keep the interest. That's your commission.'

'Can I ask how much?'

'You can count it.'

He must go and collect it at once. It would be a bag or a package, small enough for a left-luggage locker, and for a man, he hoped not too strong a man, to carry away. As he walked to the underground station he wondered briefly how the Irishman and his son were getting on. He'd like to see Liam Noonan after all his trouble in finding him, have a face and form to go with the name. But now he must keep his mind on his own problems and make sure he wasn't observed. After all, if the Police had any suspicions they might be keeping the locker under what they would call surveillance. Then as he turned this thought over again he realised that in truth there was nothing he could do to protect himself. He had to walk naked up to the bank of metal doors, find the one that matched the number on the key, and open it. For even if the Police weren't watching, they, those others, surely would be. Among the dozens idling about, waiting for trains or seeming to, would be a watcher to pass the word that the drop had been successfully picked up or not, as the case might be. The knowledge that he was being observed, probably by someone with a gun in his pocket, made Orazio's legs weak and shaky and his head buzz. It needed a real exercise of will to force his feet to follow each other through the echoing arcade. His hand too was trembling as he stabbed at the lock. He'd had to get out his glasses in order to make quite sure of reading the numbers correctly. He mustn't fumble: he must try at best to look unconcerned. The little door swung open. Inside was a black cloth bag, the sort he'd seen being sold from a stall in the market: anonymous, ubiquitous. He put a hand into the locker, got hold of the handles and drew it towards him. It was undoubtedly full and heavy. Orazio heaved it out, got the long strap over his shoulder and turned towards the exit. There was no question of his being able to go home by tube or bus. He would be lucky if he got as far as the taxi rank without collapsing. Thank God the bag seemed brand-new and unlikely to break. He had a vision of ill-gotten gains blowing away like confetti.

The money would have to stay in the house for the weekend. Then perhaps he would be able to pay it into the new account on Monday.

'What ever have you got in there, Mr Carbonny?' Mrs Heamans said as she helped him drag it into the house.

'It's something my daughter asked me to pick up. Something for the children, I think,' he lied easily.

'She ought to have more sense. It weighs a ton. Pity it's not gold bars.'

'We'll put it in my old office. She and Stephen will have to come and collect it with the car.' Orazio closed the door on the bag, glad that Ruby Heamans hadn't been curious to see inside.

'I'll just feed the cats before I go. That One-Eye's that crafty he never shows his face while I'm about but I'll have him one day. It's for his own good.'

When she had gone, Orazio made himself a cup of coffee and went back into the office to unzip the black bag. All he could see was something that looked like an ordinary plastic bin-liner in muddy grey. Some instinct stopped him merely tearing it open. He felt around for an end, a neck he could peer into and when he found and untied it, he was confronted by a series of oblong bricks wrapped in sheets of newsprint from one of the more scurrilous tabloids, each held together with a rubber band.

Taking one out he unwrapped it, disclosing a stack of used five-pound notes inside another rubber band. Orazio began to count them carefully. There were five hundred notes in the first stack; two thousand five hundred pounds. He counted the stacks. Sixteen. Forty thousand pounds in all, if the blocks of notes were uniform. He couldn't just assume that. He would have to count them all. With growing irritation he worked his way through the packs, putting each aside as he checked it. He felt his own hands being soiled by the hands that had fingered the notes before him. He reached the bottom row and pulled out another pack. It seemed much heavier than the earlier ones. He unwrapped it, disclosing an ordinary brick. The rest were the same. Now he understood the arm-wrenching weight. It meant there was only thirty thousand pounds. But why? It made no sense unless the purpose had been to slow him down or suggest there was more money in the drop than there was. He put the bricks aside to take into the yard, checked the stacks and put the whole lot back into the bag. Then he went and scrubbed at his skin with a nailbrush until his hands were stinging clean.

The money gave him no sense of excitement or desire. He tried to imagine how some people might kill for it but the thought filled him only with contempt. Was that another example of the coldness, the arrogance, the lack of ordinary human feeling that Catterina had charged him with? Was the worship of money part of most people's emotional baggage? He couldn't believe it was just his arrogance that made him impervious to its attractions. Puritanism perhaps: the spoiled priest in him. But then, wasn't that what the Fathers had called spiritual pride? I thank the Lord that I am not as other men.

And this money in particular must represent at least an equal sum of misery and fear parcelled out in small individual lots. It came from drugs or prostitution or gambling. It was fool's gold, the payment for dreams that poisoned the dreamers and sleepwalkers. Why should he feel any lust to possess it? His mother would have said tainted money could only bring bad luck. 'God sees,' she would say, believing that one day the scales would be balanced and retribution would fall on his father, but the only time this happened with a dose of clap his father had recovered quickly and after a few months of caution was back to his old ways. Hearing his parents rowing in terms he only half-understood at the time, Orazio too waited for the divine hand to fall. It was seeing his father's self-pitying old age after his mother had died of cancer of the cervix that put paid to the last remnants of Orazio's belief, that and Catterina's reproachful grief. Those who'd entrusted the money to him would never understand his lack of desire for it, his contempt. They would expect him to be looking for ways to make it his own and this thought, that they prized so much what he despised, gave him a sense of power.

He would have to take the notes into the bank a few stacks at a time. Perhaps he should change them up into higher denominations before trying to pay them into the new account. He, maybe with the Irishman's help, could change the fivers at different banks. He wished Noonan would telephone, then they could make some plan. It was hard not knowing what was happening. Perhaps now he had his son back, Noonan would think that was that, the end of the game, of the partnership. Orazio poured himself a glass of wine and began to study the television listings. There was a schools programme on dinosaurs. He might watch that. He knew it all of course; all that would be offered to children on the subject, a favourite one among youngsters. He wondered why. Popular as dragons must have been once, dinosaurs were their modern manifestation in scaly scientific dress. They had lingered in human consciousness, even though they and our ancestors had never overlapped, as symbols of old evil and bloody power.

It was thought, the narrator was saying, that some of them had been warm-blooded, upright and fast. Lizards and birds were all that remained of them. The earth's heavy tyrants had evolved into creatures of air and song, just as the mythical beings in Ovid's *Metamorphoses* were changed, though in his stories the traffic was the other way: humans, and gods in human form, were shape-shifted, usually by lust, in pursuit of the forbidden, like his namesake Horace, warped into unseemly tears by Venus and the boy who wouldn't.

The dinosaurs, those that hadn't taken to the air or water or shrunk to pygmy size, had vanished and the great trinity of mystery about them now was why and when and how. Perhaps their very vastness had made them a burden to themselves and to the earth which had finally given a great heave and shrugged them off. How far had their intelligence progressed before they were snuffed out? Orazio had a picture of chess-playing dragons sitting up on their haunches to move the mighty pieces between delicate front paws on a nibbled green board, or bowling rocks at spillikins. They had left no artefacts or at least none that were recognisable, but birds gathered materials and wove nests and their forebears might have done the same. We called them bird-brained and believed their architecture was just a matter of genetic programming while being sure that ours was something more consciously reasoned, but how could we be certain? Our degenerate descendants, millions of years hence, might appear to the intellects of the day, as they pondered in their teeming cellular cities, simply as a reactive species that had been unable to survive the famines and plagues their growing numbers had caused, and instead of co-operating for the general good, had begun to destroy each other until only a few pockets of miserable wretches remained, picking over the huge waste mounds their ancestors had left behind.

Would the boy yield if Orazio went after him; would he be grateful to be taken off the streets and given a place to stay, like Liam, or would he struggle like a wild thing on a silken leash? And what did he want of the boy anyway? If his guess was right and the boy couldn't hear or speak, how would they communicate except by dangerous touch? If you stretched out your hand to a wild animal it shied away as One-Eye and the little tortoiseshell did, not believing in the doctrine of 'for their own good'. Even the animals, at least our fellow mammals, didn't want their autonomy violated, were conscious of self-hood, of their existence as units in space and time: an innate apprehension that made them chary of a trap, the cage.

On the other hand the boy might be longing for rescue from the streets, jump at the chance, no price too high. And then Orazio wouldn't want him or at least only briefly. He would quickly sicken at his own body and turn away. With Catterina he had told himself at first that it was because they were both virgins: that if he or she had been more experienced, the one might have helped the other. He'd gone with high hopes on a business trip to Milano which had ended with a private party where girls were provided: *fanciulle* rather than *puttane* so there was no coarseness that he could blame. He managed as he managed with Catterina, but it was still a duty, what was expected of him this time by his associates. The second night he pleaded an appointment, with a laugh and a wink, and went instead to see Napoleon's floodlit cathedral façade and look surreptitiously at the *giovanotti* in their sharp grey suits and pearly shoes, with dark glossy helmets of hair and thin faces, ragging each other as they strolled arm-in-arm.

Could this boy be Italian? He was dark enough. He didn't look English. Northern. But then no *italiano* would be on the streets of London selling soap and dusters. Almost overnight, the boy had become an obsession. Orazio found himself unable to keep still, wandering from room to room, and then out, taking the bricks which he'd loaded into a plastic bag, to the yard where it had begun to rain, giving a sheen to the dying Gaul's stone skin as if it had been oiled for combat.

All his life since the war he had lived quietly, respectably. Now through no choice or fault of his own he had been forced over the edge. Technically he supposed he had become a criminal, receiving money got through some kind of illegality, and he and his family had been put in danger, a danger he had compounded by refusing to submit, by embarking even if only in his head on a passive resistance, silently shaking his attenuated fist at them, biting his thumb in the old gesture of defiance behind their backs. Perhaps his obsession with the boy was a way of keeping his mind off all this or perhaps it was merely the last grasp at life of the dying animal.

It would be winter soon. Orazio thought of the others he had encountered in his search for Liam. Those in the benders of Lincoln's Inn Fields were probably best off. Those under arches, in doorways, beside a transitory blaze on a waste lot would try to endure till the opening of pubs, doss-houses, day centres. He couldn't save them all but he might take in one if that one could be persuaded. He could offer him his own room, Agnese's old room, or even turn one of the storage rooms into somewhere habitable. He would go and look at the possibilities now and try to think of some way to explain his actions to Ruby Heamans and his daughter before committing himself to a search for the boy which might end in failure and the loss of his dream. Like him, too much of the house had been shut up under dust-sheets far too long. Gradually the rooms would be, were being, opened up.

Pearse woke without a hangover. It was only half-past seven. He wondered how early their surveillance might begin: not the Police of course. They could keep it up around the clock from a neighbouring flat. But those others would have to sleep, wouldn't have the facilities for an all-night vigil. They would probably see him home and, the lights safely out, give it another half hour and then call it a day, knowing he wasn't an early riser after a drink or two. So if he got himself shaved and dressed with a cup of tea inside him, he might be away before they turned up. It being Saturday morning too, there'd be few people about for them to hide amongst. He tried a few bars of 'The Rose of Tralee' as he scraped at his stubble with a blue plastic throwaway razor and dunked a couple of teabags in the big cup.

Inching open the door he peered down over the balustrade. The sky was soggy with rain which should help to keep unwanted followers off his back. The clothes he'd sorted out last night were packed in a plastic bag, and in his other hand he carried a lightened version of his tool-kit. If anyone asked he was going out to do a job. These were his work clothes. Ducking down, he scrambled crabwise along the walkway where his neighbours should still be sleeping off Friday night behind closed doors. His bulk made the ungainly position hard for him to maintain let alone move in, and he was breathless and sweating by the time he reached the far stairs and lowered himself, squatting, down the first few till he was sure his head was below the sight-line of any watcher. He scurried through the emergency exit into the road behind, empty of even an early reconnoitring dog, and keeping his body as flat to the wall as it would go manoeuvred himself round the far corner of the next block and along until that ended. Beyond lay the maze of nineteenth-century brick terraces, with their fancy icing of porches and moulded stone lintels, that fringed the estate.

Scrambling on out of breath he reached the bus stop by the baths and began a nervous wait. He needn't have worried: the grey puddled world, where even the leaves in the little park were darkly glazed with rain, had been swept clean of people. He might have been the last one alive till the bus came with its yawning conductor and carried him away. It was still too soon to present himself at Lady Pritchard's though he suspected she was an early riser. Besides he had to buy Liam some jeans and trainers too. His shoes had obviously been through a lot. By the time Pearse reached Notting Hill the world was beginning to wake. He found a coffee shop where he could sit munching toast while he read the *Mirror*. On his way he'd passed a charity shop selling old clothes. He would try that as soon as it opened. He reckoned he could ring the bell in Huntingdon Gardens at quarter-past nine.

Nicole was up but still in a flowing dressing-gown, a kind of kimono he thought it was, in blue silk embroidered with birds and flowers like a painting. She looked younger, just awakened with her hair loose. When she bent forward he was excited by a glimpse of one white breast with a little veined marbling, smooth with none of the wrinkling in her face, and he was surprised at his sudden arousal.

'I looked in just now,' she said. 'He was still asleep. How old did you say he is? He looks very young and thin.'

'He must be thirty-four or five even. I'm not sure.' Jessie had always attended to the birthdays and the dates of things. He hadn't needed to bother, could live in an eternal present, knowing the chronicle she kept in her head was always on hand to be referred to. Since she'd been gone he'd lost that framework. Past events existed as a series of unsequenced images. When Liam had said his date of birth Pearse had had to take it on trust.

'Old enough to know better,' he heard her saying now in his head. And to drown that voice, said aloud, 'I hope the clothes I've brought will fit him.'

'I'd better get dressed myself. Will you be all right if I leave you for a bit?' She picked up the plastic bag. 'I'll put these by his bed for when he wakes up.'

Pearse's thoughts followed her out of the room. There'd been no sign of her stick this morning. Maybe she had good and bad days. It was that had thrown him. She'd seemed like other people: not set apart by illness. It had given him a bit of a start too to hear her saying Liam's name as if she had known him for years, was even related. In some way he felt guilty, as of a betrayal.

While he waited for her to come back he moved about the room, looking out of the bay windows into the back garden that was full of shrubs he couldn't put a name to, and blue and purple drifts of Michaelmas daisies and lavender that he could recognise. The room itself was full of objects, china figures, crockery and precarious lamps that if he'd been a clumsy man would have filled him with dread. As it was he touched them with fingers that had been trained to delicacy by a lifetime of fine wires and subtle connections and that belied his bulk.

'Hello, Dada.' Liam was standing in the doorway, his face still sown with granular auburn stubble and his hair tousled from sleep.

'That fit you then?'

'They're fine. What time is it? I slept like the dead. Did you stay the night?'

'She asked me to but I had things to do. I came away early.'

'You weren't followed?' His face had gone suddenly translucent as if the blood had all rushed out of it.

'I don't think so. I tried very hard not to be.' For the first time he realised the full depth of the boy's fear.

'It's just that if they find me they'll kill me. Whatever they said or pretended to you.'

'Not the Police?'

'Not them. They'll just try to squeeze me dry before they lock me away. Maybe inside is the only place I'll be safe from the others.'

'Surely a girl wouldn't . . .'

'Even more. You don't understand, Dada, how these people think. It's not like romantic Ireland, like the old stories you used to tell me or even the old-style Volunteers. It's a different world now, harder. There's so much I can't tell you. So much they didn't tell me. They never really trusted me, you know. They saw I was soft inside.'

'We have to talk about the future. Where you can go to get away from them.'

'They don't let you go. Not if they think you betrayed them.'

'What about Kevin Clancy? He gave it all up and said so. They didn't harm him.'

'That was different. He'd been a hero. He never co-operated with the enemy. They saw it more as he'd got religion while he was in Long Kesh. It ruined him for the Army but it didn't make him a traitor. He was old by the time he was in his twenties, with ten years' service behind him. It'd worn him out.'

'Did you betray them?' Pearse asked, hoping he knew the answer.

'No, that's the irony of it. They only think I did because they never really trusted me. They sensed the lack of belief in me even though I never actually did anything. I was always a traitor at heart.'

'Suppose you met her and talked to her, maybe you could convince her you never meant, don't intend, any harm. They might just let you go.'

'The thing is, Dada, part of me doesn't care. It's as if a bit of me's died or was never quite alive.' By now, he was sitting in a low spoon-backed chair: his elbows on his knees, his head of uncombed hair, that was like damp feathers, resting on his hands.

'That's a terrible thing to say.' Hadn't the Church taught him when he was a boy that it was the ultimate sin, the sin against the Holy Ghost, despair, and although he no longer believed in Heaven or Hell or that God of his mother and the Fathers, Pearse still felt it kick him in the gut as the sin against life. Again he experienced the need to reach out and touch the boy, offer him the comfort of physical contact but his hand shrank back from it, shying away. He's like the Don, Pearse thought, recognising a kindred bleakness of spirit he'd never been able to put a name to but had often sensed in the other man. 'You're young enough to start again. You've had a good education. You could go to America maybe or Australia. You'd be out of their reach then.'

'There are branches everywhere, Dada. Brigades in every country where the Irish are. How can you live your life on the run?'

'It's better than not living your life. There must be a corner of you that doesn't want to give up otherwise you wouldn't have run from them. You'd have stayed where they left you and waited till they came back. Running shows a kind of hope.'

'Maybe it's just a reflex, like any other animal.'

'You're not an animal unless you behave like one.'

'We're all animals, Dada.'

'Maybe you're too clever for your own good.' He heard himself growing impatient. Liam was too like him. That was the trouble. If he had more of his mother in him now he'd be fighting back. Fleetingly he remembered that all the old stories ended in sorrow but pushed that thought to the recesses of his mind. He wished Lady Pritchard would come back. She might be able to talk sense into Liam where he couldn't. If the boy wouldn't fight and he wouldn't run what was Pearse to do? Perhaps the Don would have some ideas. They should have a council of war. He wondered what Carbone was up to today. In his excitement and anxiety last night at finding Liam he'd forgotten to ask. Was it only last night?

Lady Pritchard appeared framed in the doorway, a full-length portrait in black jeans, an emerald jumper and red patterned neckerchief. Her hair was drawn back in a ponytail showing two small, smooth ears that dangled silver earrings. The rich colours made her seem vivid, like a sunlit figure in a stained-glass window or that painting that had once been so popular everyone had had it over the mantelpiece: the windswept young woman with a dog straining at the leash. She stood there with the light behind her, her face shadowed so that Pearse saw only the fine bone structure and the slash of lipstick, the alive blue eyes. The map of lines drawn on her skin had been painted out by that trick of the light.

'Breakfast for us all I think,' she said. 'An army marches on its stomach.'

There would be no rest for him, Orazio realised, until he had found the boy. He looked out into the courtyard for the nth time and saw that the rain had stopped. He would put on his raincoat and hat, take an umbrella in case, and go out now on his quest like a latterday Quixote without his ambling nag or Sancho Panza, a rôle the Irishman could perhaps have performed had he been to hand. But then would Orazio have dared admit such weakness? He had no idea how Noonan would respond to a man his age in pursuit of a waif with whom he couldn't claim even the most distant or vicarious kinship. Lights from shop windows spilled on to the wet pavement and slopped their iridescence into the gutter. The rain-darkened tarpaulins over the remaining market stalls flapped dismally in the wind. He remembered his mother telling him that when she had first come to England the stalls had been lit by naphtha flares. She had suffered inside from the dark and cold and rain of those first winters, that seemed chill symbols of his father's infidelities, as well as from the physical discomfort of this bitter climate. Her pain came back to him now as he set off for the station, compounded by the pain he had given Catterina in his turn as if that icy miasma his mother had known had replaced the marrow in his bones, leaving him hollow, thin-blooded. He caught sight of himself in a passing window and for a moment didn't recognise the lean elderly man in his long mac and pulled-down trilby that made him look almost a caricature of those others, the Dons of his nickname.

The station flowed out to meet him with its stream of homegoing commuters. He bought an evening paper from a paperboy nearly as old as himself and a ticket from the machine. The paper was meant to give him something to do, a kind of camouflage from the rest of the world, and to steady his nerves. He left the train at Victoria and went first into the main station to see if the groups he had seen before were still there, but the rush of human traffic was too strong to allow anyone to stand around, and Orazio soon wandered out again, following the route he had taken before, down Victoria Street. This time however the doorways he passed were taken up with more would-be travellers spilled from the blocks of offices, huddling out of the wind while they waited for buses that sailed up full and away without stopping.

He must have been mad to set out on such a hopeless search. Well, he was a little deranged, *pazzesco*, off his head. He would walk as far as Westminster and either join the damned at the bus stop, abandoning hope, or be sucked down the tube. He had reached the piazza in front of the cathedral. Perhaps he would go in and sit for a while out of the cold. He turned towards the ornate façade whose fake Romanesque seemed even more out of place against the aluminium sky that was now being eroded by tides of a sulphurous yellow. As he moved towards the steps Orazio realised that several of the benches were occupied by anonymous figures lumped under some form of covering: an old coat, a plastic sheet, a piece of blanket. He felt a trembling rush inside his body. From a state of complete hopelessness he was transported at once to one of utter conviction. He was sure he would find the boy among them. He must be careful. He didn't want to frighten him away, and an approach to the wrong person, a drunk sleeping off *un' orgia* for example, could land him in trouble. He would take a seat himself and watch for a bit while he tried to penetrate under the coverings of the crumpled shapes, knees drawn up, an arm over the face, and decide what he would say.

His best yardstick, he decided, was the feet that stuck out from under the covers. There was a duo of gnarled old boots he thought he could eliminate as unlikely, and a pair of lace-ups that had once seen better days in a ladies' shoe-shop. The most promising were the sometime-white, scuffed with deep black creases yet still recognisable, trainers. He was sure he had caught them running away in the beam of his torch. He moved to a bench that was nearer and waited.

After another five minutes Orazio began to give up hope that the figure would wake until he made some move himself. Unless he was to sit there, perhaps all night, growing progressively colder he would have to do something and risk the wrong reaction. Trembling he stood up and walked across to the other bench, bent over the recumbent shape and shook its shoulder. At once it sat up pulling the cover up to its chin. It was indeed a boy of about the right age, but the wrong one.

'What the fuck . . . !'

'I'm sorry. I made a mistake. I thought you might be . . . I was looking for someone.'

'Haven't I seen you before, nosing around? What you after?'

'I'm looking for someone . . .'

'Don't give me that. Who you looking for?'

'My nephew. I promised my sister. He's run away from home.'

'Then he don't want to be found or he'd a been in touch. You could be cops or the SS . . . How do I know?'

'No, I'm not. I'm nothing to do with either of them, any of them. Look, are you hungry? I was going to buy him a meal if I found him. Maybe you'd like it instead. Maybe you could help me.'

'What's his name, this nephew?'

'Richard. He's about your age.'

'Which is?'

Orazio did a quick calculation and plunged: 'Eighteen? He told his mother when he rang her that he was selling things.'

'What about this grub then? You could give me the money instead.'

'I'd rather buy you a meal. Maybe I'll give you something too. It depends how helpful you turn out to be.'

'If I go in somewhere with you, people'll think it's funny, you know. You in your gear and me in mine.'

'Well, it isn't,' Orazio said firmly. 'Do you want to eat or not?'

The boy considered for a moment. Then he stood up, thrust his arms into the dirty jacket that had been covering him and stuffed the plastic bag he had been resting his head on into his pocket. 'Why not? There ain't much going on here. You gonna buy me proper grub or just a pie or something in the station?'

'What do you like?'

'Fish and chips or lasagne.'

'All right. We'll find an Italian place.'

'I know a good cheapo. If it don't cost you much you can give me the change.'

His face was pointed and hollow-cheeked. He reminded Orazio of the *scugnizzi* he'd seen begging in the streets of Naples after the war, the same sharpness, the same frantic speech and movements like a jerked puppet.

'You got any stuff?' the boy asked as he led the way back towards the station.

'What sort of stuff?' Orazio asked, thinking he knew the answer.

'Smokes, poppers, dust? You know.'

'I don't carry that sort of thing.'

'Crafty, eh? This is it.'

The sign above the steamy window of crinkled opaque glass read *Anna's Trattoria. Pizza e pasta.* Inside was small and dark but it smelt reassuringly of garlic and fresh parmesan, like old post-war *ristoranti* he remembered, along with the street boys, from those days when everything came to his senses sharp and strong to be imprinted on his memory forever.

They sat down at a corner table with its central candle in a straw-cushioned chianti bottle and a handwritten menu whose dishes were fading under the plastic cover.

'What will you have?'

'The lasagne's great. You get a lot of it.'

Orazio wondered who had paid for his last meal in here. 'And to drink?'

'Beer.'

Somebody's young cousin, brought over as cheap labour and to learn the language, took their order. 'My nephew,' Orazio said when she had flip-flopped away in her thin flat shoes, 'he told my sister he was selling things.'

'He'll have to have one of these then, either a real 'un or a fake.' The boy took out an identity card and held it up for Orazio to see.

'Can I look?' Orazio stretched out his hand but the boy withdrew the card away from his reach.

'As long as you give it back. They cost, they do.' He handed it over for Orazio's inspection. Unwillingly Orazio put on his glasses.

The boy's picture was on it, name and age and place of origin. Turning it over Orazio saw that it was a pedlar's licence, for which someone had paid twenty-five pounds, authenticated by the West Mersey Police. It said the boy was seventeen and his name was Scott Barrett.

'Means you've got the right to go round selling things if you want and they can't touch you. And you get the right to be on the streets.'

It seemed a strange thing for someone who was little more than a child to be carrying in a capital city at the end of the twentieth century: an archaic document, something he would have attributed more to Papageno or the gypsy woman who came round the streets in his childhood selling clothes pegs and lavender.

'Course, if you're blind or deaf or something like that, you can work for one of the charities. Not blind I don't mean, cos you couldn't see what you was doing; just a bit disabled. But the rest work for a firm. They provide you with the goods and you get a cut off what you sell. It used to be a good pitch till too many got in on it and now people have got too leery and won't part with the dosh.'

'Where would he be staying?'

'Either on the streets, or if he's a bit flush in a bed and breakfast.'

'Isn't that too dear?'

'Not the way they do it. They stack you up the walls in bunks, as many as they can get in. It dun' half pong in the morning. Then you collect your bag of gear and start walking. Sometimes you walk all day from eight in the morning and don't sell nothing. They don't like that, the Fagins.'

'Fagins?'

'Geezers who runs the business. Sometimes they supplies the licences or you can buy one off of someone who's given up the game or needs the money. Take your picture at the station, stick it in and you're set up.'

'So this isn't your name?'

'It might be. Why should I tell you? I'll tell you one thing: the age is right. Here, can I have another beer?'

Orazio reordered a Peroni for the boy and a mineral water for himself.

'You have to learn the patter, how to stop them shutting their doors as soon as they see you. You can try the hungry, walking all day bit, or the first time out bit, or the trying to earn a living, self-employed not taking public money bit, depending on what sort of a touch you think they are.'

And what would come next? Drugs, drug-running, prostitution, petty and then more serious crime. Prison, followed by more of the same until something broke the cycle. There was nothing Scott, if that was his name, could do, no job that was within his untrained capacity, no apprenticeships because there were no industries that weren't already shedding labour. Italy had always had a pool of young men who hung about the beaches and bars in summer, kept by their parents, or worked as waiters and ice cream vendors. They weren't turned out of their homes except in the destitute south, and the climate was kind enough to give them at least jobs in the sun for half the year. They were expected to play *pallone* on the sand exploiting their looks while they were young and svelte before marriage and responsibility thickened their waists along with those of the girls who were eyeing them. But here the long winters ate into everyone, making parents harsh and cold while the puritan ethic demanded that everyone work at jobs that didn't exist any more in running-down Victorian industries.

Scott was tucking into a syrupy rhum baba. 'Course,' he said, 'sometimes you put it on that you're a bit disabled. That's always a good pitch. Specially if people look like turning nasty.' He scooped up the last of the syrup.

'Coffee?'

'Yeah. Cappuccino.'

· *Agnese's Aria* ·

It was always Papa I wanted to please, to be his little princess, perhaps because I realised, though without being able to put it into words even in my own head, that he hardly noticed me and that he would have preferred a son. That should have made me closer to my mother, but it didn't. When she put her arms round me I didn't hug her back. I looked over her shoulder to see what my father was doing, whether he was watching and when I saw he wasn't I would just stand there with her arms round me until she'd be forced to drop them. I knew quite early, when I was still a child, that he didn't love her, that she was always trying to force love from him as she did with me and that our shared coldness, his and mine, often reduced her to tears. She should have left him of course but then Italian women of her generation didn't leave their husbands. Where would she have gone? Back to my maternal grandmother, an old woman in the dusty black dress that all women put on after the age of forty, in perpetual mourning for some distant relative, in whose house she would feel nothing but her failure when the married women called to gossip until she too took her permanent dress of dusty black.

Mama would have had to take me with her and then I would have grown up there and I would have been a different person. If she'd gone as soon as I was born of course, I'd have spoken only Italian instead of the mix we always used at home because my father preferred me to speak English and my mother Italian. She'd never learned to pronounce the language except as an émigré. In my wicked moments I called her accent icie-creamio. Later, when I was a teenager, I said it to her face in a moment of frustration when she wouldn't let me go to a disco. 'Other girls' mothers . . .' I shouted.

'*Non sono italiane.*'

'Well, I'm not Italian. I don't talk funny like you do. Why don't you speak properly?'

It was as if I'd struck her. For once she didn't cry. She shouted back at me, '*Scostumata, ignorante!* You like your father.'

'Yes, I do like my father,' I cried, deliberately misunderstanding. Then she began to cry and I felt myself turn as cold as little Kay with the splinter of ice in his heart. I knew that if I'd been a boy I'd have been allowed to do what I liked, that all my mistakes and failures would have been smiled at. When we used to go to Italy on holiday I'd see them careering about on their Vespas, out late at night chasing the girl tourists while I had to stay in listening to the meandering gossip of the older women, intercut with their criticisms of anyone who stepped outside the norm, comments on my hair and clothes and make-up, and how pale I was, while they sipped at their tots of Strega. I needed building up, they would all agree, meaning I wasn't plumply sexy and no one would want me. I should eat more pasta and drink red wine that 'made blood'.

My young cousins would laugh at my pronunciation and say I spoke like an *inglese* or pretend not to understand what I was saying and that I couldn't speak Italian at all so that I dreaded the long summer holidays, part of which would always be spent in visiting Mama's family. The only thing I liked about it was being able to boast when I got back to school of glamorous encounters with golden boys, days on the beach and warm nights drinking at little white tables under a canopy of bougainvillaea. My skin tanned very quickly and gave a glow of conviction to the exotic tale I served up to my audience. 'You should see my cousin Gennaro. He's a real dish. We really had something going.'

'Cousins can't,' Theresa O'Malley, who sucked up to the Sisters by pretending to have a vocation, objected.

'Yes, they can. It's not as if we grew up together or I wanted to marry him.'

Then there was Alessandro from Rome: a great sophisticate who would be coming to London to perfect his English and had put his tongue in my mouth French kissing.

'Yuck! What was it like?' they all wanted to know.

'Sort of warm and alive,' I invented slowly as if remembering. 'Of course he only did it because he thinks of me as English. They find foreign girls very exciting.'

'A pushover, you mean.' Theresa was pretending to be contemptuous. 'Just slags.'

'What word did I hear you use, Theresa O'Malley?' Sister Theophane had come up silently on her rubber-soled sandals with the big doughy white toes showing between the brown thongs. 'You will come with me to the cloakroom and wash your mouth out with disinfectant this instant.' That was the punishment for 'unclean speech'. Unclean thoughts were only known to our confessor, if at all, and brought the much less painful punishment of a novena, or three if they were really steamy.

I never understood my parents' marriage and there was no one to ask. There still isn't. Perhaps one day I'll get up the courage to speak to my father about it but what sort of answer would I get and do I really want to know? It could only be his side anyway although maybe with his strange regard for reason, one of the things that drove my mother to distracted weeping, he might try to give me a balanced view or even take all the blame on himself. All I know is that my father went back to Italy for a wife and returned with my mother, ten years younger than him, a simple girl as they were in those days who'd never left home before, one of four sisters. And maybe that's part of the answer, that she was married off like someone in a Jane Austen novel because there were so many of them and girls still stayed at home, gaping chicks, all mouths to be fed until they married. Even I would never have been able to leave home and live on my own or with a friend like the truly English girls at school did. Perhaps, too, the constant fear that I might want to, might actually do it and that she would be left alone with my father, contributed to my mother's illness, to her dying.

I thought after she died that my father might speak then. His mourning surprised me: shutting himself up and then filling the house with antiques he pretended to sell. She loved the house and it couldn't reject her. She cleaned and washed and kept it painted like a palace. Several times he suggested getting someone in to clean. Now he has that terrible Heamans woman, the Kittycat. But always Mama would say that no one else should lay hands on her things: that the house was her hobby, her province. He had the Castel Grande and she had the Palazzo as she called it. She grew flowers, shrubs and herbs in pots and troughs in the yard, her *terrazzo*, that's given over to mangy wild cats now and those creepy statues that look like people turned in an instant to stone who might come alive again at the wave of a hand. I saw them once by moonlight when there'd been a noise in the yard. Stephen and I were visiting Papa and we all went out to see what it was. They reminded me of *Don Giovanni*, of the murdered stone father coming to supper. There was nothing there in the yard except them, poised to wake. The noise must have been one of Kittycat's little pests.

When Stephen began coming to the house once a month to do the accounts with Papa, I saw him at first as grey and unattractive compared with the golden boy cousins and their friends I'd observed on holiday. Mama was suspicious of him at once, I could tell, even though she obeyed the ritual of offering and making cups of her own, freshly ground coffee for him as they pored over the books and, probably at Papa's insistence, asked him to stay to lunch. I could tell too that my father thought well of him. He was more relaxed, drank a couple of glasses of wine, enquired into his family and education. Mama's hostility caused me, perversely, to look at Stephen with eyes prepared to see more in him than I had at first. When you got over his colouring, or rather the lack of it, he had quite a handsome face. His shape seemed quite good too, as far as I could tell under the formal suit. At least it went in and out at the right places. There was no sign of a pot. Like me, he was too thin and tall for an Italian mama's taste. It was the summer holiday of my last year at school. Officially I'd left the Sisters and was waiting for a course at secretarial college when we came back from our annual trip to Latino where her family lived. This year I was going to insist on being allowed out alone or, if not, that Mama should at least come with me. I had no intention of spending two weeks shut out of the sun with the heavy garish furniture that filled the *salottini* of relatives and neighbours while they went through the roll call of births, marriages, deaths and emigrations since our last visit.

That night I asked Papa if I could spend the next two weeks, before we went, working at the Castel Grande.

'Working?' He put down his paper. 'What work?'

'*Che specie di lavoro?*' My mother cut in. 'You useless in the 'ouse. *Non fai niente qui.* You want to work, you can work here.'

'If I was a boy you'd have made me go to catering college and then sent me to a hotel somewhere to be trained. Why shouldn't I run the business one day? After all, you don't need to be big and strong. You're not,' I said to Papa. 'Anyway, I'd like to try. Perhaps I won't like it.'

'What do you want to do?'

'I want to see it all, try it all: washing up, waiting at table, helping in the kitchen.'

'You don't even make the toast.' My mother tried again.

'That's because you always do it all, Mama. You won't let me.' The truth was I'd been brought up just like a princess who never soils her hands and has all the pretty things she can think of. Sometimes we would go to Sunday lunch at the Castel Grande, me holding my father's hand, dressed in white and pale yellow, a delicate spring flower, and I'd be treated like a precious china doll, the boss's daughter, teased, lifted on to a table to be admired, given cakes and sweets.

'I don't know if Aldo would let you into the kitchen.'

'He will if I ask him.'

So I went to work for the first time. It wasn't a fair trial of course because I was the proprietor's daughter and the staff indulged me and made things easy for me. After all, they'd seen me running about since I was a child, but they weren't obsequious as British staff might have been. It was in a way a kind of family and they *tutoyed* me as if I was still a little girl but that was better than them sucking up to me because of my father. It made it easier for them to correct me, too, when I made mistakes as I was bound to do. The first week I did the hard dirty exhausting jobs. It was the first time the Castel Grande had ever had a waitress but I was only allowed to wait on lunch, not dinner. Then the second week I spent as my father's trainee assistant in the mornings before helping to lay the tables for the evening and polishing silver and glass. I found I got great pleasure out of the ranks of gleaming cutlery and the tumblers, balloons and schooners like massed soap bubbles. But I liked the administrative part even better: ordering, anticipating, overseeing everything. My father might have been captain of a liner moored beside the Thames. If it sank, I suddenly understood, we all went down with it. I was sorry when the two weeks were up and I had to leave with Mama. My going to work for Papa had made her unhappy and afraid of losing me. She stared into the future and the loneliness she saw ahead frightened her. Suddenly I wasn't her little girl dressed up in pretty clothes, to be fussed over and spoiled, but an alien with a life of her own.

I looked at the golden boys differently that year. Perhaps because of my show of independence, I got my way about being allowed out alone or rather with Gennaro and his sister Costanza. I won the same freedom for her so that we could chaperon each other. Lying under a green-and-white parasol with my eyes closed, I could let my thoughts drift without everyone asking me what they were. When I'd had enough of them I'd run in among the brown bodies and throw myself at the flickering surface of the water, breaking it into flying salty fragments brilliant with sunlight. In the evenings I persuaded Mama to come for a walk with us in the warm twilight and to sit watching the passers-by at a little table, drinking almond milk. I think she began to relax a bit, even to enjoy herself, and I felt closer to her than I'd ever been able to before.

Gennaro's mother spoilt it all. 'I find you a nice Italian husband, not cold like the English, like your father. Why don't you stay here when your Mama goes home?'

'Yes, darling. Why don't you?'

Suddenly there was a conspiracy to run my life. 'I've got to do my secretarial course. I've already enrolled and Papa's paid.' The money he'd invested was my lifeline.

'I can pay him back,' my mother said.

'You know how angry he'd be.'

She did know: not raging, the big operatic Italian performance of raised voice and gesture, but a chill that made our blood run cold, that she would have to face alone if she went back without me. So the threatening moment passed but I'd seen the danger. As long as I was unmarried the scheming would go on and my own body might betray me. Gennaro was only too happy to escort his cousin to the beach and instead of playing beach football with the other boys to lie beside me and Costanza where our hands and legs would occasionally and inevitably touch, to insist on relieving Costanza of the task of rubbing suntan oil into my back. His skin when it touched mine was warm, gritty with fine sand and salt, firmly flexible with the tensile muscles visible beneath. His hand on my back rubbing, smoothing in its glove of hot oil made my ears buzz and my crotch clench and unclench as I lay on the sea-smelling towel with my face turned away, when what I wanted was to roll over on my back and open my arms and even my legs too.

There were a couple of girls in my class who'd already done it and were the bearers of news from that distant shore the rest of us hadn't reached yet, that irrevocable crossing beyond which we could never be the same again. They were our avant-garde but we had no means of knowing whether their rhapsodies were anything like the truth. We regarded them with a mixture of envy and horror but above all with fascination. They had dared pregnancy, the loss of their souls, and Mother Superior's disgust and contempt. Of the list of terrible consequences it was hard to decide what was the worst, since even a joke giggled from mouth to ear in the domestic science lesson as we beat up our mixing bowls of Victoria sponge mixture, about the nun who was caught doing press-ups in the cucumber bed, attracted confession and punishment for impure thoughts, though we were never very precise to Father Doyle, the visiting school priest, about the nature of the impurity.

The worst effect, I had decided for myself, was pregnancy which couldn't be hidden and would trigger many of the other consequences that might otherwise be avoided by an efficient secrecy. If I gave in to Gennaro or any of the others and fell, I would be trapped for ever. So I flirted like the rest; we were all cockteasers, leading the boys on and backing off at the last minute in the belief that they also knew the game's rules. When we'd driven them too mad, they'd zoom away to Naples on their scooters to pick up a real blonde foreigner, American or Scandinavian, who'd only come there because Northern men hadn't the passion to satisfy them. Everyone knew that. They took care of the contraception too so that the boys needn't feel any guilt. In the off-season when there was a shortage of tourists there were always the Neapolitan prostitutes, some of them quite young and fresh, some older and more experienced whose job was to perform the rights of initiation when the boys were brought to the brothels by their older brothers and cousins.

One day the boys would marry the respectable local girls and everyone would settle down but first there was this wild spring to be run through, repeated in every generation like a never-ending erotic movie watched by the elders with nostalgia and indulgence. My father must have known how at risk I was but he said nothing. It was women's business. The only man who took an interest in such things was Nonno, my father's father; that is, he took an interest in me. He was living with us then. Nonna, his wife, had died a few years before and he had moved into our house. My father didn't like it, didn't like him, but there was nothing he could do. The family was still a dead weight, demanding obedience to its ancient rules and ways of behaviour. My grandfather sold his house in Golders Green and brought his great belly to lean against our dinner table so that my mother could cook the foods he'd always been used to: sauce his pasta and roast his meat with rosemary. That smell of herbs and fat became a symbol of his stay with us.

At first I'd felt sorry for him all alone, until I found him looking at me. I thought I must be making a mistake, imagining things, that I couldn't see his eyes properly because of the light caught in the thick lenses he wore. My grandfather smiled a lot in an ingratiating way, almost as if he was rubbing his hands together. I hadn't been used to locking the bathroom door: everyone always knew where everyone else was in our house because there were so few of us. But now you never knew where Nonno was. The first time he pushed open the door and caught me sitting there, I didn't know what to do. To get up and pull at my knickers seemed impossible so I simply sat on. And he stood smiling with the door half-open, instead of shutting it at once with some murmured apology and going away. I think he'd have stood there forever if he hadn't heard a noise from below where my parents were. When he did shut the door I still sat there unable to move and sick with fear and disgust. At any moment it might open again. I managed to tear off some paper from the roll and wipe myself before creeping over to the door to shoot the bolt across. Then, and only then, I pulled up my pants and sat down on the cold edge of the bath to recover. After that I was always careful to secure the bolt. Even so, Nonno often tried the door just to see, hoping I suppose that I would forget one day, and I would have to sit there like a mesmerised rabbit, watching the handle silently turn. Then he took to opening my bedroom door.

Once again the first time it happened I was completely caught off-guard. I opened my eyes, woken by some instinct or sixth sense, and saw him silhouetted against the passage light that was reflecting off his bald head. I closed my eyes and prayed desperately for him to be gone when I opened them again. When he was, I wondered if it had been a nightmare. Until the next time.

I was dressing to go out when the door opened and he was standing there with his terrible smile. I had reached the bra and pants stage.

'You're a lovely girl, Agnese.' He said it in Italian and the word he used for me, *ragazza*, had somehow different connotations from the English I automatically translated it into. It seemed sexier, coquettish even, with a swish of flared skirt.

I snatched up my slip and held it against me. I was amazed that he had dared to speak, that he hadn't at least tried to make some excuse. What should I do? Tell either or both of my parents? What if they didn't believe me? What if he said it was my fault? I thought of how I'd led Gennaro on by passively accepting his attentions. Had I encouraged Nonno in the same way by not speaking out until now it was too late? There would be a terrible row if I told my father or mother. And yet if I didn't he would have somehow drawn me into a silent web of complicity.

I could get away from the whole problem by asking to be sent to Italy. Suppose I said I felt ill and needed a holiday in the sun? But then my mother and her sisters would think they had won and set about serious matchmaking. Yet I knew I couldn't stay in the house with him. Sooner or later he would get me alone in some compromising situation where he would go further than just looking, so far that I would either have to submit or tell. I imagined him advancing on me and my fists beating at him as I screamed and screamed, bringing the house down around our ears. I went in such constant fear of some confrontation that I really began to feel ill and was afraid my mother would notice and pack me off immediately for some sea air and sunshine.

I could never have spoken to my father about it because he might well have killed my grandfather. I'd heard rumours about Nonno in the village. My aunt was grinding pepper at the kitchen table when my mother had told her that he was coming to live with us. The pepper mill turned furiously. 'That old – – – – – – –.' She used a word I hadn't heard before and didn't understand.

'Be quiet,' my mother said. 'The little girl . . .' Meaning me.

'Not so little. Anyway she has to know some time.'

'Why? It's not necessary.'

I should have asked my mother what they'd meant when we were alone but I was so concerned at that time not to give her any hostages that I let the opportunity pass and pushed the question out of my mind. Now I thought I understood. I began to observe my father with his father. His manner was even colder than with the rest of us. He hardly ever spoke to Nonno and he would leave any room soon after my grandfather came into it, except for those meals which we had to take together when he couldn't escape but would behave with scrupulous politeness, filling his father's glass and passing him bread, though I sometimes wondered if this was to prevent him helping himself. There was something sickening about his sallow sausage fingers reaching out for things across the table, endangering his glass with his elbow, sopping up sauce and gravy and carrying them not very accurately to his mouth so that they ran down his chin and spotted his tie. I tried not to look at him eating in case I should be unable to go on with my own food and my mother should notice. One day I caught my father eyeing him with an expression of disgust and hatred as he forked tagliatelle into his mouth, dripping with sauce the colour of drying blood, the flat ribbons of green and white pasta like knots of tapeworms. I was nearly sick and then I saw my father's face and I realised that he felt the same. After that I watched him more closely whenever my grandfather was around and came to the conclusion that he detested the old man as much if not more than I did. At first this was comforting. I felt as if I had an ally. Then I realised that it would take only one thing to tip him over the edge of his hatred into violence and that I held that one thing.

With this realisation I knew I could never tell my father because of what it might cause him to do. It also made me love him more and want to protect him. The strain of it all had made me fail my first secretarial exams. My father was very disappointed.

'Let me try again, Papa. I won't fail this time. It's because I had flu for so long and I lost speed in the typing exam because I had to keep blowing my nose.'

He agreed to pay for a second attempt and this time I did it easily and asked again for driving lessons as my next step to freedom, although I didn't put it that way. I got them at last as a reward for passing the commercial course. All this took me away from the dangerous house where I might bump into Grandfather alone during the day. But when I saw my second driving test coming up, after I'd failed the first, and thought that this time too I would probably pass, the question of what to do next became urgent.

When I got home with my newly-acquired freedom of the roads, Mama was resting. I made some coffee, all I was ever allowed to do, and took her up a cup. I sensed that my grandfather wasn't in the house. She was propped up against a pair of crossed pillows reading *Deo Gratia*, a Catholic magazine that came every month from Italy and seemed, on the rare occasions I'd dipped into it, to be mainly about missions or the current Pope. She looked exhausted lying there and I felt a spasm of anxiety and tenderness for her. Before I knew it I'd started on a sentence I'd never meant to say.

'Mama, I don't like the way Il Nonno looks at me sometimes.'

'Looks at you? Why should he look at you? He's your grandfather and he's got a grown woman of his own over in Willesden. That's where he's gone now.'

It was too dangerous, I could see, to go any further and I at once changed the subject, asking her if she had any news from Italy.

'Gennaro wants to come over and study English and the catering with your papa.'

That somehow made things worse: I was to be pursued on my home ground. But it also gave me an idea. When my father got home that evening my mother told him I had passed my driving test. I knew that she was both proud of me and frightened of the new licence it might give me.

'We must celebrate,' he said with more enthusiasm than I'd seen before, perhaps because my grandfather wasn't coming home for supper. He left the room to return with glasses and a bottle of *spumante* which he opened with a celebratory bang.

'First the secretarial, now the driving. What next?' he said, raising his glass to me.

'I want to go to catering college, Papa.'

'But your cousin is coming, Gennaro.'

'Oh Mama, he's just a kid. I want to go to college and study the whole thing: nutrition, hygiene, management.' I cast around desperately for what I thought might be suitable components of such a course.

'You don't need to go to college to study our business. Gennaro . . .'

'Gennaro can wait at tables and learn how to serve wines and all that at the Castel Grande. I can't, and anyway I want something different. I want to do it properly, Papa, please.'

He looked at me as if he could read my mind. 'I think she's earned it, Catterina. Where would you go?'

'I'll go to the library and look up all the different courses tomorrow. They may not be able to take me at once. I thought I'd do some temping, earn some money to buy a secondhand car.'

'A car.' My mother looked stunned. 'What do you want a car for? Your papa doesn't have a car even.'

I don't know how I'd got this idea into my head. After all, no one else from my class had a car. But then no one else had taken their driving test. 'Why you want to learn to drive?' my mother had asked suspiciously when I'd first told Papa I wanted driving lessons as my reward for getting seven 'O' levels. I think it must have come from American college movies where girls drove around in open-tops with their hair streaming in the wind, or the freedom of my cousins on their Vespas and Lambrettas, though that was only the boys of course.

'Oh Mama, everybody does it these days.' But they didn't. At first I hadn't thought of buying my own car, only of having the freedom, the power of knowing I could drive, but once I was safely through the test it became not just logical but necessary to be able to use my new skill.

'You kill yourself in a car.'

'It's safer than a motorbike and if I was a boy you'd let me have a Vespa.'

'That's in Italy. In Italy it's safer.' She knew this wasn't true, that the last time we'd been there her sisters had been lamenting the toll in young lives the new freedom to burn up the narrow hairpin coast roads at night had brought with it.

'The young have to take risks,' my father said. 'Nature intends it as part of the survival of the fittest. In the same way Nature intends weak babies of any species to be weeded out.'

My mother looked at him in horror on the edge of one of her fits of weeping that so angered him. '*Frigido!*' she shouted at him. He opened his hands and shrugged indifferently as if to say: 'That's how things are. What can I say? I can't change the facts.'

When she left the room he said, 'I will match whatever money you earn. That way you'll at least have some decent brakes and your mother won't kill me.' He seemed pleased at my outbreaks of independence, half-amused too, but I couldn't tell if it was on my account or because of the eternal subterranean struggle between them.

I temped for six months going from job to job, often being asked to stay on, to become permanent, but there was nowhere I wanted to be for good, to settle. In those days there were plenty of office jobs just before the oil price-war. None of us felt like settling down. There were so many things to make us look free and pretty. In the mornings the streets were full of suited men, some still with bowlers and long black umbrellas, and girls like butterflies darting among them. Most of the others had to pay money to their parents for board and lodging, or rent towards a shared flat, but I could keep all mine for myself. I'd found a course for the autumn and all summer I watched my savings grow in my new bank account that was also a symbol of freedom.

Mama of course was longing to be off on her annual visit home but I refused to commit myself though I thought I should probably have to give in, in the end. She needed these times away and she needed me to go with her. At the end of July I knew I couldn't hold out any longer and looked for the chance to speak to my father alone. I decided to visit him in his office in the Castel Grande.

'Mama wants to go to Italy next week.'

'And are you going with her?'

'I think so.' I couldn't let her go alone; she would be shamed in front of her sisters and I would be thought too grand and anglicised. Even though I wouldn't actually hear the comments, I could fill them in for myself from long experience, and they would hurt both of us.

'How much money have you earned?' I told him. 'Well, I'll do as I said and match it. Do you want a cheque now or when you come back?'

Working in offices had taught me about interest. 'Now, Papa, please.'

'Have you decided between an Alpha and a Lamborghini?'

'I thought I'd have a Triumph or a Morris Minor.'

'Very English,' he laughed. 'And you'll bring Gennaro back with you. I hope he intends to work. Then you'll be off to college, out of his way,' he added to show me he understood, but it wasn't really Gennaro I was escaping from.

For a moment I had the crazy idea of driving to Italy, putting the new car on the ferry and then roaring all the way south through France and under the Alps, but I knew this would look too grand. Besides, a new car, especially a secondhand banger, couldn't be trusted on such a journey. The last thing I intended was my independence to end in a humiliating breakdown from which we'd have to be rescued by a satirical mechanic full of quips about women drivers.

These days we flew and that was another reason why my mother needed my company. The flight terrified her but she had come to hate the discomfort of the train and as soon as she left our house wanted to be there, longed for the magical Cinderella change to take place with a wave of a wand. In the village she was a different person from the weak and weeping woman we saw at home. Among her family she had the status of the traveller who returns with tales of exotic lands and people. What was drab Deverham commonplace, in Castel Grande glowed with otherness. Even the rain and the cold seemed romantic: 'Like Dickens,' one of her brothers who'd never seen it said once. Briefly on our return I'd see it like that too and then that way of seeing would be dulled by everyday and I'd lose it again. Even my car-to-be was brought out by my mother as a source of wonder and status.

'I'll be able to drive it, Agnese,' Gennaro said.

'No you won't. You don't have a British licence.'

'I can drive my own machine.'

'It's only a scooter. It doesn't count. Anyway you wouldn't be insured and I shall be taking my car to college.'

This too was a marvel: that I should be going away from home instead of studying locally. 'You have to work hard, Gennaro,' his mother told him. 'Your uncle is very strict. You work hard, you learn a lot. You've got a good opportunity. The Castel Grande is a top class place. He isn't soft like me. He'll put some discipline into you. No more lying in bed in the morning and spending half the day getting dressed up to go out.' It was strange to hear her speak of Zi'Orazio and know she was talking about my father. Suddenly his difference was a weapon she could use to turn her son into a breadwinner, the husband and provider of grandchildren he had to become. I almost felt sorry for him. All my previous envy for his freedom melted away as I saw how ephemeral it really was.

My mother's personality change came as the plane rolled to a halt after landing. She took off with the same state of agitated terror she lived the rest of her life in and flew with it across Europe to drop it like a discarded old dressing gown as she stood up and began to direct me in getting our bags and coats out of the overhead locker, and then moved along the gangway, saying a gracious '*Arrivederci*' to the stewards' guard of honour. The last vestiges of that other person fell away as she gathered a great breath of Italian air into her lungs at the top of the aircraft steps. I wondered how she would manage with Gennaro in our house, whether she would be able to keep her Italian self with her under his influence or whether once she was back she would wilt as she always did into the émigré who had never felt at home? Suddenly I felt very protective of her. I didn't want her weakness exposed in Gennaro's tales home to his mother and I was glad I wouldn't be there to see it.

'Perhaps you should stay here, Mama. It suits you better: the climate, the way of life.'

'What are you saying? Who would run the house and look after your father? And now Gennaro. You won't be there.'

I had known I would be punished for my attempt to break out. When it came to it of course I was frightened though I was determined not to show it. I'd never been away from home before or looked after myself. I couldn't detect whether my father knew how I was feeling. My mother simply thought I was hard and cold like him. We were all gathered in the dining room with its two heavy sideboards loaded with her glass animals, plaster saints and framed snapshots all reflected in the glass behind so there seemed to be three or four of everything, under the Sacred Heart exposed on the wall above the fireplace, with little ornate thimbles of sticky Strega in our fingers to toast my going. I drank it quickly, refusing a refill. Now it was time to kiss them all goodbye. Grandfather's plump cheeks were bristly grey and he smelt of hair lotion and a sweetish aftershave. In some ways they seemed younger than my father's thin features that were like those of one of the bony saints he didn't believe in. Gennaro made the most of his kisses, holding me tight against him so that he could feel my whole body. I felt I was just getting away from him and Grandfather in time.

'Eh, what shall we do without our beautiful little girl,' he had said as he had kissed me.

Now it was Mama's turn. I expected she would break down and cry but since we had brought Gennaro back she had been more restrained as if some of my father's own bearing had eaten into her at last, stiffening her limbs and calcifying her heart. Gennaro himself had been a model of punctuality and hard work. I wondered how long they could both keep it up. She kissed me formally and I caught a whiff of reproach. How different her embrace would have been if I'd been setting off on honeymoon with Gennaro. Yet this time I'd gone so far that my body no longer responded to the closeness of his. Then I was going out of the house, down the steps with Gennaro carrying a couple of my bags, and the stiff envelope Papa had given me digging into my leg through the pocket in my new white flares. When I looked back the three of them were standing there framed by the doorway as if in an old photograph of Mama's perched on the piano that was never played. They all looked so fragile in the sunlight which had that autumn mistiness, that their world seemed unreal and as if it might just vanish like a reflection in water, so different from the haze of summer with its promise of solid heat to come.

Afterwards it would have been easy to remember this moment of looking back and their apparent fragility as some kind of premonition if I hadn't been a sceptic like my father. I never saw my grandfather alive again. When I came home for Christmas he'd taken Gennaro back to Italy to spend it with his family. He'd also taken his ageing girlfriend with him. I always thought of her as Ruby, like the Heamans woman, Mrs Kittycat, but perhaps I'm wrong. On the other hand, my dislike of Kittycat may go back to that memory. My mother was shocked and affronted even though it was the remembrance of her mother-in-law, not her own mother, that was being insulted. Her anger caused me to wonder if she'd been fond of my maternal grandmother whom I only just remembered.

I was slicing mushrooms in the kitchen when I decided to ask her. I'd been determined that this holiday I wouldn't be shut out and treated as a child or someone completely useless while she slaved herself into exhaustion preparing meals my father would only pick at. After our first meal together I had begun to stack the dishes and scrape the leftovers into the pedal bin. Immediately she'd got up from the table and tried to take the pile from me.

'Sit down, Mama. I'm doing this.' To my surprise she sat down again and picked up her coffee cup. She did look tired. Feeding and looking after Nonno and Gennaro was wearing her out. 'You need a rest.'

My father lowered the newspaper he was reading or hiding behind. 'I've offered your mother to get somebody in to help now there are two more. But she won't hear of it. I've also asked her to send the washing to the laundry but she won't do that either. What more can I say?'

'They tear the clothes. Nothing lasts as long once they get their hands on it. In Italy I could get a washerwoman to come in where I could keep an eye on her,' my mother said in Italian.

'Ah, *in Italia!*'

Later he said, 'Shall I tell you what's really wrong with your mother? She's upset because the old man has taken his fancy woman on holiday with him. It's I who should be upset but she's being upset for me. I'm not allowed to feel my own emotions. She's afraid I won't bother.'

As my knife bit cleanly into the white fungal flesh (we were doing *rognoni trifolati* and my mother was slicing the kidneys into slippery brown trefoils), I asked her about Nonno, my question letting loose a flood of fluent invective always so much more forceful in Italian, drowning both him and 'that prostitute'. I tried to imagine what the Jezebel must be like.

'Perhaps he'll marry her.'

'Why her more than the others?'

'Did Nonna know about her?'

'Of course. How she suffered all her married life. She should never have been married off to him, a young girl from a good family sent away from her own relatives.'

She might have been speaking of herself and so she was, in a lament for how many women of those generations, hers and grandmother's and probably others before, stretching back in their mourning dresses, a procession of ghosts.

'Where are they staying?'

'Who knows? In a hotel. No one would have them. He shames us all. *Che brutta figura!*' The term was untranslatable even to me who went in and out of the two languages perpetually. It wasn't 'dishonour' though that was the closest I could come, more an oriental concept of losing face that maybe the

English with their phlegm never allowed themselves to suffer. 'Your father doesn't care.'

'What could he do? If his own wife couldn't stop him while she was alive . . .'

'He should take notice of his son whose house he lives in, whose food he eats.'

I knew it was no good to argue with her but the more she said the more she painted my grandfather as a rebel, a daredevil, refusing to be bound by the very conventions I myself was kicking against. Yet it was impossible for my own struggles to be identified with those lecherous puffy hands and cheeks, that smell of hair oil.

'He gets on well with Gennaro,' she said bitterly, betrayed. 'Two goats together or an old goat and a young donkey. I hope Gennaro doesn't gossip about this house back home. It's very good of your father to have him here and try to teach him the business.'

After that she let me help her more and more and by the end of my holiday she was rested, almost cheerful. 'We'll go over together in summer,' I said to reassure her though I'd half-formed plans of going to France or Greece, camping with some of the other students and I didn't intend to spend all my summer at Gennaro's mercy. Being one of only two girls on my course I had plenty of boys to pick from if I'd wanted them. They couldn't pronounce my name at the school and I wasn't prepared to become the English form: Agnes or Aggie, so I had renamed myself Lolla, after Gina Lollobrigida, which the students and the staff changed again to 'Lola' as if any Latin or Romance language were interchangeable with any other. I knew it meant that they saw me as exotic, Southern, and I was happy to play up to this, never telling them that I'd been born in St Martin's Hospital, Deverham.

One spring evening I got back to my shared flat to find a message that I should telephone home. I was nervous at once. No one from home ever rang me. Once a week I rang Mama but I knew she wouldn't telephone me, however much she might want to. Her only calls were to Gennaro's mother,

her favourite sister: 'To hear my own language,' she would say, meaning not just Italian, which she and my father often spoke together at her insistence, but the language of her heart.

'Your grandfather is dead. Can you come back for the funeral?'

I felt a sudden lightness as if a flat iron sitting on my chest had been lifted away. Then I didn't know what to say. I couldn't say I was sorry; the words wouldn't come, and the knotted words in my chest took the place of the flat iron, restricting me again. 'I don't know if I can miss college. I'll have to ask. I didn't know he was ill.'

'Neither did anyone else.'

'How did it happen?'

'He died in that woman's bed. *Che vergogna!* Not enough to shame us with his life but with his death too! She had to call the ambulance to take him to hospital but he was dead when he got there.'

Again I found my reactions were divided. It seemed an act of defiance to die in your mistress's bed 'unhallowed and unaneled'. I thought how shocked the Sisters would have been. I didn't want to admire him in any way but I couldn't stop this sneaking feeling that he'd put his fingers up at us all. Then the thought of the ridiculous spectacle of the flabby flesh being hauled out of a sordid bed by burly ambulancemen dispelled any sympathy that might have been undermining my fear and dislike, replacing them with disgust.

'I'll come if I can.'

The drive to the Catholic cemetery from our house through dismal streets past the notorious prison was as silent as I'd expected. Mama had decided that the thing had to be done in style and I wasn't allowed to cram them all into my Morris. Instead, my parents, Gennaro and I trooped into the funeral limousine behind a black-suited and capped driver. I was glad that at least we were meeting the coffin at the chapel and not going in a cortège. His dying away from home, not even in the local hospital, had given us this advantage and we had to be grateful to the Jezebel for that, although no one acknowledged it aloud. There were a surprising number of people gathered when we drew up and got out, all in a mourning we none of us felt, I was sure. Some of the others I recognised as the present staff of the Castel Grande, some much older were unmistakably émigrés of an earlier generation who greeted each other in Italian and were introduced by my father. 'What a beautiful girl! You have a lovely daughter,' they said, but I knew these were formalities that had to be gone through. If you weren't positively *brutta* then you were pronounced *bella*.

'He was very generous, your grandfather,' one old man said to me, holding my hand. 'He never forgot his own people.' I looked about me at these, his people, as we waited in a grey wind that denied the promise of May. Then I heard my mother's intake of breath.

'That's her. She's come.'

I followed the direction of her stare. 'How do you know?'

'She came to the house once. He insisted.'

'Who's the young man?'

'Maybe her son.'

She was a little woman, neatly dressed in a navy coat with matching hat, gloves and shoes; neither fat nor thin, the colour fading from what had been at best mousy hair. At home I suspected she wore a cardigan. Perhaps there were others like this woman, unidentified among the spread-out group that was now moving together, standing back to let us pass as the chief mourners, any one of whom might have loved him more than we had. I began to wonder if I'd imagined it all or misunderstood his appearances at my bedroom door, the softly-turned handle, and if so what this said about me. One thing I was certain of: if this was what arranged marriages, however subtly it was done, led to I was going to arrange my own. Then at least I should have only myself to blame.

She cried quietly during the ceremony, I noticed, and hung back decently at the graveside as Grandfather was lowered into the earth. My father hadn't put his shoulder under a corner of the coffin but had paid the professionals to do it as if he couldn't bear to be so close. I too found the thought of the body in the box hard to take. The words that were meant to be comforting struck me, standing between my parents, one disbelieving and one hoping against hope, as even more inappropriate than usual. At my grandmother's funeral the tears had run down my father's face and my grandfather had blown his nose into a cream silk handkerchief. That time, I was still able to believe my grandmother, who at the end of her life had become almost transparent, might rise in some spiritual form, but that Il Nonno's flesh should be resurrected was monstrous because it was that flesh which had caused so much suffering, and had gone to the grave unrefined.

My parents had invited some of the mourners back to our house; they had to. I found myself taking round plates of sandwiches and pizza slices my mother had spent all morning, since dawn, making and arranging. 'How you've grown,' those who hadn't seen me for years would say as they stretched out their hands.

'You won't remember me. You were only a baby when I saw you last. I really came to see your father not to mourn that old rogue.' This was the view of Nonno I was used to and it was somehow comforting. 'There aren't many of us left.' He was a man a little older than my father, short and bald with the sallow skin of someone who spends a lot of time indoors. My father who was going round with a bottle of wine came over to fill his glass.

'*Come sta*, Adriano?'

'Orazio! I was telling your daughter there aren't many of us left. But then we're lucky to be alive at all. Your father would never have made it. It was a good thing for him he wasn't around.'

'Lucky or clever,' my father said. I couldn't follow their conversation at all.

'Clever or crafty. Ah well, we mustn't speak ill of the dead. Who knows which of us might be next. It's good to see you. If it hadn't been for you . . . I never forget.'

'Who was that man, Papa?' I asked him later.

'Which man?'

'Adriano. He said he'd come just to see you.'

'The best Italian chef of his day. He's retired now.'

'What did he mean about "lucky to be alive"?'

My father looked at me as if wondering if he could speak. 'It's an old story. Maybe I'll tell you one day.'

As soon as I could, I drove back to Norwich, pleading my course. Gennaro would be back for a few more months and then he was going on to Switzerland to work in a hotel. When he went my parents would be alone in the house until I came back which I would now be free to do. But I'd grown used to being away, to a life among my equals, the freedom to come and go as I pleased. It would be hard to settle into home again. Even though Mama now accepted that I couldn't sit around all day she didn't like me to go out in the evenings. I'd kept up with Siobhan from school and when I was home I'd pick her up in the Morris and beetle off somewhere to a dance or for a day out, harmlessly shopping and gossiping, but my mother was never at ease when I was out of the house and I in my turn resented having to tell her where I was going, almost having to ask her permission. But there was no way round it: if I wanted the Castel Grande for myself one day I should have to convince my father that I was capable of running it and I could only do that if I spent some time there. First, however, as soon as I got my Diploma in Hotel Management and Catering, I took a summer job as Assistant Manager at a medium-sized hotel in Jersey, to gain more experience. When that ended with the season, I felt ready to face being at home for a bit.

This time it was Mama who asked for a job to be found for me in the Castel Grande because she knew that if I didn't get it I would find one elsewhere. Surprisingly, Papa agreed. I was to be his assistant. 'You'll be able to go on holiday,' I said.

'Where would I go?'

I realised that being unable to leave the business had been his let-out, his excuse for not accompanying her to Italy. Perhaps they neither of them wanted it.

'Maybe you'd like to go to Africa, see all the animals you're always watching on TV. Or the Barrier Reef. Didn't you once go to Australia?'

'A long time ago. We'll see. I'll think about it.'

It was an episode in his life I didn't really know about; I didn't even know when it had taken place. Once, when he'd been watching one of his wildlife programmes he'd said over his shoulder, 'They're strange creatures, kangaroos, much more intelligent than the Australians give them credit for, that is the whites. When you see a group of them in the bush, if you creep up quietly so that you don't disturb them, you realise at least one is on guard duty, and they're all conscious of each other and the guard, even though they seem to be just feeding.'

'Have you seen them then, Papa?'

'Yes, I've seen them. A long time ago. When I was a boy.'

Occasionally now he would take a half-day off. I think he went to lectures at some museum or other, because I would sometimes find a leaflet of forthcoming 'attractions' among his papers with a particular event marked in biro but he hadn't been persuaded to take a holiday by the time I became conscious of Stephen.

Mama caused me to begin to look at him more favourably after my initial judgement that he wasn't as attractive as Gennaro. Gennaro, she said, had been asking after me. He'd been back in the village visiting his parents during her last trip. He was doing very well in Switzerland and was thinking of trying for a place of his own. It would be a great help to have a wife who knew the business. 'You know he's always had a liking for you. *Un gusto,*' she said, as if I was a dish for tasting.

'He's my cousin, Mama. We're like brother and sister. I couldn't marry Gennaro.'

'Who you going to marry then? You got so much choice? I don't see them coming round in their hundreds knocking on the door. You don't go anywhere to meet anyone. You don't come to Italy with me.'

'Well, I can't come if Gennaro is waiting to pounce on me.'

'So where you find somebody to marry you?'

'Maybe I'll stay single.'

'*Zitellona*? The old maid!' She laughed harshly but I knew this forced bitter laughter was always a form of reproach and close to angry tears.

She was in bed with a cold the next time Stephen came. I had decided to stay home even though Siobhan had tried to entice me out to the cinema with John Travolta and *Grease*. It fell to me to make the coffee and take it with a plate of *amoretti* into my father's office where they sat to do the books. Stephen stood up when I came in.

'You've met Agnese, my daughter.'

'Yes, just once, about a year ago I think.'

'Perhaps you should stay and listen,' my father said to me and then explained to Stephen: 'Agnese is my assistant manager now. I think she wants to push me out and take over one day but she'll have to wait a bit.' He laughed, and Stephen and I did too, while all the time we each knew there was truth in what he said, that Papa had taken this public opportunity to tell me he understood what I was after, and that as long as I went about it tactfully he didn't really object. I wondered if he had discussed it with Mama.

'Agnese has more qualifications than I've ever had. I was always intended to be a priest.' Now he was telling me something else, in front of a comparative stranger, he'd never even discussed with me in private, something which helped explain some of Mama's incomprehensible allusions.

'But Papa, you always say you don't believe in God.'

'No. That turned out to be an insurmountable difficulty.'

I went to fetch another cup for myself, wondering about the person my father had chosen for this revelation, and then joined them for their discussion. Stephen, I discovered, wasn't just the book-keeper. He was my father's financial adviser. It turned out that, like Papa, he was a chess player. They had met at a tournament where they'd drawn. Papa had taken to him because of the way he played. They had kept in touch. The business was growing and needed a more sophisticated financial management than my father could provide. When he decided to raise a loan for refitting, instead of the usual immigrant network, he used Stephen to deal with an English bank.

The oil crisis had hit us badly with fewer people willing to throw their money down their throats in food and drink.

'Don't worry,' my father said, 'the English like to go out to eat. As soon as things improve they'll be back. Meanwhile we have to hold on.'

'You could reduce staff.'

'Then when things pick up you've nobody left. If you lose your cooks you never get them back and a restaurant without its chef is a nothing. You have to treat it like a family, not so much as a business.'

'What do you think, Miss Carbone?'

'Oh, I agree with Papa. I think we can find some economies here and there but not get rid of the staff.' What Stephen couldn't know was how it would rebound, would be chewed over 'at home' by the families there so that when you were ready to hire again, no one would work for you and any attempt at a holiday visit would lead to angry confrontations until you hardly dared show your face. But I liked the way he included me.

The next time he came was on a Sunday morning and Mama asked him to stay to lunch. Sundays was a set buffet at the Castel Grande and, feeling that they could manage without him, my father had the day off to work at home or take himself for a walk about the empty streets or to the park by the river where he could wander along, pausing to look over the parapet between the railings at the mudbanks when the tide was low or the opaque oily swell when it was full, and the skiffs and longboats put out from the rowing club on the far bank to hover over the water. Sometimes I went with him. The unspoken rule was that we didn't talk. Mama never joined him or us on these expeditions. Other times I went to the Castel Grande in his place to enjoy the sensation of having it to myself. The staff had begun to get used to this, to the idea of a girl as Assistant

Manager who might one day be the owner, but I had to tread carefully.

Looking back, I've often wondered why Mama connived at bringing about the last thing she wanted.

'I hope you like Italian food?' she said as she carried in the bowl of pasta.

'Oh yes, Mrs Carbone, I do very much,' but he looked at me as he said it almost as if he was winking and we were part of a conspiracy. And this I hadn't expected: that the staid Englishman in his formal clothes would be just as eager as Gennaro once you understood the language, and I was still surprised when he rang me at the Castel Grande and asked me if I'd like to go to the cinema. Did I fancy *The Godfather II*? I laughed and said yes, I liked films, but that one might not be very authentic and anyway it had been running forever. Could we see *Murder On the Orient Express*?

I told my mother I was going to meet Siobhan at the cinema. I parked my Morris at the back of Deverham Road. Stephen was already waiting outside the Odeon in the light of the street lamps with the crowds going in, closing and then opening around him while he stood there, calm and fixed, more solid than I'd remembered. He'd already bought the tickets and we went straight through the foyer, past the anxious pushing queues. He asked me if there was anything I'd like and did I mind if he smoked, very polite, and didn't try to hold my hand or lean all over me as Gennaro had on the rare occasions when I let him take me to a film.

Afterwards he asked me if I'd like supper and said he felt nervous of suggesting anywhere to someone who knew it all from the inside. But he didn't seem nervous. I aired my knowledge a bit, saying there was only one decent pizza house and we could walk to it. Over the round plates of *Quattro Stagione*, my recommendation, in the dining room that was like a fish tank everyone could look into from the street, but where they used real Italian mozzarella and black pepper, which wasn't so common in those days, Stephen told me a bit about his life: the widowed mother in the South Coast town, the asthmatic younger brother he felt responsible for, his love for rugby, that so-English game, and how he'd studied accountancy at London University because it was safe but also because he saw it as the thing of the future rather than the old-fashioned professions of teacher and doctor.

He told it all lightly, throwaway, as if it might be about someone else, laughing at himself as a student, telling me of his mistakes, not needing to pretend to be perfect, not afraid of a little *brutta figura*, encouraging me to laugh too. Afterwards I offered him a lift home but he said it was too far. He had a studio flat in Maida Vale. He walked me to the car and for the first time took my hand and said he'd much enjoyed the evening and could we do it again? When? Next week? As we stood there in the dark with that first physical contact of hand on hand, I felt my body respond. I desperately wanted him to be carried away and to overwhelm me with kisses but at the same time I knew if he tried I'd push him off and it would all go wrong. So I simply said yes and he said he'd telephone. I got into the car determined to do everything perfectly, not to stall or crash the gears but to draw smoothly and decisively away. And so I did, waving and honking the horn though my heart threatened to choke me or jump out of my mouth.

I soon realised it was my otherness that attracted and excited Stephen. With Gennaro I was just another *lazzarella* like all the rest until he suddenly saw I might also be useful as a co-worker, a married drudge who'd further his business and bear his children while he did what? Became my grandfather, forcing me to be my grandmother? Surely he'd realised that things weren't like that now, that girls weren't as long-suffering as their mothers, that if I had married him I'd have insisted on complete fidelity. He still sent messages asking when I would next be in Italy and my mother began to matchmake again. I hadn't told her about Stephen even though we met every week and he telephoned me at work every day.

One evening after we'd been out three times he seemed a little preoccupied. I suggested a drive to Battersea Park instead of our usual supper and a walk by the river. I knew it was dangerous, that I was being deliberately provocative but I was now beginning to feel that if we didn't break this strangely chaste pattern we'd adopted we'd be caught in it forever like some fairy tale of enchanted lovers barred from touching by an invisible wall, the sword between Tristan and Iseult.

We sat in the car facing the river promenade. Beyond, the tide was flowing full, the light summer night sky making its surface towards the far side milky under the moon.

'Do you mind if I have a cigarette?'

'Not if you give me one too.'

He offered me the packet and then flicked his lighter. I knew the flame would be lighting up my face when I leant towards it as I'd seen so often happen in the movies. Instead of putting a cigarette in his own mouth he kept the flame alight looking at me. I blew a stream of smoke out of the window.

'Are you worrying about something, Stephen?'

'Not worrying exactly.' He paused. 'I want to marry you, I mean I want us to be married. I want you.'

'But we've only been seeing each other for a month.'

'I knew it the very first time I saw you. Then you went away and I had to wait a year before I saw you again. So you see, I feel it's a year and a month, as if it's forever.'

He was proposing and we still hadn't kissed. 'Stephen . . .' In the darkened car he leant forward across the narrow space, took the cigarette from my fingers and threw it out of the window. Then he kissed me.

I'd been afraid that nothing would happen, that I wouldn't feel anything, that perhaps because of our long build-up it must be an anti-climax. But it was all right. In fact I felt I might explode at the gush of sensation that ran from what seemed the root of my responses, the tingling, burning between my thighs, up my stomach and down my legs, as if our joined lips, where I felt nothing, were simply a kind of switch to let the new passion flow.

I couldn't let him know how much he had moved me. I had to pretend and draw away though I hoped that as with Gennaro, who'd once pushed me back against a wall and thrust himself against me, I could have felt his arousal, hard and full. I'd shoved my cousin away almost spitting in his face. 'You're like a dirty old man on the bus in Italy.' He'd laughed and said it was only natural. Girls were fair game. They liked it in reality though they had to pretend otherwise. The foreign girls couldn't get enough.

'We hardly know each other,' I said to Stephen.

'I feel like I've always known you.'

He didn't of course and neither did he want to. He wanted the dark-haired Agnese of his fantasies, with her car and her distinguished father and his flourishing business. Not that he was 'after my money' in any crude sense. It was more a part of my otherness. For Stephen I was indeed a princess of his imagination. He wanted me to be passionate like Magnani or Lollobrigida but also, I suspected, to be a virgin. My brief spell as Lola was over but as far as I was concerned she lived on inside me, like those Russian dolls that open to disclose another, identical yet smaller, and so on until you reach the solid figure at the core. I'd never stretched that far down into my being and I wasn't sure what I should find there or if the layers, the other women I sensed inside, were indeed identical or whether each one was different and should be given another name like Lola. At any moment, if I wasn't careful and in control (I, the top, the surface Agnese), one of them might force her way up and assume my appearance or rather that skin the world saw. For I had to admit they were all me. Only, what was at the centre, the heart? Did I have a heart at all or was there just a stone in the middle, a little hard olive pip or an emptiness, a hole? Could any and every man turn me on like Stephen or Gennaro? If so, I ought to marry Stephen as soon as possible. For I was in danger; I could see that. Not my immortal soul as the Sisters would have said but me, my freedom. One mistake, the lowering of my guard, where the enemy was within as well as without, and I was a traitor to myself and I would be lost; at the mercy of my mother, my betrayer, my world, the scorn of my mother's sisters and their children, especially Gennaro, whether he was the one who defeated me or not.

'We have to give each other more time. You have to give me more time. You mustn't rush me, Stephen.'

'I'm afraid of losing you.'

'You won't, I promise. But if you try to rush things you might. It isn't simple. My mother wants me to marry my cousin, Gennaro.'

'The boy who was living here while you were away? I met him once. He's just a kid.'

'He's doing very well in Switzerland now. Starting his own business.' Stephen looked down, sulking as I'd intended. 'I've known Gennaro forever. He's like a brother.'

'He doesn't think of you in a sisterly way.'

'It isn't what he thinks that matters, it's what I think.'

'Your mother wants you to marry him.'

'That's my problem. She doesn't want me to marry someone who isn't Italian. It wouldn't matter where you came from, what country I mean. If you were an Italian from America or the South of France or here, that would be okay. Best of all in her eyes would be someone from Italy, her village even. But that isn't what I want.'

'And your father?'

'He usually keeps out of things like this but I think I can get him on my side. First though I have to be sure. When I am, if I am,' and there I laughed and touched his hand, 'we can be engaged, for at least a year. That will give everyone time to get used to the idea.'

'I thought long engagements were out of fashion these days.' He was still sulking.

'A year isn't long. Anyway, I haven't said I will yet. My mother doesn't even know we've been out together.'

When I told her she cried out angrily at first, calling me, *'Perfida, ingannevole, falsa!'* Then she wept. It was pure Puccini, whom she loved and would play to herself alone in the dining room when Papa was in his office, the high arias of lost love and despair filling the house. When she reached the stage of tears, she said, 'It will make your father happy to see you with a cold man like himself.'

'Stephen isn't cold, Mama.'

'He's English, isn't he? Anyway, you won't know until you're married.'

I didn't know then that it would kill her, not quickly, the last act of *Tosca*, but slowly over the months of our engagement and even during my pregnancy and Richard's first year. Now I have to wonder, when our lives, my children's, and our living are threatened, whether it isn't some kind of punishment. Not that I want to go back to believing in the God of the Sisters and my mother but perhaps there's some kind of justice, a weighing in the balance, some principle like that which governs the world. I'd like to ask Papa what he thinks, sees; if all those programmes he watches of animal life and death have taught him anything about the laws that control the universe and if the books are finely balanced, as Stephen sees it.

I have what I wanted: my freedom and his adoration, a comfortable life, my children. Halfway through our engagement I decided I should find out what sort of a lover he was and deliberately seduced him so that it appeared as if it was him who'd been unable to resist making love to me, and was irresistible. I didn't want my wedding night spoilt by bloody fumblings. Siobhan and I took ourselves to a pregnancy advice service. She'd decided she couldn't wait any longer either though she didn't see her current boyfriend as permanent. I didn't want to be pregnant on my wedding day.

Once Stephen asked me what my name meant and I laughed and said she was a virgin saint whose symbol was the lamb, that the name meant pure and he was to remember that. 'And what about my name then?'

'He was the first martyr. He was stoned to death for love, but not your sort.' I was teasing him again. There were so many things he didn't know from his practical schooling that was all maths and science as far as I could tell. I found there was a lot I'd simply absorbed from the Sisters like a sponge without knowing what I was doing, and if I had, I'd have probably rejected it but now it added to my exoticness in Stephen's eyes, gave me more power over him. He complained that he wasn't doing his work properly because he was thinking about me all the time, lusting after me. I began my countdown with the tinfoil strip of little pink pills, each one marked for its day. I was determined there would be no mistake.

'Have you done it yet?' Siobhan asked.

'Not yet. Have you?'

'Uh-huh.'

'What was it like?'

'Better second time, even better the third.'

I found my palms sweaty as I picked Stephen up and set out to drive us to Barnes Common where I'd decided it should happen. My hands were slippery on the plastic driving wheel and I hoped I wasn't sweating all over. It was a warm day for England. We parked in a side road overhung with lime trees giving off their scent from their pale drop earrings of flowers. I'd brought a picnic that Stephen was carrying. We passed an abandoned over-grown graveyard and for the moment I considered that as a place to eat. We could still see cars in the distance and far away on the fringe of the common two women walking dogs, and so I led us further on until we found a place in the middle of the common where high dense grasses formed a screen around us. 'Babes in the wood,' I said.

'Some babes.' Stephen lit a cigarette and I began to unwrap the food. He was already sulking with frustration.

'I brought us a bottle of wine. You can open it.' I passed the corkscrew and dug out a couple of tumblers wrapped in serviettes. Stephen had told me his childhood hadn't included wine, just an occasional Christmas glass of port or sherry. He thought even his father, whom he remembered patchily, had only rarely drunk a glass of whisky. Stephen had learnt about beer playing rugby. I knew he still went out for nights with the boys when he would drink what seemed to me an unimaginable number of pints. It was something I wouldn't tell my mother.

Wine, I knew, was still special to him, glamorous. I allowed every gesture to be an enticement, filling his glass, feeding him cold roast chicken and olives, Italian rolls and *dolcelatte*, taking the cigarette out of his mouth and drawing on it before giving it back, so that when we lay down side by side he soon raised himself above me on an elbow and began to trace the line of my lips with a grass stem, before translating this soft brushing into a kiss that I let become longer and harder and be succeeded by others until he was lying over me and I could feel him hard against my stomach. His hand reached up under my skirt to caress my bare thighs. By now we were both breathing hard. The wine had done its work. I knew I was safe, and suddenly I wanted him. Instead of pushing his hand away and murmuring caution, I kissed him hard, holding the back of his head with my hand, leaving his free hand to begin to pull at my knickers and then to unzip his flies. And suddenly there he was: hard and yet soft and smooth, pressing between my thighs, parting the lips, pushing against me while I moved under him to help, pushing back, putting down my own hand to ease my flesh around his and feeling myself suddenly give with a sharp pain and he was inside me, thrusting with something I'd never even seen but thought of as like a blunt-headed snake. It hurt like hell each time he half-withdrew and thrust back. And the pain damped down my pleasure but I held on to him and soon, almost too soon, I saw a change in his face: it was emptied of everything. His mouth opened and he began to half-grunt, half-cry and I held on to him saying, 'Darling, Stevie,' and then I felt a gush that stopped the pain. I realised afterwards it was because that gush had stopped everything. He lay there on top of me half-dead while I was just painful and unsatisfied. But there was nothing to be done. I had to look after him, take care of him. It was the last time. After this I would take my pleasure too. Siobhan had said it was better the second and third time.

'Christ, Annie, I'm sorry.' He still found my name hard to pronounce in Italian, although he was trying to learn a few words and could say *cara* quite nicely.

'I'm not.'

'What a mess.'

I stretched out my hand and picked up the two serviettes that had been round the tumblers. 'One each.' He wiped the blood and sperm off himself while I made a pad to put in the crotch of my knickers. I felt very sore and swollen. Walking was going to be painful. But it was done. Stephen was an effective though unimaginative lover. I wondered if Gennaro would have done any better. He wouldn't have apologised after. He would just have been triumphant. I'd made the right choice.

My wedding morning is fine and clear. Yesterday it was raining and I felt a despair that surprised me. I hadn't known how important the occasion had become. I don't feel nervous. I set my alarm for six o'clock but knew Mama would have been up for hours. I was determined to sleep and I have. Now it's here: the moment in my life, never to be repeated, when I'm the princess who enters on her father's arm with everyone looking on. The house is full. Gennaro and his mother are here for the wedding. Yesterday the sisters were cooking and ironing for hours even though the reception is to be at the Castel Grande. I have only one bridesmaid: Siobhan. My mother wanted some of the younger girl cousins but I refused. She won on the wedding itself. I wanted a quiet English affair, perhaps at Chelsea Town Hall, but I could see as soon as I mentioned the date that I would have to give in. So today we shall drive to St Peter's in Clerkenwell for a full Italian ceremony, and it will make a magnificent setting. Stephen and I have been there twice while Father Roberto explained it all to us, the rite and its meaning, and we've both agreed to go along with it for Mama's sake.

I've even enjoyed the fittings of my dress as I saw myself in the long mirrors gradually being transformed. Mama of course is exhausted and tearful, intent on perfection and afraid of the least flaw. I slip the dress over my head and Mama begins to button me in. Everything is apricot and cream, colours that suit my skin and hair. The dress is ivory silk, ruched and flounced, with leg-of-mutton sleeves. It's as if I'm in a bowl of stiff whipped cream. Mama pins on my veil with a chaplet of apricot rosebuds. She's in a navy silk suit. Siobhan is in very pale apricot, shading to peach. My aunt appears to announce the first car. Mama and Siobhan kiss me. Gennaro is waiting downstairs, not allowed to come up or he would have kissed me too.

Suddenly the house is quiet. It's time to go down and find Papa. He looks up as I come into the lounge.

'*La principessa*,' he says. It's all I hoped. And he's handsome and upright enough for a king. We go out to stand on the steps. The cream limousine with its fluttering white ribbons slides up beyond the gate. We go down. The drive takes half an hour through the traffic to the city. A small crowd has gathered like a guard of honour as we get out of the car and cross the pavement. A bell is ringing in the tower. I'm holding Papa's arm and we fall into step with Siobhan behind us. I feel him tense suddenly. He's looking up at the memorial above the church door. Then we're going inside, carried on a burst of music from the organ, and Father Roberto is there to meet us. We process round the church.

Everywhere I look is like a vast bouquet of roses, freesias, carnations in my chosen colours because even the ends of the pews are hung with them. And as far as I can see there are faces turned towards me. The whole Italian colony seems to be there. Then I dare to look at Stephen waiting by the first pew on the far side of the aisle where his family are, reassuringly impressive, filling his hired morning coat, and standing very straight. I wonder what the ceremony means to him. We can never really know how other people see things, see inside their heads, and because he doesn't talk much I often don't know what he's thinking. Father kisses me, shakes hands with Stephen and hands me over. Now we're going up to the altar together and Father Roberto is beginning his address in Italian on the sacredness of the family. I'm glad I can't catch my father's eye. Then Siobhan reads from St Paul in a clear calm voice: 'Love suffers long and is kind . . .'

Stephen speaks up clearly in the responses and I feel proud of him in front of all these people. My aunt will be making comparison with her darling Gennaro who looks handsome enough in his dark lounge suit. Stephen has one of his friends from his rugby days as best man. I know they were all celebrating his stag night yesterday, and this morning his skin is pale and his eyes dulled. Now the rings are being blessed and exchanged, and our hands are touching. I have some difficulty getting Stephen's over the knuckle and he nearly drops mine. We each say our piece and Father Roberto, who's been encouraging us with little jokes and chats in English and Italian all this time, pronounces us husband and wife. The best man stumbles through the prayer on behalf of the congregation. We sit for the singing of the *Ave Maria* from the organ loft. After the *Pater Noster* in English from everyone, the first part of the service is over. Stephen kisses me and then I kneel before the altar for the nuptial mass. We had to rehearse this part twice because he'd never seen or done anything like it before. 'Why do we have to have the extra bit?' he asked.

'Because it will please my mother. She won't feel it's proper unless we do.'

So he has to wait while the communion wafer is put into my mouth and then the priest goes to my mother and Siobhan. I know my father will be staring firmly ahead with his mouth shut like a trap whose jaws would have to be prised apart. But Father Roberto is used to this, though perhaps he hoped that Papa would relent and repent on this occasion, and he turns away after my mother has received communion. At first I had difficulty swallowing the host and I was afraid I might choke but it's gone down now and it's time for us to go backstage behind the altar and sign the register.

Siobhan comes forward and so does Stephen's best man. This is the part that means most to Stephen, I suddenly realise.

'There we are then,' he says, putting in his signature with a quick flicking of his wrist that shows off the writer of cheques and signatory of accounts. This is the last time I shall be able to use my own name unless like Italian widows I go back to it one day. But I won't become Annie Harrison. 'You must learn to say my name properly or I might become more of a tiger than a lamb and start calling you Stefano.' The organ music swells in the wedding march and Stephen and I lead the procession back down the altar steps where the watchers break out into applause as we process arm-in-arm right round and up the aisle again, the faces turning towards us smiling, the hands pattering together as we go by. As we pass our parents we pause to kiss them and shake hands. Father Roberto comes up for a final friendly exhortation. We pose in front of the altar in different groups for the formal pictures. I'm glad now that Mama got her way. An English wedding would have seemed cold and brief. Now we're out on the church steps with everyone flowing after us. The guests douse us with confetti and take snaps. A breeze has got up and whips my veil about.

It's growing colder as we stand here, or is it me? My excitement is wearing off. I need a glass of champagne. At last the car's here to take us away to the Castel Grande. As we enter on the red carpet under the dark canopy, the staff who've been left behind to make it all ready clap us again and the band begins to play. The whole restaurant is done out in my colours, both as a compliment to me and as a gift box enclosing me where I can be on display. Every piece of silver and glass is gleaming. The flowers are softly brilliant, the napkins folded into perfect cuffs. I feel as if it's already mine. The long windows look across the water whose usually dull surface is whipped into small sparkling waves. I clink my glass against Stephen's and bury my nose thankfully in the pale golden bubbles. I'm emptying the glass in great gulps of delicious fizz and stretching out my hand for another. There are the speeches to be got through and I want to be as oblivious of them as possible without falling under the table.

Later Stephen and I get up to lead off the first dance while everyone claps again at the handsome couple whirling in their midst. My head is beginning to spin too but I don't care any longer. Even Mama looks pleased, dancing with Stephen's young brother Christopher while Papa and Stephen's mother waltz sedately and Siobhan is smiling up at the best man. Now it's my father's turn to dance with me. We hold each other formally, stiffly apart. I can't tell what he's thinking. He's given me away and I don't know if he cares. I dance with David, the best man, who rolls like a sailor and now it's Gennaro holding me too close, a little drunk already and whispering in my ear, 'You should have married me, *cara*.'

· *Rough Play* ·

Liam couldn't stay at Lady Pritchard's for ever or for ever in hiding, Pearse thought. People did of course, under threat of assassination or in a war, living for months or years even away from the light in lofts, or cellars, to be caught, so many of them, in the end, dragged out for an only too easily imagined finish they must have suffered, gone through, again and again in the months before. That was the trouble with us humans, our all-seeing, the before and the after. When you were on the run you tried to keep your mind off them, the glances forward and back that could undo you, keeping your mind on putting one foot before the other. That's what Liam had been doing to survive. Now he'd stopped running they would crowd in on him from both sides and bring him down to that despair he was showing at present. 'We look before and after and sigh for what is not,' he heard Jessie repeat from her schooldays.

They'd kicked around the problem, its possible solutions, over breakfast in Nicole's kitchen and came up with nothing that offered even a smattering of hope. 'You're exhausted,' she'd said to Liam, 'you can't expect to be thinking straight. Just take it easy here for a few days. Something will come to you.' After, when he'd gone to sit in the garden with a newspaper to fend off any more discussion, she said to Pearse, 'It'll come back. He's too young to give up.'

'I'd better be off to get him some more clothes and shoes; that's what he needs most.'

'I'll make him rest this afternoon. That's what he needs most. Rest and food.'

'When should I bring his other stuff?'

She touched his hand resting on the pine kitchen table. 'You must come any time you want. I'll give you a spare key.'

'I don't want us to be a nuisance, moving in on you when you've been so kind. I'll ring before to let you know when I'm coming.'

'You mightn't always be able to. Anyway, come to supper this evening. And Pearse . . . take care.'

It was the first time she'd used his first name instead of 'Mr Noonan'.

'I'll bring a bottle of wine.' He could ask the Don what best to buy when he telephoned him, as he must. Just because he had Liam back he mustn't be neglectful, ungrateful.

There were shops along the street market where he could buy jeans and shoes. He thought a pair of the trainers that he saw shoeing everyone's feet but his own and the Don's would be just the thing to keep a runaway light on his toes. The small shops lined the road with only the pavement between them and the barrow's abacus displays of fruit, veg and greenery, eggs and fresh fish and the banner hangings of bright-coloured clothes, flash for a short season, fragile as lacewings. These shops didn't frighten him as the big stores did. They still had a human scale like those he remembered as a child, with a bell behind the door to announce a customer, or, in the grander ones his mother sometimes took him to, overhead pulleys with the little cylinders rocketing money and bills to and from the cashier in a central glass cage. He often found clothes for himself in the indoor market at the boys' club on Saturdays where the junk of all the borough fetched up to be recycled and you could still buy a pint glass for twenty pence or a pair of trousers good enough for work for a quid. Sometimes he was shocked by the intensity of the faces above those scrabbling hands, picking over the jumbled heaps of the cheapest clothes that didn't warrant being displayed on a hanger behind the stallholder's head. 'As if their lives depended on it,' he'd said to himself once when an old woman in a ginger knitted hat had snatched a faded blue jumper from under his nose. He had Liam's new things in a dangling plastic bag; he'd pick up some chips and a couple of cans on the way home. He passed the half-open door of the Sally almost self-righteously.

'What have you got in the bags, Mr Noonan?' The man stretched out his hand for them while the girl stood with hers in her pockets where she might have been concealing anything. 'Aren't you a bit young for jeans and trainers? Not quite your style, I'd have thought.'

'I'm a bit of a silly old fellow about me clothes. I like something dandyish from time to time. If I was a woman now they'd say it was mutton tickled up lamb.'

The man, Pearse thought he remembered he was called Fergal, held up the jeans by the waistband against himself so that their narrowness showed. 'I'd like to see you get into these.'

'Well now, what a shame. I'll have to take them back and change them. I must have picked up a small pair by mistake.'

'Or maybe they're the right size for Liam. What would you say, Tessa, you're the expert?'

'They look about right to me.'

'Me chips are getting cold,' Pearse said.

'Chips, is it? You'd better invite us in to share them.'

'I only got a small portion. There wouldn't be enough to go round three. But you're welcome to them. I can go back for some more.' He offered the carrier bag in which the hot packet rested against the cans of Murphy's.

'We want to come in for a bit of a chat.'

They had stepped out on him at the foot of the stairs. It was his own fault. He'd allowed his thoughts to wander, not been on the *qui vive*. Now he'd have to climb up the stairs with them behind, every second expecting a gun hard in his back, or be shut in the lift, all three together where they could easily duff him up, even if not kill him outright. He saw the doors opening and his body being turned out slowly by a leisurely foot. There seemed to be nobody else about. Better to die suddenly on the stairs. Pearse took hold of the banister, cold metal under his hand, and began to climb between the grey graffiti-covered concrete walls. There were dark splodges on the treads under his feet that could have been ancient dried bloodstains. The muscles of his thighs ached with weariness, compounded with fright.

As he paused before his own front door, he felt an unmistakable steel pressure in his spine. 'Don't try anything silly, like shutting the door against us. This shoots through doors like a hot knife through butter, especially doors like that bit of plywood.'

'I'll just get my key out.' Pearse transferred both bags to one hand and fumbled in his jacket pocket with the other. No inspiration came to him. His mind ran around the flat, a caged rat frantic at the bars. There was nothing he could do to keep them out. He turned the key and pushed open the door. The man put his foot in the doorway, and then he kneed Pearse in the back and sent him sprawling into the narrow hall. The cans of Murphy's clattered away into the corners. As he lay there he heard the door close. Then the toe of a shoe struck him in the ribs making him grunt and gasp.

'You were in the British Army.'

'It was wartime. I was only a kid.'

'Once a traitor always a traitor, and a breeder of traitors. Where's your traitor son?'

'I don't know. I've been trying to find him. I think he might be on the streets somewhere with the down-and-outs.' The truth, a little outdated, couldn't hurt Liam now. 'The clothes are for if I find him.'

'He won't need clothes when we find him,' the girl said. 'We think you've both been giving us the runaround. You're not taking us seriously. But you will.' He saw a foot draw back at his eye level and instinctively covered his head with his arms but it was hard enough still, even a girl's foot, in a running shoe heavy as a boxing glove, to jar his skull back on his neck. And it was only the first. He lost count before he lost consciousness.

*

The darkness when he came to added to his confusion. For a moment he thought the blows to the head had blinded him and then he saw a narrow crack of light at the edge of the door where the draught came in in winter and Jessie had once nailed a strip of felt he'd taken down so that it shouldn't remind him of her. He realised he was still lying in the hall and the faint luminescence was from the lights on the walkway outside. It gave him no clue to the time or how long he'd been unconscious there. He wondered if he could move or if something was broken and found himself unwilling to try, to face the truth. Somewhere he'd heard or read that if you could wiggle your fingers and toes and turn your head it wasn't all that bad. There was a real danger that he might simply fall asleep. It was so easy and restful just lying there. But then if he fell asleep he might die while he slept. People did: blokes in police cells for instance choking to death or just stopping breathing.

He tried his fingers. His brain, dissociated by the dark, had difficulty finding them and issuing the right order. Then he tried his toes but this was harder, encased in his shoes. The slight movement of his big toe seemed hardly enough to justify optimism. It was when he moved his head that he knew he was alive, from the fierce stab of pain. He must try to sit up. He felt for the wall he knew should be just there beyond his hand, dragged himself the few inches to it, rolled over on to his side and managed to prop himself up like a dumped scarecrow without its supporting pole. He was one pounding ache all over, apart from those areas of acute pain where the boot had gone in.

With luck nothing was broken. They were skilled operators who knew just where to thump and when to stop. He must try to stand up now. On his backside he shuffled to the kitchen doorway and used the door handle to pull himself upright. Nothing was broken then. He could stand. He took a deep breath and nearly shouted with pain. Well, maybe a rib or two. He felt along the wall to the light switch and turned it on. The flat was devastated. After he'd passed out they must have done it over very thoroughly. The concealing poster had been torn from the wall and the faces of the dead underneath looked out at him. Drawers were emptied on the floor and the beds. The new jeans had been slashed to ribbons with his own Stanley knife from his toolbox. He wondered what they'd made of his gallery of the dead of both sides. At least they'd left it alone. He hoped they hadn't taken any of his tools away.

Painfully he groped his way to the bathroom. His trousers were soaked. He must have pissed himself while he was unconscious. Pearse ran water into the basin and then dared to look at his face in the mirror of the medicine cabinet. One eye was blackened and swollen and his left cheekbone was badly grazed. There was blood matting his hair. He splashed warm water over his face and soaped it. That felt better. He patted it gently dry with the towel. He must get changed out of his trousers and underpants, but when he tried to bend, pain engulfed him and his mind's eye filled with the picture of broken jagged rib ends piercing the dark spongy tissue of his lungs. He sank down on the closed lavatory seat and took several shallow breaths before he tried a new tactic. Sitting down, he could lever off each shoe with the other foot. Then he undid his belt and his zip and, bracing himself with one hand, was able to ease the wet clothes over his hips and drop them to his ankles where he kicked them away.

Pearse lifted his shirt and looked at his own white skin. The bruises didn't show yet, only blotchy red patches where they would be. The old man seemed shrunken into himself, a wrinkled deflated balloon. 'I'm surprised they left you alone,' he said aloud. He couldn't see his back but he felt it gingerly with each hand in turn and the sore flesh winced under his fingers. An internal ache suggested they'd given his kidneys some attention. He hoped it was nothing more.

He dipped a flannel in the basin beside him and washed and dried himself as best he could still sitting there. Then he levered himself up on the edge of the bath and went to sort among the scrambled clothes for pants and trousers. He sat on the edge of the bed to pull them on. It was only when he was dressed again that he remembered to look at the time.

Eight minutes past eight. He should have been at Nicole's by now. But he couldn't go in this state. They mustn't see him like this. Still, he needed company. He needed to talk. he couldn't phone Nicole from here. He could phone the Don.

'I wondered if you were busy this evening. Someone came to call and showed me some new moves I'd like to discuss with you.'

'No, I'm not busy. It would be very interesting to try out a few new ideas. I'll expect you as soon as you can get here.'

On the way he found a telephone and rang Nicole. 'I'm sorry to be so late. I'm afraid I shan't make it for supper. I've had some visitors. I have to go to a friend's house to talk over a few things. Is Liam all right?'

'He's very listless still.'

'Don't tell him about the visitors. I'll call if I can.'

'Pearse, are you all right yourself? Do be careful. Keep in touch.' She sounded really concerned, he thought, and would have smiled if it hadn't been so painful.

He didn't know if he was being followed. He ached too much almost to care. But in any case his visits to the Don were known about, on file. Only he hoped no one would catch up with him tonight. He didn't think he could take any more. He wouldn't think about coming back. 'Sufficient unto the day,' he murmured to himself, a saying of his mother's, as he made his slow painful way towards the Don's gate.

'I see they left their calling cards.' Orazio studied Pearse's battered face as he let him in. The Irishman had clearly had a very bad time. His own wounds, bruises, were internal.

He had known instinctively who it would be even before he lifted the receiver.

'This time,' he said, 'leave the bricks out.'

'It was a little joke. You got no sense of humour?'

'You want me to die laughing? I'm an old man; I don't need to carry bricks.'

'You ready to send the stuff when you're told?'

'I'm ready.'

'Okay. We send you a parcel this time, recorded delivery, so we know it gets there and you can't say you ain't received nothing.'

It was too soon; even a less vigilant Irish bank might be suspicious and inform the Police as they were supposed to do of any unusually large sums being deposited. He would have to keep this lot in the house for the time being and if they asked for payment find it somehow, perhaps with a mortgage or a loan. But then they would be back again and again; he saw himself taking up floorboards to stash the wads of unusable notes. Maybe he should open another account abroad, take a suitcaseful to Geneva, send himself a parcel to a foreign hotel. Their greed was making the whole scheme he'd been so pleased with impossible. He could risk this next payment as the second tranche of his notional redundancy, but after that?

As he looked at Noonan in the dim light of the hall, his own flesh crawled. He felt sick with fear, knowing he would never stand such pain.

'What did they do?'

'The buggers jumped me and give me a kicking.'

'Not the Police?'

'No. Those others.'

The characters were different but the plot would play the same. And he had hostages that the Irishman hadn't. Noonan's son was safe for the time being but Agnese and the children couldn't be hidden forever without a complete disruption of their lives. He hadn't realised how important they were to him. Or was he behaving just like an Italian *paterfamilias*, defending his own as all the animals did, even Ruby Heamans' wild cats? Ultimately, by all the unwritten rules, it was up to him to protect his family, but his enemies and theirs were riding high. If an outraged state and its people couldn't control them then how could one old man? He caught sight of himself in the long hall mirror and almost laughed out loud at the thought.

'You need a cognac and so do I.' He led Pearse into the study where the Irishman lowered himself into a chair and closed his eyes while Orazio poured the drinks.

'They say sweet tea's better for you but this feels like it's doing you good. *Slainte.*'

'*Salute*. Perhaps you should spend the night here.'

'I'd be grateful for that: a couch somewhere will do, or a couple of chairs. I don't think I can face any more today.'

'And tomorrow?'

'I don't know what to think. That's why I needed to talk. I'll have to get Liam away somewhere but at the moment he seems to have lost all interest in living. I don't know what to say to him to get him going again. Anyhow, enough for the moment. I haven't asked you about your problem?'

'Like yours. It doesn't go away. That little scheme we set up won't work.'

'Why's that?'

'They're too greedy. They want me to pass too much through the account. I could do it if I was using the Castel Grande but then I'd have to involve my daughter and son-in-law and they have to be kept out of it. There has to be another answer.'

'Two answers: one for you and one for me.' Perhaps it was the effect of the kicking or the cognac but Pearse was beginning to feel cheerfully light-headed.

'No. Occam's razor. One answer.'

'Occam's razor? What's that, then?'

'Something I learned when I thought I might become a priest and was studying mediaeval philosophy.'

'Oh, philosophy, is it?'

'William of Occam was an Englishman who said you should strip everything away to get at the simple answer and that'd be the right one.'

'Well, that's right enough. You can't make a good connection without stripping down to the bare wire. Would he have been one of the old monks?'

'They were the only ones with any knowledge in those days.'

'So our two problems have to be stripped down to one, you'd say?'

'They're basically the same after all.' Orazio refilled the

glasses. 'It's like chess.'

'Ah, now I'm with you. We've got to work out a game plan, then our moves. If they do this we do that. A strategy.'

'A strategy for survival.' The world was an interlocking network of consuming and being consumed, from the smallest particle to the biggest extinct dinosaur. What appeared so steady was really in constant flux and within that flux each unit had its individual manifestation before it dissolved into its constituents to form part of something else. That unique existence took form, however briefly, in time, and everything that breathed, and maybe even those that didn't, strove to keep themselves in being as long as possible before the great flux broke each one down and re-absorbed it. But it has been, and therefore it was: not *cogito ergo sum*, but perhaps, Orazio dug around in the dusty schooldesk of his memory, *ero ergo sum*. Orazio found himself struggling and yet elated as he used to feel when he tried to grasp Aquinas or, though the Fathers would have seen it as blasphemy, like Jesus on top of the high pinnacle with all the kingdoms of the world beneath his feet. Not the material kingdoms he was sure, that would have been too crude, but the kingdoms of knowledge, that old temptation, and power. At any moment the veil would dissolve and he would understand everything.

Survival of the individual unit, that was the principle of life, and the fittest were those who survived longest within their own time span, whether it was the day of the mayfly or the hundred years of the giant turtle. All the time the flow or soup was all around, waiting to claim you back for reprocessing, but it was your job to hold out as long as you could. He understood it now. It was so simple. Now all he had to do was translate it into a plan of action.

'We need a scheme that will deal with them both in one go.'

'Suppose we could get them somehow to frighten each other off?'

'Or kill each other off.'

'That'd be murder.'

'Would it? Who would the killers be? Not us.'

'Ye're responsible, can be, even if you don't pull the trigger, even if you only give the order.'

'Then it's the Police.'

'We've been through all that.'

'*Dunque*, you tell me.'

'I've never liked violence.'

'Do you think I do?'

Pearse looked at him. It was hard to imagine the Don involved in anything as intimate as a punch-up, hot flesh on flesh. But there were other ways: the chill directing hand could sign the paper; the puppet-master who set up Punch and Judy.

'I saw too much of it when I was young.'

'Violence was done to me. You never forget.'

Pearse wanted to ask what had happened but in return he would have to tell his own story maybe, and he wasn't ready for that. Nobody knew. Not even Jessie.

'As long as they are still alive they won't go away,' the Don was continuing.

'Wouldn't there be others to take their place?'

'In theory, yes, but I believe that in practice no one would.' He thought of the battling males of so many species, the clash of antlers, claws, fangs, until one withdrew. It wasn't a fight to the death or a war of attrition. The loser acknowledged defeat and slunk away. Instinct told them it was time to quit. Reason should do the same in humankind. And no alternative presented itself to him that didn't contain the notion of violence with all its risks.

'I don't know. I can't see it myself.'

'We don't have to decide tonight. We can sleep on it. I'll show you the bathroom and your bed. No doubt you'll be glad of an early night.' He could see the aching weariness that was overwhelming Pearse as the cognac did its job.

After he had seen the Irishman to bed, Orazio sat on, cradling the golden bubble in his hands and turning over possible solutions. He would have to think of two intertwined schemes or one capable of two outcomes. In either case he would keep the alternative to himself, even from Noonan. There was a softness at the centre of the man. He didn't understand yet that they had no choice, that the world itself, or the human layer of it, had become starker, more uncompromising. The retreat of both religious and secular liberal humanism had left it to the warring factions of competition and territorialism, as red in tooth and claw as the cat-fights he heard being played out at night, between the parked cars and in the back yards behind the houses. The men who had come to him had no concepts of compassion or equality. Their codes were those of mediaeval brigands who lived beyond the rest of society in their enclosed strongholds, coming down into it like Attila's hordes only to prey on the defenceless. And those Noonan had tangled with had shut themselves off too, using the rest of the world only for their own ends. Both in their way typified this changed state where the appeal to reason and humanity no longer had any resonance, and the weakest, instead of being objects of compassion, were kicked into the gutter.

He should find the boy and force him into his power, according to this new code that was only old ways rewritten, given respectability by the raising of basic animal imperatives to the dignity of a philosophy, grounded in doubtful economics, where everyone either had his back to the wall or his hand raised against his neighbour. His whole life had been spent in conformity to a set of moral principles enforcing that self-denial which had soured his spirit, and which were now regarded as outmoded idealism, swept away by the simple doctrine of competition: kill or be killed. Whichever way he turned the problem it came back to that each time, a loaded dice that always fell blackest side up. What had Noonan said about getting the two aggressors to frighten each other off?

There would be poetic justice in that and it would satisfy the principle of Occam's razor. Sometimes he imagined it as an actual razor, an old cut-throat like his father used to use. He saw the bright blade held up to the light slicing through a single hair to show the stomach-turning brilliance of its stropped edge. In his mind it sliced at wrists and throat, letting the trapped blood out in a rush, paring down to the bone.

If the two groups could be brought together they might be induced to drive each other away. But how and where? Could he and Noonan take them on? Pawns could win a game against rooks and bishops. But not against a queen. Was there a queen among them? Did that girl, what was her name, Tessa, constitute a queen? Men were so much easier to deal with. Lately he'd realised that he loved Agnese but he didn't understand her. He'd understood no one in his life. No, that wasn't true. He understood Father Torre's hand on his hair and his grandmother with her pet hen.

Twice Pearse woke in the night wondering where he was and then the ache in his bones which had awakened him in the first place reminded him he was sleeping safely in the Don's house, in what had been the daughter's room, and he allowed himself to drift off again. When he woke in the morning it was daylight. He wondered if he'd be able to get up, and lay there for a bit turning things over in his mind before he tried his reluctant limbs.

Last night, coming back from the bathroom, he'd passed a door ajar, and knowing the Don had gone back downstairs after showing him where he could sleep he pushed at it and peered inside. The room was full of heavy ornate furniture that included a big double bed. For some reason he suddenly had a picture of the Don lying in the middle of it, eyes closed, face waxen, with candles burning at the head. Pearse almost blessed himself, something he hadn't done for years, and backed out of the room. Now he lay in the girl's delicate bedroom of ruffles and white-painted spindly furniture, unwilling to face the day's undoubted problems. She'd have got married from here and maybe never come back. It must have been the mother kept it like this as Jessie had kept Liam's things clean and folded in drawers.

What would they have made of his chart under the poster, he wondered? They'd been armed, at least one of them anyway. Unless they'd been bluffing and stuck something else, the neck of a bottle for instance, in his back. At the time he hadn't been eager to find out. He'd believed unquestioningly in the gun. He thought of the Don's cold words: 'Or kill each other off.' What would Jessie have said, and Nicole Pritchard? Liam, now, would he want them dead? But he wasn't to be relied on in his present state.

They'd had no qualms about kicking an old man what might have been nearly to death. If his heart had been bad he might have snuffed it. And if they'd done that to him, what would they do to the boy if they ever caught up with him? He must pull himself together and face the day. Pearse lowered his legs over the side of the single bed. Overnight the bruises had begun to appear. His legs and arms were stained with the juice of some dark fruit. A soak in the bath would maybe help. The glass of his watch was cracked on the wrist that had tried to shield his head, and the hands had stopped at five o'clock during the night. He had no way of knowing the time but he lay in the bath until the water began to scum. Then he put his dirty clothes back on, remembering his mother's words about never putting clean clothes on a dirty body, and made his aching way downstairs.

He heard a movement from along the hall and went towards it. Pushing open the door he looked inside. The Don was standing beside the kitchen table looking down at the biggest stack of notes Pearse had ever seen, lying demurely in the brown paper skirts of their wrapping.

· *Orazio's History* ·

They came for his father on the night of the tenth of June. 'He not at home,' his mother said in her halting English.

'Where is he, Mrs Carbone?'

'He go in Italy. His mother sick.'

'We're at war with Italy.'

'*Madonna mia!*'

He had been standing, up in his room. Now hearing his mother cry out he hurried downstairs. 'Who's this then?'

'He my son.'

'How old are you, young man?'

'Seventeen.'

'Where were you born?'

'He born Italia.'

'He's not on the list,' the second policeman said.

'We'll take him instead of his dad. After all, it's only a matter of time. Everyone from sixteen to sixty.'

'Only if they've been here less than ten years.'

'Oh, they'll alter that if things get rough. What's the matter? You want to be sent back again, find he's scarpered and be put on the mat? Get your coat.'

'You don't take him. He done nothing wrong.'

'Your husband's a member of the Fascio Club. You're all tarred with the same brush. Friends of Musso.' He nodded at the second policeman. 'Go with him to get his coat and pack some clothes while I have a look round.'

The second policeman followed Orazio upstairs to his bedroom. 'Don't worry, they'll probably send you home when all this is sorted out. Take something warm; you never know where you might end up.' They went downstairs again with a small cardboard suitcase he had packed, just in case. He was still studying to be a priest one day, perhaps.

'It's all right, Mama,' he said to her in Italian. 'Don't worry. Go to the Fiorinis and tell them what's happened. Get one of the daughters to come and stay with you. I'll write as soon as I can.'

'Stop that wop jabber. You might be passing secrets. Now come on.'

His mother was clinging to him, crying that they couldn't take her only son. What would she do alone in a country not hers? Gently he disengaged her with the help of the second policeman, afraid the first was merely looking for an opportunity to let loose his aggression. Her cries followed them out of the house and down the path. They pulled the door shut behind them because of the blackout, shutting in her cries. He hoped she wouldn't try to open it again and run after him.

'Emotional lot, the Eyeties.'

He had decided at once that he would be very calm and 'British', very co-operative. They blundered down the path to the gate. The first policeman swore as he caught his finger on the catch. A car was waiting at the kerb with only two pin-points of light in its blacked-out headlamps, like cat's eyes gleaming in the dark. He was pushed into the back and driven away through streets he couldn't recognise, with the hard edges of the suitcase digging into him at every bump.

Eventually the car drew up and the boy was told to get out. Sandwiched between the two policemen he was marched up a pathway beside a big building he thought he almost recognised; a door opened, he was half-pushed through the stifling felt of the blackout curtain and into the light of a large entrance hall with a soldier on guard. There was a trestle table to one side with a seated Receiving Officer where he was handed over. His name, address, date and place of birth were all noted; his suitcase and himself were searched. Then he was marched along a stone alleyway and down moist stone steps past another sentry.

'There you go,' his guard said, pointing along a dingy corridor, 'you'll find more of your lot down here. They'll show you the ropes.'

He was in a long basement where the air seemed stale and unmoving. From the end came a sound of voices and music. Orazio made his way towards it. On the way he passed two open doors. When he looked in, each room was crowded with camp beds. He reached the room at the far end and hesitated. It was full of men of all ages, talking, playing cards and on one side engaged in a haphazard game of ping-pong. A gramophone with a worn needle was grinding out a scratched tune. 'Orazio!' a voice called out, '*anche voi!*'

'Adriano, *come sta?*' It was one of the young men who had come over from his mother's village to work in the kitchens and train as a chef. A few years older than the boy, he'd now moved on to his first job as an assistant chef. Orazio put down his suitcase to shake hands.

'Have you just arrived?'

'Just now.'

'Have you found a bed yet? No? I'll take you to my room and see if there's an empty one before any more turn up.'

'What will they do with us?' Orazio asked when he had been found a bed and put his suitcase under it to mark it as his.

Adriano shrugged. 'Who knows? Send us back to Italy or to an internment camp. Where's your papa?'

'He's over there visiting my grandmother. She's ill. He's been there a couple of months.'

'Your papa is as crafty as a fox. He probably saw this coming and got out of the way.'

'They, the Police, said he was a member of the Fascio Club.'

'Who isn't? It doesn't mean anything. Just somewhere to dine and dance. What if they drink a few toasts to the *Duce*? All it means is they want to keep in well with the Embassy because of a little bit of land back home.'

The next day he was taken to a small office upstairs for

interrogation. Where was his father? What were his father's politics and his own, the officer asked, coldly but politely.

'I'm not interested in politics. I'm going to be a priest.'

But he found it was impossible to pray in those surroundings. Even to read. He sat on his camp bed with St Jerome open on his knee but the words passed in front of his eyes without impact even though he'd discovered that the place they were housed in was the Oratory School, and the scuff marks were from the shoes of hundreds of boys, many of whom had gone on to be priests, and the spirit of Newman, the founder, should have been an inspiration and guide. He realised that his faith, his desire for a vocation had been grounded in nothing but an image of himself in a soutane, set apart. As soon as it was tested he found he was empty of even the simplest belief. This was a dark night so infinite he had nothing to hang on with or to try to drag himself up by. God had vanished not just behind a cloud but from the universe.

A few days later they were told to pack up their belongings. The basement they were held in had become impossibly crowded as more and more bewildered cooks, waiters and hairdressers were brought in. They were to be moved to a camp. 'Let's keep together,' Adriano said as they put their few possessions into their suitcases. 'Maybe there will be a chance to get away.' They were closely guarded to the gate where a row of buses waited. A few passers-by had gathered to watch, not understanding. Orazio wanted to call out, 'Help us, it's all a mistake,' but the faces were blank. At night and by day bombs fell on the shipping in the English Channel. The remnants of the British Army had paddled home from Dunkirk.

The fleet of buses drove north out of London through fields where the hay harvest was still being stooked by boys, old men and women. Many of the internees had never been out of London except to travel by train from Victoria for the ferry across the Channel. After a couple of hours they stopped at a village outside Northampton where they were let off the coaches and herded into the local school. Orazio looked at the sentries and remembered the countryside they had driven through. Even if they could get away from the guards, where could they go? No one would give them shelter or help. Away from the cities they themselves were more conspicuous, and country people everywhere more suspicious of strangers. The Red Cross had set up trestle tables in the school hall where there were urns of tea and plates of English biscuits. They were taken in groups to the lavatories which were outside in the playground and for those whose bowels had turned to water with fear there was a new hazard in the pans low to the ground for infants and juniors. Then they were on their way again, passing through towns where the signs had all been removed and even when they spotted a name that had escaped censorship, some of them, like Leicester, they couldn't pronounce.

Towards evening they were skirting through a big manu-facturing centre, looking down at opened factory gates and a sea of caps like the tops of mushrooms going home, walking or carried above push-bikes and interspersed with turbans.

'Birmingham?'

'Or Manchester.'

Half an hour's further travelling through suburbs and then a brief stretch of country, and they drove in through a gate in a barbed wire fence, heavily guarded, and then another, and pulled up outside a group of what seemed to be derelict buildings. Many of the men were so sick from the day's travel that they were only too glad to stumble down from the coaches and towards the huge brick structure, hoping for a hot meal and somewhere to lie down. The cotton waste littering the yard and the entrance hall told Orazio they had stopped at an old mill. The evening meal was a lump of bread, a piece of cheese and a cup of rank-tasting tea. They collected a couple of blankets from a pile. One or two lucky ones, the firstcomers, also got a thin mattress. Orazio and Adriano put a blanket under them on the floorboards and sat on it to eat their supper. There was no light except what came through the broken panes of the roof. At the back of the huge floor the remains of the abandoned looms had been pushed to one side.

'They can't keep us here,' Adriano said. 'Tomorrow we'll be taken somewhere else.'

The coach had been stiflingly hot but the huge empty shell of the mill was dank, with old rain that had leaked through the broken roof and puddled the floor. 'We'll be warmer if we put our blankets lengthways and sleep together,' Adriano said, '*in letto matrimoniale.*' Orazio looked at him in the last evening light. His first bloom had been brushed away by the heat of the kitchens and he was pale and beginning to be a little heavy. They lay down side by side, not touching.

'Sleep well, Orazio. Maybe tomorrow they'll take us to a five-star hotel.' He turned over with his back to the boy and was soon breathing deeply. Orazio too slept at last, to be wakened once in the night by a noise of scuttling among the broken machinery. He was glad of Adriano's solidly sleeping presence beside him.

There was no attempt to move them on in the morning or the day after. Instead, more and more were bussed in to share the inadequate number of cold water taps and the filthy lavatories. It was almost a relief when, three weeks later, by the tally Adriano scratched every day on the brick wall above their bit of floorboard that did as a bed, they were called out of the morning's line up and told to collect their belongings again for an unknown journey. They were so glad to be sent out of the mill that they sang on the way to the station and even waved from the train window.

'Perhaps they're going to send us home, back to London,' Orazio corrected himself. In the camp he had become confused about where home really was. Mostly they spoke Italian as a sign of solidarity and to keep their thoughts private from the guards, not because they were planning anything that needed secrecy but simply to set themselves apart and preserve a sense of individuality.

'I tell you we're going west, maybe to Liverpool. They're probably going to exchange us for some British who got caught by the war in Italy.'

It was humiliating to be marched under guard through the

station swarming with servicemen and women and those who'd come to meet them or see them off. No one will be weeping for us, Orazio realised, because no one will know.

They went on through the dismal blackened streets. 'We must be going straight to the docks,' he said to Adriano marching beside him. The Italian repatriation theory suddenly seemed less likely. There was an even bigger internment camp on the Isle of Man. Perhaps they were going there. They were taken through the dock gates onto the quay. Moored alongside was a huge ship, as big he thought as the *Queen Mary*. Perhaps that was what she was. Then he saw the name under her stern: *Arandora Star*. The portholes when he looked up stared down sightlessly in their coverings. A deck high overhead was boarded up and barbed-wired and two gun barrels poked out of the ship's grey sides at the back and the front.

They were marched up the gangplank, counted by the guards at the top, split into two groups, and one sent down below to A-deck. Orazio and Adriano were among the second lot allocated to D-deck, the highest, where they found an ornately-panelled cabin with one bunk, already occupied. There was nowhere else to sleep but the floor, but there were glass wall lights still in place on the mahogany walls and after the deep gloom of the unlit mill it seemed like paradise.

'Where are we going?' they asked the stout man lounging in the bunk, who had introduced himself as Caprese, a waiter at *Luigi's*.

'Canada. For the rest of the war. I hope you've brought some warm clothes.'

For the moment it was enough to be out of the camp. The engines were already shuddering in the ship's belly. 'Shall we go up to see the last of England?'

'Who cares? They don't care about us. I'm going to have a shower if I can find one.'

Later, when he was clean for the first time since he'd been taken from home, Orazio relented enough to go up on deck but men were still coming aboard, only now the language that passed between them was German, and they soon went down again in search of food and information. There seemed to be no restrictions on board.

'Where can we get something to eat?' Adriano asked one of the soldiers.

'Along in the dining room, mate.'

They found the bar first, open and selling drinks and cigarettes. 'How can you believe this,' Adriano said, 'after such a nightmare? Everything's going to be fine now.'

Orazio woke on the cabin floor at four o'clock in the morning as the liner finally cast off and drew away from the dock but the steady beat of the engines soon sent him back to sleep.

When they went up on deck in the morning the long zig-zag of the wake streamed out behind to the south. 'That must be the coast of Wales.'

'Isn't that a submarine behind?'

It lay low in the water like a seal, or a dog flattening itself to the earth, herding sheep. 'Let's see if there's more of that food.' Soon they were passing the Isle of Man on the right, so they weren't going there, and they began to believe Caprese's story of Canada. The sun shone. Ireland fell away on one hand, Scotland on the other and they were heading out into the Atlantic. Perhaps a new month really meant a new life. He tried to remember what he knew about Canada but could only find stock pictures of Mounties and Indians out of some largely-forgotten geography lesson. That evening Orazio got drunk for the first time, on pink gin. It had begun to drizzle so there was no incentive to go up on deck star-gazing while the gramophone played and they had a glass in their hands in the liner's still luxurious bar as she continued picking her course round Malin Head.

'Look,' Adriano said, indicating two middle-aged men playing cards on the other side of the bar. 'Langiaconi and Zavattoni: the Ritz and the Savoy.' About midnight, he and Adriano went unsteadily to their hard bed that throbbed with the vibration of the ship's big engines far below. They were still asleep when the torpedo blasted into the aft engine room tearing a huge hole below the waterline and putting out the lights and the tannoy.

The explosion juddering upwards through the ship's bones jolted them awake. 'We must have hit a mine. Come on, let's get out on deck.' Orazio pulled Adriano to his feet. Caprese was scrambling out of his bunk in his pyjamas and fumbling for his trousers.

'Don't bother with those,' Adriano said. 'We might be sinking.' The older man picked up his suitcase and followed them to the door. The main deck was in confusion with people rushing everywhere. There had been no time to organise a boat drill and with the tannoy out no orders could be heard.

Orazio caught the arm of one of the stewards who'd served them last night. 'What is it? What's happening?'

'Torpedo. She's going down. You'd better get into a boat. Put these on.' He thrust a couple of life-jackets at them and hurried away to where a lifeboat already crowded with people was hanging in its davit over the side. Orazio saw him put his hands to the ropes to lower it. 'Not that one,' he said to Adriano. 'It's full. Come on.' He pushed through the crowd to the side and looked over. It seemed a mile down to the dull grey water. They helped each other into their life-jackets.

'We must find another lifeboat,' Adriano said. They ran to where one was about to be lowered but as they reached it the ship lurched and the boat tipped, spilling its cargo into the sea which was filling rapidly with floating debris and bodies, some striking out, others already still.

'We'll have to jump. It's going down,' Orazio shouted.

'I can't swim.' Adriano's terror made him pale and sweaty.

Orazio looked around and then up at the bridge where the captain was standing with his officers. 'Don't be afraid,' he heard the captain call. 'Jump.'

He saw a rope hanging from one of the davits. 'Look,' he said, taking Adriano's arm and pulling him towards it, 'We can slide down this. I'll go first and wait for you. Come down as soon as I've gone over. I'll be there waiting.' He grasped the rope and swung his legs over the side, his hands blistering as he slid down too fast. He hit the water hard when the rope ran out, went under, down and down, tasting the oily swill before he surfaced again and lay on his back in the life-jacket, spewing out seawater and paddling with one hand to stay in the same spot and not be swept away.

'*Vieni*, Adriano,' he shouted up, but his voice seemed weaker than the mewing of a kitten. With his free hand he waved and beckoned at the dark blob of Adriano's head. A figure appeared beside it, paused a moment on the rail and tumbled over, hurtling towards him to smack into the sea close by. Despairingly he waved and shouted again: by now the ship was listing badly. A rope ladder hung out from its side further along, with several figures clinging to it. He could see that some of them were still clutching suitcases and wondered if Caprese was among them. When he looked up again he saw a figure on its way down the rope and prayed that it was Adriano. He paddled in close from where he had drifted out a bit and kept up his cries of encouragement. 'Let go, let go!' he shouted when Adriano hesitated at the end of the rope. He was afraid the ship would go down before they could get far enough away and they would be sucked below with it.

A dead man drifted past, the puffy yellow oval of his face held up by his life-jacket and bobbing above the waves as if its owner was still alive. They were lucky it was summer and the water no colder. Even so, he could feel the chill beginning to numb his limbs. He must get himself moving soon or he would die of cold. Adriano let go of the rope and splashed down beside him, nearly sinking Orazio in the wave. He waited until the life-jacket brought Adriano to the surface then grabbed him by the scruff of the neck and began to tow him on his back away from the ship.

As they got further away he could see there were still many little black figures aboard, on deck or dangling from the sides on ropes. He felt his strength beginning to run out, his own legs becoming heavy. 'Let me go,' Adriano said. 'Save yourself.' Slowly, they overtook another figure in the water with only its head still showing, dipping under the surface, coming up and then suddenly gone. Orazio clung on to Adriano's collar, treading water for a moment and looking back towards the ship.

As he watched, gasping for breath, it began to tilt, the stern settling into the water, the bows reaching up towards the sky. The little insect figures were scrambling up the almost vertical deck, losing hold, tumbling back. A sudden explosion blew out steam and flying furniture and a huge plank that swiped the men from the ropes like a giant fly-swat. Then the liner slid almost silently, stern down, into the sea, leaving only the floating wreckage and the spreading stain of oil.

'What's that?' Adriano said, as a strange sound crept towards them over the water like the calling of sea birds.

'I think it's those who are dying,' Orazio gasped as a wave swept into his mouth. He spat and kicked out strongly, dragging Adriano after him. He could see an empty life-raft ahead. He wondered whether even if they reached it they would have the strength to climb on board or even to hang on to it. His strength was gone. He couldn't go any further even without Adriano.

As they got alongside Adriano hooked his own arm through a dangling loop of rope and seized Orazio's collar. 'Now I shall hold on to you.' Somehow, having reached some kind of help, it seemed harder to stay afloat. He hung on to the rope handle aware of Adriano's grip and the leaden body that it was supporting. From time to time he tried to bicycle with his frozen legs. He lost count of how long they'd been clinging there, and the overcast sky gave them no clue to the passing time. Orazio found himself becoming drowsy. Almost he wanted just to slip down below the surface and stop struggling. His head went under. His eyes and mouth were full of water. Adriano was hauling him up again. He wished he would just let go. 'A boat, Orazio! A boat. They're coming to pick us up.'

The raft bobbed precariously as a man was lowered aboard so that they were in danger of losing their grip and sinking at the last minute. Orazio felt a rope being passed under his armpits, tightening painfully, and he was being hauled into a ship's boat, the breath squeezed out of him. He was dumped on the deck; the rope was untied so that he could breathe again, and passed back over the side for Adriano. With a blessed sense of relief he allowed himself to lose consciousness.

When he came to he was lying wrapped in blankets on the lower deck of some ship with Adriano watching over him anxiously. 'At last you decided to wake up.'

'Where are we?'

'On a Canadian destroyer. They're taking us back to Scotland. We are lucky. Many people have died.'

By the time the ship docked at Greenock he was well enough to march with the other Italian survivors to a local school where they were given tea and mattresses. As he lay there in the dark of the first night he found himself going over and over the sinking each time he closed his eyes, and when he fell asleep it was to start awake, crying out as the water flooded into his mouth and he went down and down. In the morning he remembered that it was his eighteenth birthday.

For a week they were fed and comforted by the local Italian community. Then they were told to gather their few belongings together, clothes donated by the Red Cross and their comforters, and marched to the station. They were going to be sent to London and released, to Wales, to the Isle of Man. The train drew in to Liverpool Station and buses took them to a camp in Birkenhead. They were to be sent back to sea.

The dreams were so vivid he no longer knew the difference between sleep and waking. When the rumour began to spread that they were to sail for Canada again, he looked for a way to kill himself, but there was Adriano who watched him all the time as if he guessed his thoughts. And how could he leave him alone? He tried to tell himself that they were young; they had survived once, they could again. It was the old men who had died, overweight from a lifetime of tasting, unwilling or unable to jump.

Rain was falling as they marched into the docks. They were lined up and roughly searched, many losing most of the clothes they had been given. Orazio felt a numbing hopelessness settle on him as they were driven up the gangway at bayonet-point with a small crowd jeering at them, into a barbed-wire enclosure on deck and finally down to the lowest level in the stern, where they could see nothing but knew that on the other side of the flimsy bulkhead was just water. The narrow stairwell, their only way of escape, was closely guarded. They knew when the ship sailed by the change in its motion and the increased surge of the engines.

Orazio lay on a table unable to sleep for dread. The latrine buckets were already full and the dark hold stank. He heard a man vomiting from sea-sickness. From time to time he dozed on his table. Adriano was underneath. They had agreed to take turn about. He had no watch. He supposed they would be called in the morning if they lived.

Adriano slept better. He had hidden his watch during the search and so still had it in his pocket. When he woke and looked up Orazio was staring down at him over the edge of the table. 'What time is it?'

'It's seven-thirty.'

'I've been awake for hours. I have to pee.' He climbed down from his hard bed and picked his way between the sleeping men to the nearest bucket.

'I wonder where we are.'

'Somewhere out there again.'

Others were beginning to stir now like the dead in one of the lower levels of *L'Inferno*, Orazio thought. Some just turned, groaning in their sleep.

As he stood wondering whether to climb back onto his makeshift bed he heard a strange noise begin: a rasping and grating along the hull and then a dull thud. At once everyone was awake, on their feet and rushing at the stairs. Adriano jumped up, hitting his head on the table. 'Come on!'

'What's the point? There's a door at the top of the stairs. They'll never let us out.'

There were cries and shouts from the stairwell and a pounding that showed his guess was right. 'Sit on the table with me. Maybe if fate's on our side we'll float away together.' He no longer cared. It was as if he was already dead.

Cursing and shouting, the men gradually returned from the stairs. One had a bloody wound. He had almost succeeded in breaking down the door and a bayonet had been thrust through by a soldier on the other side, gashing his arm.

That was the only attack on the ship. They learned after that the German torpedoes had miraculously passed by. The voyage settled into a grim monotony while the men speculated about their destination. During their daily fifteen minutes of exercise on deck they tried to work out the ship's direction. After a week at sea Canada was given up as a possibility to be briefly replaced by the Caribbean. By now they were all lousy and stinking. Adriano went down with an attack of the diarrhoea that had spread through the ship making conditions even worse.

One night Orazio became afraid that Adriano might be slipping into unconsciousness. He was weak and thin, his plumpness pared away by the months of confinement, bad food and now sickness. Orazio cradled him in his arms against the bulkhead, feeding him sips of stale water and talking to him until he fell into a natural sleep. When Orazio woke in the morning he was stiff from holding Adriano all night to stop him from rolling around with the motion of the ship but he was rewarded when Adriano opened his eyes and looked at him with recognition. The worst of the fever was over.

A week later they anchored off the coast of Africa and fruit was brought on board for distribution on fruit days: bright globes of oranges whose juice ran into their beards, bunches of small green bananas like the hands of aliens, and scented mangoes. The next month passed almost as if in a dream with stops at ports they could only glimpse in twenty-second turns at the few portholes that were uncovered. Orazio began to believe that they would survive but when Adriano said, 'Surely God wouldn't let us drown now,' he couldn't answer.

'We must be getting near,' he said when they were issued with razors and extra soap. Adriano, who was still weak, was allowed a full hour's exercise with the older men. One afternoon he came down in great excitement, calling out, 'Trees, Orazio, a port, people and cars. Lights everywhere.' They had arrived.

· *Endgame* ·

This morning the air tasted of autumn. Pearse poked his head out of the Don's front door as nervously as an animal expecting a gun to go off. He thought he could manage Nicole and Liam's questions better today after the cups of good coffee and the toast the Don had filled him up with.

'What will you do with all that?' he'd asked, staring at the stack of notes.

'Here, have some.' The Don took a pack off the top and thrust it at him.

'No, thanks all the same. It's got through misery and it can only bring misery.'

'It's only money, a way of exchange.'

'But what would I exchange it for?'

'A ticket to Canada for your son. Or Australia. It's an interesting country. I spent a few years there when I was young.'

'He says it's no good: that they're everywhere. I don't think it would bring him any luck. I'd best be getting along to see how he is. We'll talk some more later.'

'You can always come back here. But think about what we said. We need a plan soon.' Orazio wondered when it might be his turn. Noonan seemed to have recovered very quickly though he still looked a mess. He wasn't so sure of his own powers of recuperation.

Pearse dodged across the road into the market, surfacing beside the wet fish stall with its blend of old and new, fishes he had never seen when he was a boy: red mullet, squid and snapper, and those the fishermen had thrown on to the quay in Arklow: herring, crab and cod. He moved quickly through the ambling crowds and along the patient queues. Passing a charity shop he had the sudden inspiration of a hat that would disguise him and his bruises a bit.

'Shall I put it in a bag?' the volunteer on the till asked, looking doubtfully at the sandy corduroy cap.

'No, I'll wear it, thanks. I think it might rain.' The cap made him feel invisible like the fairy caps in the stories, dissolving their wearers from sight. He jumped a bus going in the opposite direction and got off beside the allotments where dahlias and Michaelmas daisies burned in front of dense green and red tapestried curtains of runner beans. No one had got off with him. No following car drew up or poked a blunt snout out of its window. How long could he live like this, heartstoppingly? He caught another bus. Nearing Nicole's house he got off a stage early and jinked among the turnings until he was sure he was alone and could ring the doorbell.

There was no sign of a stick when she opened the door. She seemed to be going back in time while he stood still or ran on. 'Where's Liam?'

'He's in the garden. Your poor face.' She touched the graze on his cheek.

'Sure, I'm better today. I was a right mess last night. Does he know?'

'I think he guesses something. I'll bring you a drink. You look as if you could do with one. Beer?'

'That'd go down a treat.'

The boy was sitting with a book on his lap as if he'd been reading, but his eyes were closed. 'Dada, what happened?'

'Nice people you've been mixing with. They held me up and then gave me a kicking.'

'That's why I didn't come to you in the first place, why I didn't want to involve you. I should go away now; then when they come again you can tell them I've gone and they'll leave you alone.'

'You mean kill me off as no further use. You forget: I know who they are.' Even as he spelled it out he realised the hopelessness in what he was saying. They could never leave him alone now. Only if they could be made to believe that he or Liam was dead. But then to do that they'd have to go away, change their names, disappear. Nicole came through the French windows with a tray of filled glasses.

'I know it's early but I feel we all need a drink.'

After the Irishman had gone Orazio set out the chess pieces and played himself a long game of attrition. He needed the problems and strategies to fill the forefront of his mind while he waited for some way of dealing with those of real life to crystallise behind in the recesses of his brain, where the animal instinct for survival might operate, rather than try to solve them as he had before, by conscious reasoning.

Both sides must be brought together on the board. The queen had to be lured out of her position of safety before she could be taken. He took a white pawn with a black and then sent the white bishop diagonally down the board in retaliation. Where should it be? Shoot-outs in Westerns took place in saloons or under the sun in the centre of town. For a moment he played with the idea of the Castel Grande itself as a suitable setting but it might be damaged or even destroyed in the process. These days the multi-storey car park had replaced the crossroads as a suitable venue for the last frames to be shot. Could he think of a way to get them all to such a place? He advanced the black queen to a position of menace knocking off the bishop. Black was doing too well. He must be showing favouritism. He doglegged with a white rook.

Then there was the boy. He'd heard nothing from Scott. Perhaps he'd never hear from him again. Surely self-interest would take a hand if his smart streetboy's wits thought there was money to be made. And there was the pile of money itself. After the Irishman had superstitiously refused to take any, the Don had hidden it at the back of a sideboard, behind the wine glasses. He anticipated that they would ask him to pay out soon just to test him. He must make sure Ruby Heamans didn't suddenly get the urge for a 'good turn out' before winter closed in. He manoeuvred himself towards stalemate to prove his impartiality and sat back to look at the board.

He could decide what pieces represented themselves and their opponents, set them out and play them off against each other. Himself and Noonan would be white of course: a bishop and a castle maybe. That made him smile. And the blacks? A queen and three pawns. He'd like to see them as that. And the kings? They were abstractions, positions to be defended. He was getting nowhere.

The boy probably didn't exist, was a fantasy of his own invention. He had left it all too late, been too timid and spoiled other people's lives, Catterina's life especially, in the process. The mention of Australia to Noonan had brought back the whole episode, as his dreams did, including that moment of the greatest tenderness in his life when he had cradled Adriano through the night against the roll of the ship.

Adriano had been sent home before him. Because Orazio had become a spokesman for the internees, he was regarded as a troublemaker. He found that from the start he had inherited his father's category 'A' classification and he'd perversely set about earning it. Adriano, who had been only a 'C', had taken the chance to join an Australian Pioneer Corps and had gone away to build roads while Orazio stayed on in the corrugated iron huts of Camp Tatuna where dust blew in every day from the winds swirling around the hilltop. Only at night when the wind rested was there a clear sky, coldly brilliant with its strange Southern stars. Lean and brown now, Adriano had come to say goodbye.

'You saved my life: I'll never forget. When it's all over we'll meet again. Even if you do become a priest.' Most of the inmates thought he must because of his reading, his arguments, the lectures he began to give from the books he read. But he knew he never would. It was best if Adriano went. His nearness was too much of a temptation. Orazio was afraid that if he stayed, one day some gesture or look would give him away.

It was only after Adriano had gone into the whirling dust-cloud set up by the departing truck that he began to really study the other animals. Humans were too chary: their behaviour clouded by imagination and consciousness, too erratic and dangerous. From time to time aborigines came to the camp, boys about his own age or younger. He wondered about them: whether they were innocent and spontaneous or as convolute as he saw himself and those around him to be. When they met again in London after he came back to set up the Castel Grande and Adriano was looking for a job, he was able to see him without the stirring of the old emotion. That had faded with his years in Italy as his anger against his father, whose place on the *Arandora Star* he'd been forced to take, had swelled inside him.

Orazio had gone to Adriano's funeral alone. He hadn't made old bones. Soon after Agnese's wedding he had first felt a little not-well and then a little ill. Who could say how what had happened to them when they were *giovanotti* might have left scars that would open up again with time. He was surprised at his own longevity. Adriano had seemed an old man when Orazio had visited him during his last illness. Adriano had asked him to go and see him. It was as if everything, marriage, work, children, that had happened to him since the war had left no mark. He seemed to want to go through those distant terrors almost as part of making his will, as if the memory was something he wanted to be sure Orazio had intact, in his keeping, the only legacy he could leave him apart from the watch.

'I've kept it all this time. I want you to have it.'

Orazio remembered him cleaning it one day at Tatuna. 'It's stopped. I think the sea water must have rusted it.' Orazio could see his brown fingers delicately picking among the minute parts with a feather dipped in oil.

'I'll keep it till you're better if it will help you to rest.'

'It was good of you to come, Mr Carbone,' Adriano's wife had said at the funeral.

'If there's anything you need. Any way I can help . . .'

Adriano had looked as old as his own father before his death. Orazio was shocked to find as he noticed every wrinkle, the shine on the sweaty bald head, how completely love had died in him. Perhaps the boy could have, indeed had, rekindled it but he couldn't bear that the boy should see him as he had seen Adriano.

When he picked up the telephone he was expecting to hear the Irishman's voice or that other. 'Yes?'

'It's me, Scott.'

'Scott?' He was confused. He had forgotten for a moment that he had given the *scugnizzo* his number.

'Yeah. I ain't found him, your nephew.'

'No?' He was relieved and disappointed together.

'Yeah. I could do with some dosh though. I ain't 'ad a square meal since yesterday breakfast.'

'What am I supposed to do?'

'Well, if you want me to go on looking you better keep me alive.' Orazio was silent, considering. 'Eh, you still there? I ain't got any more money. I'm on a payphone.'

He made a decision. 'Reverse the charges and ring me back.' The telephone returned to the dialling tone. He replaced the receiver. 'Yes,' he said when it rang again, 'I will accept the call.' And to Scott: 'All right, I'll give you some money. But I can't come out. You'll have to come and get it.' He had accepted a responsibility, made a decision that carried the seeds of the future in it. 'I'll give you the address. Can you get here?'

'I'll get there. 'Ere, what's your name?'

'Why do you need to know?'

'I gotta call you something.'

'You can call me the Don. A lot of people do.'

He had forgotten it was Ruby Heamans' afternoon. 'I'm going to get them two, Mr Carbonny. You see,' she announced as she plonked down her bag on the kitchen table and took her apron from behind the door. 'Their time has come. I've got some stuff to knock them out. I know some people would say it was cruel but you have to be cruel to be kind sometimes.'

'I'm expecting a visitor.' He wondered what she would think

of Scott. 'A rapscallion,' probably, since that was the word she used for erring cats and people. One-Eye was a rapscallion.

'You be careful, Mr Carbonny. He'll go off with the spoons, that kid,' she said when he followed her into the kitchen to bring Scott coffee and biscuits.

Scott was certainly hungry. He gobbled the biscuits, hardly tasting them, like a hound. 'Fancy you having such a big place all to yourself.'

'It hasn't always been just me. My wife and daughter lived here until my daughter got married and my wife died.'

'You had a wife and family? I had you down for a loner.'

Aware of a miasma of disapproval emanating from the kitchen, the Don took the boy through the house. 'You could sell all this lot for a bundle and retire to Spain, live in the sun comfortable, plenty to eat, booze, anything you wanted. Or you could fill it up with dossers and have a party every night. Only it wouldn't last long then. You gonna leave it all to that nephew when you find him?'

'No, I've got two grandchildren. It's left to them.' It was true but he'd felt no emotion, no pride in the knowledge before.

'Cor, grandchildren! Lucky little sods. No one ever left me nothing.'

Mrs Heamans brought them a plate of sandwiches. 'I had a friend staying last night. He slept in Agnese's old room. Give it an extra tidy, and the bathroom, will you?' She would no doubt speculate to her husband on what things were coming to.

Later she put her head round the back door. He had taken Scott out into the yard to see the statues. 'They're really weird,' the boy said. 'I like the geezer with the pain best.' He nodded at the dying Gaul.

'I'll be off now, Mr Carbonny. I've left that stuff in the cupboard under the sink. I'll be back to deal with them two next week. Take care.' She didn't usually exhort Orazio to take care.

'What two?' Scott had asked when she'd gone with a slam of the front door.

'One-Eye and the little tortoiseshell: they're two wild cats who live in the yard. She wants to catch them, have them neutered and bring them back.'

'People do that all the time: catch each other and knacker you, try to turn you into tame old tabbies. I expect that's what you want to do to your nephew, or his mother does. I shouldn't be helping but what can I do? I got to live.'

Orazio handed over twenty pounds.

'Thanks. 'Ere, suppose I don't find him? I mean, not straight off?'

'Then you'll have to come back for some more. You know where I live now.'

'I wouldn't mind a shower before I go. You really get grotty in them doss houses and I don't like everyone bossing at me when I'm washing meself.'

Orazio looked at the boy's clothes and wished he had some means of replacing them. 'I could let you have some clean underwear and a shirt.' Nothing else he had would be suitable. His tidy suits were old men's clothes.

Scott held up the twenty-pound note. 'I can get a pair of cheap jeans with some of this.' He followed the Don into his bedroom and watched as he opened drawers and took out a fresh shirt, pants, socks and finally a vest. 'Only old guys wear them things. Still, I'll take it. Might start a new fashion.'

Orazio got him a clean bath towel from the airing cupboard. 'I'll be downstairs when you're finished.' As he turned away from the closed door he heard the taps begin to run. Scott would be taking off his clothes. The thought of the boy's pale body stepping into the bath made him feel sick with longing. *Te per aquas, dure*, he remembered, almost laughing at himself. What waters could his namesake have meant?

Perhaps the boy went swimming in the Tiber or maybe Horace had given his BC version of Scott a dip in the baths.

Scott came to say goodbye. 'Thanks for the clothes an' that. I'll see yer. He's a lucky little bugger, your nephew. I dunno what he's doing on the streets with all this waiting for him.'

What would he do now if Scott should suddenly produce the boy? His face was fading while the image of Scott himself grew stronger. The other had been a dream to set against his drowning nightmare. Reality would drive it away as it had dissolved his love for Adriano into a subdued ache, a sense of loss.

It was a relief when the telephone rang again and it was the Irishman. 'I wondered if I could maybe spend the night at your place again? We could talk some more.'

'Where are you now?'

'I'm at a friend's. But I think I'll risk going home. The place is in a terrible mess. I need to set things a bit to rights.'

'Come back, of course. I'm not going out. We could think over a move or two. I don't like being beaten.'

Pearse put back the receiver and peered at his face in the gold-framed mirror above Lady Pritchard's gleaming hall table. He looked a villain himself. He needed a bath and to scrape off the silvery stubble that had salted his chin making his skin seem dirty, a rogue's mugshot. He knew he only had to say and he could have a bath run for him upstairs but he was shy of that. It seemed somehow as if it would weaken him though he wasn't sure why.

They had had their lunch in the garden; Liam hardly eating anything, just picking as usual. 'You'll fade away,' Jessie would have said. He needed to go home to her now, to their home, and lay the sense of betrayal he felt at the memory of Jessie's things, that her hands had touched, disordered, roughly torn from their places and thrown down.

'Liam,' he'd said over the sandwiches, 'we'll have to work something out. That wasn't me they were kicking though they pretended it was. All that stuff about me being in the British Army. It's you they want and they'll stay as long as they believe you're here.'

'But if I go, Dada, they'll force you to tell them where I've gone or kill you if you won't.'

'Don't worry about me.'

'And save myself, is that it? That won't do, Dada. You don't know these people. They won't relent.'

'Then we'll both have to go. Leave the country. We could start by going up to Scotland to see your mother's people.'

'They know all about them. There's probably somebody there already keeping watch.'

'Then it'll have to be abroad: Australia or America.'

'It'd cost a lot of money. We mightn't be able to come back.'

'I think I can deal with that.' Could he begin again, cut off those roots he and Jessie had put down together, leave her lying there alone, break the habits of half a lifetime? If there was no other way and it meant Liam was safe. She'd want him to go. He would have to accept the Don's offer.

He took his usual circuitous route home with a change of bus, deciding that even that would have to be altered next time. Then he set off down the road past the church, and turned into the estate where he was at his most exposed. He looked up at the tower blocks sailing across the sky which for once was a' pale cloudless blue, as if he wasn't aware of every corner that might hide an ambush.

When he reached his own entrance he' faced again the old stairs versus lift conundrum and, because his heart was already banging in his chest against the bars of his ribs, he took a deep breath and pressed the button for the lift.

Peering round the edge when the door slid open, his key already in his hand, he made a dash for his own front door and then he was inside throwing bolt and chain into position. He sank down on the lavatory seat to still the fluttering in his chest.

After a few minutes he was able to get up and survey the wreckage, standing a fallen chair upright on its four legs to lower himself onto while he decided where to begin. His own legs were like aching putty or the rubbery creatures of television adverts except that his wouldn't bend and straighten again at will. Perhaps it would be easier to start in the bedroom he still thought of as theirs, his and Jessie's. Her dressing-table had been hurled forward on its face. He struggled to right it, fearful that the mirrors in the oval frame might have shattered. Putting his knee under from behind he pivoted the top-heavy piece on two of the spindly legs and hauled it backwards. Jessie had been so proud of that bedroom suite with its inlaid pattern of lighter wood picking out the edges of the rich mahogany veneer. They'd got it cheap, second-hand, but she'd preferred it to the modern stuff she'd said was nothing but plastic-coated chipboard. It must be even more out-of-fashion now or maybe it had come round again. He began to cram the strewn articles back into the dressing-table drawers. There was no time to try to set them to rights.

The ring at the door set his heart, which had begun to steady, drumming again in his ears. As quietly as he could he went through into the living room and then slipped briefly into the hall and through to the bathroom. From here he could call out without putting himself in the line of fire from anyone taking a pot-shot through the door. 'Who is it?' He had to know. If he'd stayed silent and they'd broken the door down it would have been worse.

'Police, Mr Noonan. We want to talk to you.'

'You've already talked to me. I've nothing more to say.'

'We can talk now or come back with a warrant.'

'How do I know you're the Police?'

The flap of the letterbox was lifted up and an ID-card poked halfway through, spread flat enough for him to identify as genuine. Pearse drew back the bolt and opened the door on the chain. It was the same two as before.

'Do you want us to shout?'

He undid the chain and opened the door. There was barely room for them to push past him through the narrow hall.

'Looks like you've had visitors.'

'Somebody else looking for Liam. They weren't very polite.'

'We still think we can help him and you, if you'll let us.'

'You see how I'm fixed. It's bad enough as it is. If they thought I was talking to you . . .'

'We can give him protection, find him a safe house.'

'In return for information.'

'What else can he do?'

'I don't know. I'll have to think about it.' He wanted them out of the place.

'Did you give him the number we left you?'

'Yes, yes he has it,' he said, wondering what he'd done with it, if it'd still been on the mantelpiece when those others had called and they'd taken the card away.

'Tell him to use it. It's for the best. We don't want to have to arrest him. If we did, we could keep him a long time. We'd prefer his co-operation.'

'I'll tell him all that. But he'd need to be sure he'd be safe.'

'You don't look as if you're very safe as you are. He shouldn't be hiding behind his old dad.'

'Who else would he hide behind?'

As soon as they were gone he began his search for the hand-written card with the giveaway number. If they had taken it and tried dialling those figures, what answer would they get except one that would bring them back more determined than ever? Pearse scrabbled about on the living room floor in desperation, turning over the cushions and books, the broken shards of a pair of vases and the oak clock that had been wedding presents. With a great heave he righted the sofa and spotted the card among a litter of other papers, electricity and water bills, his pension book and television licence reminder, a minicab number, that had been swept from the mantelpiece with the ornaments. His visitors must have thought they were all the same sort of junk and not bothered to inspect them. He picked up the card and looked at it before putting it safely in his wallet. There was nothing to suggest the nature of the information it carried and he returned more easily to his tidying.

This time it was the telephone that interrupted him. 'Is that the traitor's hideout? Tell him he can't hide from us.'

'Why can't you just leave him alone? He's no threat to you.'

'Because of his loose mouth. We've seen the British Police going in. They can't protect him. Tell him that.'

It was dark by the time he reached the Don's, after a combined tube and taxi journey to cover the few hundred yards without being followed by anyone. Even though he was pretty sure they all knew about his visits there, it was as well to keep them guessing. The Don let him in and sat him down in the office with a glass of whisky. 'I believe I begin to see how it might be done,' he said.

Pearse thought he seemed over-excited, not with his usual calm air but flushed, his eyes intent and narrowed.

'You're an electrician. Could you detonate an explosion by remote control, a harmless explosion?'

· *Pearse's Tale* ·

A year after leaving the Christian Brothers Pearse had still been kicking his heels along the sea front. It had seemed so easy. He would follow his father to sea. His mother hadn't wanted him to go of course since his father had come home from his last voyage to Africa only to die from some disease that turned his skin yellow as a guinea and wasted the flesh from his bones. He hadn't been an easy patient either, first fretting at his lost employment, then his confinement to the low rooms of the cottage and finally to bed. Pearse had always remembered him as a jolly man on his visits home, singing to his wife's piano with a glass in his hand. Now he resented the hours she spent knitting or sewing to earn a bit of bread, taking up the space, with her own mother sitting the other side working at a quilt, while he banged with an old knobkerry on the bedroom wall for attention. Pearse loved the pieces bag with its chopped-up coloured squares, and diamonds of discarded clothes and bedding, and the wool bag with the bright skeins for knitting and crochet. Wet days, when he was younger, he would sit on the rag rug in front of the fire sorting and tidying the two bags.

There was just enough in the burial club to give his father a proper send-off and Pearse wore his black armband to school, until it was torn off at the football and his mother quietly put it away in a drawer with the black-edged card announcing the funeral. The piano wasn't opened for over a year, not till the second Christmas when his uncles and aunts came round and began begging for a song. 'You can't mourn forever now, Nan.'

His mother had wanted him to stay on and take the examination that would have started him on the way to being a teacher but he wanted to be up and earning to make things easier for her. 'There's no jobs in Arklow. You might as well stay at the schooling.'

'Then I'll go to sea like Dada.' For that he'd have to go first to Dublin. He took his last walk along the shore staring out at the sea he'd soon be riding on, and then his last look back at the cottage, as his mother walked him to the station. It seemed very small under its brow of thatch. 'When I come back on leave I'll whiten it over for you.'

'Sure, I can do that while you're gone. It'll give me something to keep me busy. You remember to write now. Your father never did. I never knew when he'd be turning up.' He was to lodge with a married cousin in Dublin till he got a berth.

Two months later the money his mother had saved and sent him off with was all but spent. The whole world seemed to be running down. People said it was no better across the water. Even so he thought he'd have to try, take the ferry to Liverpool where there must be more boats that might have a place for a deck-hand to get started. He was coming back from a fruitless day hanging about the dock Labour Office when the man stopped him.

'Are you looking for work?'

'I've been looking for a year.'

'Where are you from?'

'Arklow.'

'How would you feel about going abroad?'

'I'm trying to get a ship. But there's nothing to be had even though me daddy was a seaman.' He had tried his father's last line but although the clerk had been sympathetic he had shaken his head.

'If you can keep something to yourself I can offer you a trip to Spain and twelve pesetas a day.'

'What would I have to do?'

'Fight for Holy Mother Church against the Red atheists.'

'I don't know about fighting.'

'You'll soon learn. Where were you educated?'

'With the Christian Brothers.'

'Well then, you should be keen to defend the Faith, a young man like you. I'll give you a name and address to contact. But mind, you have to keep it a secret. Our government doesn't like young men going to fight for a just cause. They don't stop them joining the army of the enemy though. Now give me your name and address.'

Pearse took the piece of paper and put it away without looking at it. Time enough when the man was gone. Spain sounded enticing. He knew there was a civil war going on there but he didn't understand what it was all about. It was hard to get at the truth between the allegations of nun rapes and priest murders and the counter-cries against fascism and old corruption. It was the first time anyone had addressed him as a man instead of a boy.

The name on the paper was Liam Walsh. He asked his cousin's wife if she'd heard of such a one. The name seemed familiar. 'There's someone with a name like that secretary of the Blue Shirts.'

'Who are the Blue Shirts?'

'You country boys. They're a political party. Cosgrave's lot.'

The address was his own name: Pearse Street. It seemed a good omen but the days passed and he heard nothing and there was still no job at the docks or on shipboard. Then one morning his cousin's wife said there was a letter for him. He expected to see his mother's handwriting across it, but the envelope was typewritten. He put it in his pocket and set off as usual on his tramp for work. The letter burnt a hole there until he was far enough from the house to open it up.

He was to tell no one and report the following Sunday at ten o'clock at night at Batchelor's Walk. A car would pick him up. He should bring only a small suitcase. He had to think of a story that would satisfy his mother and cousin: a promise of a job over the water should do it. 'If I get it,' he wrote home, 'you mayn't hear from me for a bit so don't worry.'

He left the house in the afternoon as if he was catching

the boat and hung about till it was dark and time to get himself to Batchelor's Walk. He half-believed no one would come. Then he would take the Liverpool boat anyway and try his luck over there. He couldn't go back now. But promptly at ten by a distantly-chiming church clock, a car drew up just as he had propped himself against the lamp-post under the sputtering gas light. A tall man in a soft hat and trench coat got out. His face was dark under the shadow of the hat brim. 'Pearse Noonan?'

Pearse nodded, unable to speak for excitement. It was just like the pictures.

'Have you got some form of identification on you?'

Pearse showed him his birth certificate.

'Get in.'

The only empty seat was beside the driver. There were two other fellows, with suitcases and round about the same age as himself, already in the back. Pearse sat with his case on his knee saying nothing as the Ford roared through the empty Dublin streets and out into the countryside.

'Where are we going?' he asked at one point but the driver only grunted. Pearse found himself falling asleep as the dark countryside unrolled outside the car windows. They weren't going south. He would have recognised the road that led through Arklow to Waterford and Cork. North was unlikely. They must be right out in the heart of Ireland. After a couple of hours they drove through the silent streets of Athlone. He'd been right then. They would be heading for the West Coast. An hour later the car pulled up in Eyre Square in the centre of Galway, and after unwinding their cramped legs the three of them followed the driver into the reception hall of a large hotel and through to the dining-room which was already full of young men, some of whom looked even younger than Pearse, standing around drinking tea.

He stood there uncertainly, wondering what they were supposed to do. The other two had been absorbed into the crowd and the driver had done his bit by delivering them and had probably gone off to report. For a moment, looking round at the other nervous or over-excited faces all trying to assume an expression of calm, he wondered what he was doing there. Suppose he just turned round and walked out, would he be allowed to leave? Where would he go?

Another fellow with a cup in his hand who'd been standing alone also surveying the scene, unstuck himself from the pillar he was leaning against and came over towards him. 'Hullo, haven't I seen you at the Labour Office at Dublin docks?'

'I have been there sometimes, looking for work.'

'Like a lot of us. I'm Seámus.' He put out his hand.

'Pearse. Where did you get the tea?'

'Up that end on the table.'

Pearse pushed himself through the crowd and came back slopping his over-full mug.

'Well,' Seámus said, 'we must be going to fight for the Faith. While you were getting your tea I went and asked one of them fellows by the door where we were going and he said to wait "for Christ's sake". I don't know how they think they'll make soldiers of this lot. Some of them are still wet behind the ears and a lot of the rest are just counter-jumpers.'

'Have you done some fighting yourself then?'

'I've seen a bit. Watch out now, there's some sunburstery coming. That fellow with the eleven-a-side 'tache is going to tell us why we're here.'

Instead he told them to line up with their suitcases and cars would take them to the harbour. The square was now full of people watching and cars, with no more attempt at secrecy under the blazing lights and no sign of the Police. 'Where's Dev's CID?' Seámus muttered as they waited their turn to be driven to the quayside. Other hotels had delivered up their cargo of young men and the square was packed.

They lined up again when they reached the docks to go aboard the tender waiting alongside. Pearse read the name *Dun Aengus* on her stern. The wind was rising and it had begun to rain. Once aboard they lined the rails, some waving to the crowd below, others already beginning to feel queasy from the pitch and yaw of the battered boat. As the ship began to draw away there was a ragged attempt at a song from those who weren't feeling too ill. Pearse knew the words and the tune as one his mother had played but he noticed Seámus wasn't singing and the words died on his lips.

'Soldiers are we, whose lives are pledged to Ireland,
Some have come from a land beyond the wave,
Sworn to be free, no more our ancient sireland
Shall shelter the despot or the slave.
Tonight we'll man the Bearna Baoghail,
In Erin's cause come woe or weal.
Mid cannon's roar and rifle's peal,
We'll chant a soldier's song.'

'It'll be a different story when they hear the "rifle's peal",' Seámus said. Someone began on 'Faith of Our Fathers' but the wind was blowing the words away. 'Come on, I'm sick of this. Most of this lot wouldn't be here if they had work. And neither would I.'

By this time they were soaked through and there was barely room to crouch down on the deck out of the wind. The *Dun Aengus* slid over the bar. 'We're never going to Spain in this old tub. We must be going to rendezvous with another ship.' Soon after they felt the forward movement stop and then with a rattle of chain an anchor was run out. The night passed slowly, with the tender hove-to outside the harbour and many of the young passengers hanging over the rail in the misery of seasickness, cold and wet. It was a relief when morning came: the anchor was taken in and they began to move out to sea.

'Look, there she is,' Pearse said, proud of the fact that he seemed to have inherited his father's sea legs. A big grey shape had appeared. 'She's a foreigner.'

'*Unter den Linden*,' Seámus read out.

The sun was high up before they could get alongside. Rope ladders were dropped from the big ship to the tender and they had to climb their slippery, swaying rungs with the vessels bobbing unevenly and the strip of water between them constantly changing width. Pearse remembered his father saying: 'You put one hand after the other, and one foot after the other, and don't look down.' Then he was clambering over the side and jumping, to land awkwardly on the heaving deck of the German ship. A sailor helped him to his feet and indicated that he should go down the companionway. He hung about for Seámus to catch up and then they went below where they were handed a hot dixie of unidentifiable soup and a lump of bread.

'This is the life,' Pearse said, already catching his tone from Seámus.

'Goodbye to auld Ireland.'

I've never even been to Liverpool, Pearse thought, and here I am on my way to Spain.

Later that day they were all lined up for inspection. Some NCOs had emerged among the group or had been there in mufti all the time. Now they shouted the rest into groups of fifty.

'Ten groups,' Seámus said out of the side of his mouth, 'so there must be five hundred of us. That's Captain O'Sullivan; that jumped-up corporal told me.'

Officers in smart field-grey uniforms had appeared from below. O'Sullivan jerked up his arm in the fascist salute familiar from the newsreels, and the other officers responded. He spoke to them in German and then joined the group as they passed along the rows inspecting the pale young faces and the worn dirty clothes. 'You could see from their looks,' Seámus said when they were dismissed, 'they think we're a shambles, especially the Jerries.'

The weather was still rough and even the increased size of the ship didn't stop her rolling so that the seasickness among the young soldiers was still high. When one didn't make it to the rail a German sailor gave him a bucket of seawater and a mop, indicating that he should clear up the deck, which caused him to puke again and sink to his knees, weeping. Later there was more thin soup with lumps of gristle floating in it and more hard black bread that could only be chewed and swallowed after it had been dunked in the greasy mess. 'I bet some of them wish they'd never left their mothers,' Seámus said. Pearse thought of his father, understanding for the first time what he must have endured in weeks at sea, often without sign of land for days on end.

After a further day of misery Pearse, who had been looking out while Seámus lolled half-asleep propped against the side, called, 'Come and see. It must be Spain.' A low grey cloud had appeared ahead on the water, thickening, solidifying as they gradually approached.

'Or Portugal. Maybe we'll get some decent grub once we're ashore.'

What they got was a freezing train journey across a coastal plain and then through arid mountains for half a day without hot food or drinks until they reached Salamanca. As they drew into the city suburbs the NCOs appeared again, rousing them and telling them to smarten themselves up as best they could before they arrived. They saw why as soon as they got down on the platform, into some semblance of a parade, and marched out of the station to line up, surrounded by cheering crowds, in front of the dais draped with the Irish tricolour of green, white and gold, alternating with another flag in red and gold. A band played, the dais was heavy with priests and local dignitaries.

'That's General O'Duffy,' Seámus said when an officer in a handsome uniform stepped forward, the winter sun winking back from the harp badges that closed the ends of his collar. 'He's the Irish commander.'

He began welcoming them to Spain, to a new crusade for the Faith, for the defence of two thousand years of civilisation and their brother Catholics by the defeat of those atheists who were guilty of such hideous crimes against the Church and her servants. Pearse found his mind wandering: it seemed so unreal that he should be here at all. He'd thought that Spain would be hot but a freezing wind blew down from the mountains and he was hungry. O'Duffy gave way to the local mayor who spoke at length in Spanish and then a bishop raised his hand to bless them and they all knelt in the cold dust and echoed his gesture with their hands across their breasts, even Seámus. For a moment Pearse felt a terrible pricking of tears.

O'Sullivan stepped forward and told them they would now go on to Carreras where they would be issued with uniforms and begin their training as the Fifteenth *Bandera* of the crack Spanish troops, the *Tercio*, whose motto was 'Long Live Death'.

'Long live Ireland! Viva España!'

As their train meandered south through the mountains they sometimes saw the small crosses of planes overhead against the chill blue and wondered whether at any moment they would find their caterpillar of coaches, so vulnerable as it snaked among the outcrops and rocky gorges, under a rain of bombs and bullets. 'Perhaps they're on our side,' Seámus said.

Once they reached camp they were indeed issued with their uniforms which included a green beret and the self-same harp badges to the collars as their commander O'Duffy had been wearing, though the cloth of their jackets was thin and shoddy by comparison with his. They had time to write home now. Pearse knew his mother would be anxiously waiting for news but he wondered what he could tell her that wouldn't make her even more worried. There was already talk that the youngest were to be sent home at the demand of their parents who had somehow discovered where they were. In spite of the discomforts of camp life, Pearse wasn't eager to be one of them. However hard the conditions and the German instructors who trained them under their own officers, he didn't want to be sent home the object of Seámus' satire, 'wet behind the ears'. What was there for him anyway? Nothing had changed. He would still be unemployed.

The food was terrible but that was something else he couldn't tell his mother: Irish stew, so-called, which was lumps of pork and rice, a rubbery sweet that might have been tapioca, and coffee when they were used to tea. The portions of stew were meagre for young men training hard. One day there was a riot over a second helping of pork. Moorish troops from the next barracks were brought in with fixed bayonets to restore order. Seámus was one of those court-martialled and given seven days solitary in the dark, on bread and water.

Pearse had only ever seen darkies before at the docks, and they were thin, small, harassed-looking men, lascars who worked the boats and were sometimes to be seen scurrying along ashore in blue overalls. These were tall proud men in long multi-coloured robes and turbans, dark-skinned with moustaches and beards, who handled their rifles as if they loved them. 'What is it we're supposed to be doing, fighting for the Faith with a lot of infidels?' Seámus asked bitterly when he was let out. 'And that mangy yellow hound that's supposed to be our flag, I bet that was O'Duffy's idea. He's said to be a great one for the dogs.'

Their evenings spent drinking the strong local white wines in the town bars, with some of them going off to the bordellos after, couldn't be written home about either. Sometimes the night would end in a fight with the Moorish soldiers that could only be broken up by the intervention of the Spanish Military Police. At least in the town they couldn't hear the firing in the local concentration camp where there seemed to be nightly executions.

One day the townspeople staged a bullfight in their honour and they were marched to the ring to watch. The *banderilleros* had decorated their darts with ribbons in the Irish colours. Pearse was sickened to see them quivering in the animal's flanks with blood oozing stickily through the rough hair. 'Me, I'm on the bull's side,' Seámus said. It was a relief when the matador stepped in for the kill, cutting an ear from the fallen animal to present to O'Sullivan as a great cheer went up from the local people.

At last, after three months' training, they were thought fit for the front. They were to move out next day and that morning High Mass was sung before they left at noon. There was a long delay once they had entrained while they sat in the station. Someone passed the word that the driver was a spy who had intended to jump train on a decline, leaving it to career on with no one to guide it or apply the brakes. It seemed a sinister beginning to their part in the action if it was true.

For two days and a night they travelled, the journey broken again for repairs to a bomb-damaged section of line. There was nothing to eat or drink, only the bitter cold that dissolved their bones and made them unable to sleep. When they finally left the train they marched for two hours in the dark. 'The men up front say we're being guided by a kid.' They reached Valdemara at last and were allowed to sleep on the tiled floors of a convent after an issue of bully beef and coffee. 'They say that's the blood of nuns that used to live here.' One of the others pointed to the rusty splashes on the white walls.

In the morning, still sore from the train and the hard floor bed, the *bandera* marched on to take over the defence of Ciempozualos from the troops who'd been holding it. They set out cheerfully hoping for better food and lodging once they were settled in their forward positions. They had hardly reached the little white-washed town when they were halted. A troop was coming out to meet them. They stood still while their officers rode forward. Suddenly a shot rang out.

'Christ, Pearse, they're firing at us. Get down.' They threw themselves down on the dusty road unslinging their rifles. All around shots were being exchanged. Men screamed and fell over on their sides. Suddenly there were shouts of, 'Cease firing, cease firing.' Pearse stopped at once, waiting in terror for a stray bullet to find him as the sound of shots gradually lessened and finally died away. No one moved. After a few moments he risked raising his head. Over the intervening bodies which could have been alive or dead he could see that officers from both sides had met in the middle.

An NCO called out, 'On your feet, lads.' They got up gingerly ready to throw themselves down if the firing should break out again. The other troop was picking itself up too.

'They're our own side, the silly buggers. Someone's head'll roll for this. Look, Tom Hyde's down.'

It was a bitter introduction to the front. Four of their officers had been killed by a *bandera* from the Canaries, mistaking the Irish for the enemy, in spite of the statement from their Spanish liaison who had been among the first to die with the words hardly off his lips. The town when they reached it was a wreck littered with unburied bodies from the heavy fighting. The trenches left them by the withdrawing Moroccans were flooded and louse-ridden. Rain and shells fell on them constantly and it was still only tinned beef and coffee. At night they were fired on from an armoured train so close they could hear voices speaking in English, some with their own accents. 'It's like we're fighting ourselves or our own shadows in the dark.'

They held the town for four weeks before the order to advance came. Exhausted, their wet uniforms now threadbare, they set off. 'Going over the top,' their remaining officers had called it at their briefing. Shells began to fall, pinning them down. 'O'Sullivan says we're going back to Ciempo.' They straggled defeated into the town. In the morning they stood to again, ready for another try, but before they marched out word came that the attack was off. They were to dig in. They set about delousing themselves and the trenches and loosing off pot-shots at the enemy positions. The dead were taken back to Cacares to be buried in style. 'Did you know they're saying St Mary's pipe band have come over from Dublin to play at the funerals?'

'This place is unhealthy,' Seámus said. 'If we don't get out of here soon they'll be burying the rest of us.' But it was another four weeks before they were moved and by then his disenchantment was common to them all, even when they were visited by the Spanish generals, Franco and Mola, in an attempt to lift their morale: 'Or make us see what we can't see and not feel what we do feel, which is starving, cold and wet.' The generals repeated the old song that it was the Rocos who were destroying the Faith. 'Did you hear there's two nurses come from home to hold our hands when none of the doctors would?'

Those who could still march moved up to within sight of Madrid at La Moranosa with the Hill of Angels on their flank. Headquarters was set up in a ruined factory, and field kitchens in the gulleys between the hills. It was growing hotter and fresh water had to be brought by mule from eight miles away. They were part of the besieging force and their trenches were within enemy range. Rifle-fire and intermittent shelling soon taught them to keep their heads down. 'This is a stalemate. We could be here for months waiting for the buggers to attack, and they're waiting for us.'

They were on their way back from trench duty when they came across a knot of Moorish troops.

'Let's keep out of their way.' Pearse pulled at Seámus' sleeve.

'I want to see what they're up to.' He craned his head to peer between the turbans that made the Moroccans seem even taller than they were. 'They've got a couple of bodies in the middle.' Looking between the robed figures in his turn, Pearse could see that one was an old man, white-haired, while the other was a boy younger than himself, their faces blacker than their executioners' with soot and coal dust. '*Qui sont-ils?*' Seámus asked the nearest soldier.

'*Ils sont des républicains, des conducteurs du train. Ils se sont rendus.*'

'Let's get out of here.' Seámus turned away, his face white.

'What was it? What happened?'

'The train crew surrendered and those bastards shot them. I'm sick of this,' he went on as they made their way along the bottom of a gulley. 'For two pins I'd join the other side.'

'You'd be shot if you tried to desert.'

'They'd have to catch me first.'

Pearse looked up at the ridges, barren under the pouring light from the pitiless sky that exposed every stunted shrub to the gaze of enemy and friend. Above, a bird of prey circled dropping its shadow across the bare flanks of the hills, searching out some small rodent for its stoop. There was nowhere even a mouse could hide. That night he woke in a sweat that wasn't just the heat. He'd been dreaming that he was the dead boy and he was running, jumping from bare rock to rock with the shadows getting nearer that he couldn't identify, until he stumbled, he was rolling down a slope and the bullets were thudding into him. He searched for the shape of Seámus on his straw-stuffed palliasse against the broken wall of the ruined outhouse they slept in, and when he found it hunched safely there, he drifted back to sleep.

In the morning Pearse found it hard to wake and was already sweating though the sun was barely up. 'You've got the fever,' Seámus said. 'I knew this place was unhealthy.'

'You won't go without me.' Pearse was ashamed of his own pleading.

'I won't leave while you're sick but they might cart you off to the hospital.'

'You'll come and see me.'

'If I'm let. Now I'll go and report for you. You're not fit even for sick parade.'

When Pearse tried to get up he found that his legs wouldn't carry him. A Spanish doctor came and took his temperature and he was carted away on a stretcher. He lost consciousness before he reached the hospital. When he woke Seámus was sitting beside him. 'You've been out for three days. We're going back to Cacares. They say it's all over for us. You'll get those Irish nurses to soothe your brow. They say we only signed on for six months. If you get a visit from the commander ask him for some of those Sweet Aftons he smokes.'

It was a full week after they'd been brought back before Pearse was fit to rejoin the *bandera* in camp. They had been disarmed and only waited for a ship to take them home. It was like being on holiday. General O'Duffy came to tell them how well they'd done and that Spain and Ireland were united forever in the Catholic faith because of them. They exchanged their green berets with some of the Spanish soldiers' red ones. The pipe band played and those who were well enough sang and danced. Moorish merchants came round the camp selling jewellery, silk scarves and ties, toffee and chocolate.

'Look at those silly buggers, those bold Fenian men.' Seámus nodded contemptuously at the dancing figures. 'I tell you we've been on the wrong side. Most of the old volunteers are with the Commies and I'm beginning to think they're right. The Jerry officers thought nothing of us or their Spanish chums either. They're here for their own reasons. There's going to be a war, a really big bust-up with the Jerries and the Eyeties on one side and God-knows-who on the other.'

'What about Ireland?'

'She'll be pig-in-the-middle as usual. I reckon the Jerries have just been using this for practice.'

'What will you do?'

'Soon as I get home I'm going over the water to join the British Army, without mentioning this little lot of course.'

'Can I come along with you?'

'Sure, you're still light-headed to want such a thing.'

'What's the good of me going home when there's no work? And if you're right and there's a war and Ireland's neutral there'll be even less. At least in the Brit Army we'll be fed and paid.'

'Like this, you mean?'

It was only when the same dream woke him again and again, of bare hills under the sun's eye, of pursuit and falling, that he realised it hadn't been just the fever.

· *Check* ·

They had set up their command centre in the Don's cellar surrounded by the racks of dusty bottles. Pearse had run cables for power and a telephone from above. He was coming tonight to finish his preparations, fitting up a closed-circuit monitor so that they could see who came to the front door, and other things. Orazio had told Agnese and Ruby Heamans that he was going away for a few days, which he intended to do when it was all over. He would get a train from Victoria to Geneva and telephone Agnese from there. He sat in front of his television set with a half-empty glass in his hand aware of the preparations under his feet in the belly of the cellar. They had both told their plausible tales that would bring those others to the house within minutes of each other, the black pieces to their pre-ordained squares. The Irishman had given in, admitted they no longer had any choice.

Orazio switched on the television to pass the time. For a moment he thought the set wasn't working: it appeared to be dark and soundless. Then the narrator's voice broke in with a whispered commentary and he could see that shapes were defining themselves in the gloom. 'On the bottom of the Pacific live creatures that man has never seen before, in total darkness: fish, crabs, worms, giant clams owing nothing to the sun, feeding off the bacteria that in turn feed on the sulphur spewed out by underwater volcanoes. Blind and colourless, they feel their way by touch. Against all our pre-conceptions they live without dependence on light or vegetation.'

Could that be true or was it just that we couldn't measure the infinitely weak radiance that might seep through the watery two miles to the sea bed? It must be so cold down there too, unless the volcanoes heated it like some subaqueous Hell. How did that world fit in with that earlier tenet he had heard and taken to himself: 'We are all stardust'? He had to believe in that subdued radiance. Dante had seen the ultimate circle as far below and darkly frozen. Yet there must be, if not love, procreation down there, fire of some kind, death certainly. Perhaps where light waves couldn't go particles could, dropping like pebbles of brilliance through the thick depths and tuned to a frequency our eyes and instruments couldn't yet pick up. The creatures that moved all seemed to proceed crab-wise or, if they were soft-bodied, by sidewinder undulations like the pale ribbony worms weaving themselves through the gloomy depths where the rivers of Hades had their source: Acheron, Phlegethon, Cocytus, Styx . . . Which had he forgotten? He counted them again on his fingers, remembering, smelling the ink in the white china well on the front of his schooldesk. Lethe! How could he forget that one?

'I'm going to be busy tonight and tomorrow,' Pearse told Nicole and Liam. 'I've a job to do round at my Italian friend's. Some re-wiring.'

'You won't go back home, Dada?'

'Not unless I have to. Then I'll be very careful. Now I have to go down to the pub and collect some stuff I've on order.'

He'd decided to trust the Guv'nor with his shopping list. 'No problem,' he'd said as he ran his eye down it. 'Course, it's a bit harder than it used to be when all the building sites was going full swing but I know a handy couple of blokes can knock this lot off between them. It'll cost you a bob or two.'

'That's fine. No problem there either.'

The Guv'nor was expecting him. 'All done up in a coupla hold-alls.'

'No questions asked?'

'Only silly buggers ask questions.'

Pearse locked himself in the lavatory cubicle to count out the cost from the roll of notes the Don had given him. He'd already bought the one-way ticket to Australia for Liam. He hoped he'd be able to persuade the boy to use it without him. He drank a pint of black stout while the Guv'nor curled his huge hand round a half of shandy. 'I've seen too many landlords end up boozing the profits. Now if you want any more help, just say the word. Don't drop them, will you,' he said as Pearse picked up the bags. 'That's very fragile that is, that old china.'

'They taught me to do this in the Army,' Pearse explained as the Don watched him delicately stripping and connecting the wires. 'That's where I learned my trade. Before that I was going to sea.'

'To sea?'

'As a sailor.'

'I couldn't be a sailor. I was nearly drowned when I was a boy during the War.' Even the Channel ferry repelled him and he'd been relieved when at last it became commonplace to travel to Italy by plane. This time he would have to chance it. He had spent the day before going to different travel agencies and exchange counters making the remainder of the second thirty thousand sterling block into different currencies: dollars, lire, deutschmarks, francs, even some traveller's cheques, and stowing them in his luggage with the clothes he meant to go away in tomorrow. Like the newly-married.

Pearse switched on the little monitor. 'There we are.' The Don could see his own doorstep. It was a grainy, blurred image that might have been underwater, the porch of one of those miniature follies put in fish tanks to give the inhabitants an illusion of structures, caves, reefs, wrecks. 'No one comes or goes without our knowing. Now suppose you can't catch the cats?'

'Then we'll have to think of something else.'

The telephone rang as they were eating the toast the Don had made for breakfast. 'It's for you.' He passed over the receiver and left the room.

'I need to talk to you.' It was Nicole's voice. 'Liam was out all night. He's just come back. He said he just walked the streets. Could we meet somewhere?'

'Sure. I've some things to give you. But is it safe to leave him?'

'You can't lock him up, and neither can I.'

'No, you're right, we can't. Where shall we meet?'

'There's a pub off the King's Road I used to go to, very quiet. The Trencherman. In Flood Street.'

'I'll find it.'

It was a narrow house with room for a couple of bench tables in front of the stained-glass windows, and two long thin unreconstructed bars on either side of the central serving island of mahogany and mirrors where the drinks were poured. Nicole was waiting for him outside on a bench with a glass already in front of her. Pearse fetched himself a pint and brought it to her table.

'Cheers. You seem to be much better on your legs these days.' He indicated the solitary stick she had brought with her leaning against the bench.

'That just gives me a feeling of security. Yes, I am much better. I think it must be having more to do, to think about. I don't say I don't feel any pain at all but now it isn't the only thing on my mind, it seems to have receded a bit. I've even got back my confidence to drive. But I don't want to talk about that. I'm worried about Liam. He's very . . . well, both restless and listless. I don't know what you have in mind but I don't think you're handling him the right way. Now you can tell me to mind my own business.'

'I've, we've, me and Liam, made it your business. So go on. I'm listening. What am I doing wrong?'

'All right. You treat him like a child still. It's his life, his problem, but you don't really discuss it with him. You take it all on yourself.'

'He's too tired; he's been through too much.'

'That was true at first. But he's better now. If you've got some plan I think you should involve him in it.'

'I can't.'

'Tell me.'

'I can't do that either. I'm sorry.'

'He says you're going away with him.'

'That's what I told him. I thought it was the only way. But now, thinking about it, I'm not sure. What would I do in Australia at my time of life?'

'Why do you have to go?'

'He says, and he's probably right because he knows them, that if they think he's gone they'll try to force me to tell them where and I might not be able to hold out against another kicking, or worse.'

'Then what are you going to do?'

'I can't tell you exactly. But the plan is to frighten them off.'

'Then what?'

'I've got him a ticket for Australia and enough money for a bit.'

'And you? Where will you go?'

'I haven't been too clever about thinking that one out. It must be possible to lose yourself in England, not like Ireland. Here there's enough people. Lots of them go missing every week.'

'You could simply lie low with me. There's plenty of room.'

'Oh, I couldn't impose on you . . .'

'Don't you understand: I'd like it. Company, companionship is good for me. You can see for yourself that's true.'

He felt himself being lifted up and carried away to the Land of Promise as Niamh called away Oisin, and shook his head to try to clear it. 'Promise me,' she said, 'that you won't just disappear. That you'll give it a try.'

Pearse found himself unable to answer. After a moment he said, 'I'll have to see how it all goes. I have to be getting back now. I'll be in touch as soon as it's over. Will you give this to Liam for me?' He passed over the envelope with the money and the ticket. 'If I don't turn up tell him to go. And keep this other one for me if you will.' He gave her a second envelope. In it was the chequebook in his name the Don had given him at breakfast, saying, 'You never know. I think it's probably safer with you while I'm away.'

It had been easier to set up than Pearse had expected. 'Liam wants to talk to you,' he'd said to the girl Tessa when she'd telephoned him, after his call to the contact number in the letter. 'A friend's house, neutral ground.' He knew they wouldn't be coming to talk but they'd agreed the time and place. On his way back from the meeting with Nicole he stopped to make another call.

The two cats in the trap were still sleeping off the effect of the drugged bait. Strange, Orazio thought, that he'd been able to catch them so easily where Ruby Heamans had failed, but then she'd never tried prawns, best scampi. He took out each limp harsh-furred bundle in turn, pulled on the prepared harness and put them back to recover in the cages Pearse had fitted with a remote control that would spring open the catch, making the lid fly up and detonating the firecrackers attached to each harness.

It was already dark when the first two came at seven. They watched them on the little screen, hesitating at the half-open gate, one standing guard while the other came up to the door and rang the bell. 'I'll come down,' Pearse said into the entry-phone.

Orazio continued to watch from the cellar and saw them, with a last look round, disappear into the house. He hoped the others would be on time, that it wouldn't all end in disaster, that the Irishman wouldn't panic when the business reached its inevitable conclusion.

Upstairs Pearse was showing them into a little room off the hall stacked with shrouded furniture. 'I'll bring Liam to you when he comes. But it's to talk only, you understand. Then you'll go away and leave us alone.'

'That's as may be. Let's hear what he says.'

He shut the door behind him thinking he should have wired that room for sound so that he could pick up their conversation.

They waited five minutes before the next figures swam on to the monitor. 'They're early,' the Don said. 'My turn.'

Pearse watched now. Tessa and the bearded man would think it was Liam arriving. They'd be wondering if there was anyone else in the big dark house; growing edgy.

'What's this all about, Carbone?'

'We need to talk; that's why I asked you to come. I'll just get some glasses. Make yourselves comfortable.'

'This ain't a social call. We ain't got time. Say what you got to say.'

'What harm is there in a cognac? It oils the wheels.'

The first man made a gesture of resignation and sat down.

His heart threatening to choke him, Orazio left the room. It was time to get the cages from the boot cupboard under the stairs and then go down to the cellar.

One-Eye and the little tortoiseshell were awake. They spat and clawed at him through the bars as he brought the cages into the hall. They were making too much noise. He hadn't thought of that. Suppose their visitors became suspicious and came out into the hall too soon? He pulled open the cellar door and shut it behind him, shooting the bolt they had put on the inside. 'Do it, do it. *Now!*' he called out, almost falling down the steps.

Pearse pressed the button.

From above their heads they heard first the whump of a small explosion and then what seemed like gunfire.

'It's worked! You're a genius. Now up the ladder and through the coal chute.'

But Pearse was watching the monitor. Above, the sounds had become unmistakably those of real gunfire. They were late; it was all going on too long. Suddenly what he was waiting for began to appear: shapes of men with armalites cocked running into the garden and under the porch. '*Come on!*' The Don was at the top of the ladder and pushing at the wooden doors overhead.

Pearse turned to follow. The noise above had become the sound of battle. The Police, SAS, whoever they were, had forced an entry. He began to climb the ladder. At the top he bent for a last look at the screen.

Liam was running across the yard.

Pearse struggled up into the night through the open flaps, kicking them closed behind him. The Don had disappeared. Pearse began to make his way round the side of the house towards the front. The noise of firing had stopped abruptly. Pearse wanted to run but his boneless legs refused to go faster. He felt himself lumbering, ungainly. He reached the corner of the house.

'Lie down on the ground with your arms out!' a voice shouted through a loudhailer.

'My son! I have to find my son!'

'Lie down or we'll shoot.'

A beam of light pinned him to the wall. Pearse raised his hands high above his head. As he did so Liam appeared at the top of the steps.

Orazio stumbled between the statues. He'd twisted his ankle getting out of the cellar and there was a dense pain in his chest. He grabbed the bag hidden behind the dying Gaul but he couldn't seem to lift it. He felt as if he was choking and sank back against the stone torso.

'Here, mate, you all right?'

He thought he could just make out the face of the boy Scott but perhaps it was an hallucination. 'What are you doing here?' he managed to ask.

'I came to see yer, didn't I, and there was all this racket going on. So I come round the back and found the gate on the catch.'

It had been his way out and he couldn't even walk through it. Perhaps he was dying. His legs seemed to have gone. He couldn't get up and run because the pain would hardly let him breathe or even speak. But he must. There were things he had to take care of. He fumbled for the bag. 'Yours, take it.

Everything in it yours. Now go.' The boy was hesitating. 'Get away before they come. No one else must find it. Don't try to come back.'

He never saw the boy sidle out through the gate and vanish into the dark streets. We made a mistake, he thought through the thickening veil of pain. The principle was right. Occam's razor. But we let it all get too complicated. He felt the rope slip through his hands and the waters drew him down.

Behind Liam were armed men covering him as he came down the steps. Pearse, with his hands held as high as possible, moved slowly towards him. A soldier followed, carrying the body of the dead girl which he laid carefully on the ground, kneeling to straighten it and lift the long bright hair off the blue eyes staring up. She seemed unmarked, but completely lifeless. 'I loved her, Dada. That was the trouble. I always loved her.' Tears were running down Liam's cheeks.

'We'll need stretchers,' one of the armed men covering them said.

'How many?'

'Four at least.'

'Jesus!'

'It's bloody carnage in there. Christ knows who they all are. There's even a couple of dead cats.'

· *Epilogue* ·

'I have to tell you,' Pearse said, 'because I daren't tell anyone else, especially Liam, and then maybe it'll start to go away. I tipped the Police off because I was afraid of the bloodshed. But they came too late. Or they were glad of the excuse to go in firing.'

'How else could it have ended?' Nicole said. 'If it hadn't been that way, that day, it would have been another. Do you think the Police will believe your story that you'd gone to find Liam in your friend's house because you thought the others had tracked him down? Will they believe he was staying there and not look any further?'

'As long as he goes on refusing to say anything. What I don't understand is how he knew I was there.'

'He must have followed you some time or found the address among your things. He told me he knew you were up to something and he was going to find you. I couldn't stop him. What will they do with him?'

'They might find something to charge him with in Northern Ireland but since the others didn't ever trust him, he says, or let him in on things, there won't be much they can prove. Whichever way it goes I've lost him now. I didn't understand that he really loved the girl. Even if he never finds out, and he mustn't, I've still lost him. I know it in my bones.'

'And what about your friend, the Italian? He must have died of a heart attack. I suppose an inquest will clear that up.'

'He saved his family and now no one can ever get back at him. And with the Police and all the publicity involved they'll stay away. Of course the Police don't know who the other two men were who died, just as they don't know who tipped them off. They're calling all the dead "terrorists".'

'Maybe they're right. But how was he going to avoid questions? He must have known how it would turn out.'

'Oh, the Don knew. He wasn't sure if I knew, though. He was going away somewhere, was already gone. As far as his family were concerned, the house was empty. He never told me where. He's left me thirty thousand pounds in the bank.' Pearse considered. 'He wasn't really a friend, you know. I never exactly knew what went on in his head apart from the chess. There was one thing he said though, that stuck in my mind. You know he was a clever fellow, read and studied a lot; was meant for a priest. Once after we'd finished our game and were just chatting over a drink, about life and that, he said, and I've never forgotten it: "We are all stardust".'

A man held for questioning under the Prevention of Terrorism Act was this morning found hanging in a West London police cell. Liam Noonan, aged 34 . . .

London 1992